THE WORLD UNSEEN

SHAMIM SARIF

enlightenment

First published in Great Britain by The Womens Press Ltd,
a member of the Namara Group, 2001
Second publication in Great Britain by Review,
an imprint of Headline Book Publishing, 2004

This edition published in the United States by Enlightenment Productions,
London, UK, 2008

www.enlightenment-productions.com

ACCLAIM FOR THE WORLD UNSEEN FEATURE FILM

'The World Unseen is…a sincere, beautifully realized vision of love and resistance in an intolerant world. Sarif does a fantastic job — especially for a first-time director — of bringing her story to the screen.' AFTERELLEN.COM

'The World Unseen is a touching love story… In her directorial debut, Sarif makes the transition from novel to big screen utterly seamless, depicting romantic love that transcends its racist, sexist and homophobic surroundings.' INDIEEXPRESS.COM

'I was literally on the edge of my seat. Go see this great movie. You'll be rewarded with nearly two hours of great film-making and acting as well as an uplifting story that you'll look back on fondly.' MARK'S LIST

'[Lisa] Ray is particularly remarkable as a woman who is truly torn between familiar oppression and a freedom so unthinkable that it frightens her. The film's happy ending is graceful, absent of grandiosity or too much finality. It offers genuine reassurance, convincingly suggesting that one small individual action, while not a panacea, can be the difference between hope and despair.' JUSTOUT.COM

'Slow burning and sensual, The World Unseen contains what must be one of the steamiest screen kisses of this year's Festival, but is much more than that. It's a moving exploration of forbidden love blended with a fascinating account of a shameful period in modern history.' MELBOURNE QUEER FESTIVAL

'An engaging and beautifully executed story… '
JASMYNE CANNICK, PAFF LOS ANGELES

'…a rare combination of intricate character study and engaging narrative. '
BRITISH FILM INSTITUTE

'…a compelling and complex story…done with grace and style. Fine writing, beautiful cinematography and great acting by all.'
MARK MOORHEAD, PHOENIX FILM CRITICS SOCIETY

'Subtle and rather beautiful … a touching, likeable human story.'
NOTCOMING.COM

'The World Unseen contains not one but two of this year's steamiest screen kisses.'
CAMERON BAILEY, CO-DIRECTOR, TORONTO INTERNATIONAL FILM FESTIVAL

For Hanan, who has given passion to my life, clarity to my thoughts and a voice to my words. With immense gratitude and infinite love.

.

Chapter One

Pretoria, April 1952

EVEN LYING ON the roof, with only the cheap slates in her line of vision, she could tell that it was a police car. There was a carelessness in the skid of the tyres over the sandy road, and in the way the handbrake was pulled up while the wheels were still turning, leaving a slight screech hanging in the heavy air. She stopped hammering and peered over the edge of the eaves. They had parked so close to the restaurant door that they had broken one of the flowerpots that Jacob had planted only the day before.

'Bastards,' she said, under her breath.

She left the sign half-nailed and hanging, and climbed down the ladder. Her steps were measured, gaining her time to think. A year ago she would have been inside the café within seconds, running in her eagerness to grasp and fight whatever new obstacle was being thrown in her way. But many months of struggling against rules and regulations that made no sense to her at all had blunted her appetite for confrontation, and so she walked more slowly now, curbing her natural impulse, and when she looked over at the police vehicle, her brow showed tiny lines of concentration.

One of them, the driver, was still in the car. She knew many of the local police, but this one was a stranger to her and she was taken for a moment by his looks – a square, handsome face edged with soft blond hair – until she met his cool, blue gaze, which showed only arrogance. He looked her up and down, and resolutely, she held his look for a moment.

'Never seen a woman in trousers before?' she asked, too softly for him to hear; but to her chagrin he wound down his window.

'What?'

She had no choice but to repeat herself. She spoke clearly, and his mouth gave a slight curl.

'Never seen an Indian girl in trousers, that's for sure,' he replied.

She turned away and went inside, stopping just by the door. The place was more than half full, she noted, but she could still hear the *boerewors* sausages frying all the way back in the kitchen. Nobody spoke and nobody looked up, but every pair of eyes was covertly fixed on the policeman standing at the counter. Jacob could see her, she knew, but he made no sign. He kept wiping the glass he held, nodding occasionally. Officer Stewart had a friendly arm leaning on the polished wood and with the other hand he pulled thoughtfully at his trimmed beard.

'Listen, Jacob, I mean the two of you no harm, but these laws are making life bloody difficult for the police.'

'They're not making it a picnic for us either,' Amina said, behind him. She saw Jacob give her a slight shake of his greying head.

Stewart turned and touched his cap. 'Amina. Long time.'

'Yes.'

'Guess you've been keeping out of trouble, eh?'

She gave a forced smile at his attempt at small talk. Walking behind the counter, she leaned into the squat ice box and extracted a bottle of Coke, holding it out, doing her best for Jacob's sake.

'Can I offer you a drink, Officer Stewart?'

The policeman shook his head and watched as the girl drained half the bottle. She stopped, short of breath, and smiled.

'What about your colleague? Doesn't he want to come in?' she asked.

'No, thanks. I prefer him to stay in the car. He's a little over-enthusiastic, *ja*? A little hot-headed. He has a problem with this kind of thing.'

He was gesturing to the back of the café, and as though she had no idea what he was referring to, she turned and looked at the booth where her African workers took it in turns to eat throughout the day. Doris and Jim were sitting there now, and she saw Doris's chin lift defiantly, even while her fingers shook slightly as they held onto her coffee cup. Amina smiled encouragingly at her and turned back.

'What sort of thing would that be, exactly, Officer?'

'Now, listen, Amina. You know what I'm talking about, and

giving me an attitude isn't going to help you, *ja*? You and I both know that it's an offence for Blacks to eat in the same place as Whites.'

She put the Coke down on the counter and looked around.

'There are no Whites here. Present company excluded, of course.'

'As non-blacks then. This is an Indian area. And Coloured,' he added with a nod to Jacob. 'That means no Blacks.'

'They work for me.'

'And that is fine by me,' the policeman replied, pounding the counter for emphasis. 'But they shouldn't be eating with you. It's illegal.'

'Where should they eat?' Amina asked.

'I don't care! They can eat outside. Or in the kitchen, for Christ's sake. Or when they get home.'

'Do you go without food for twelve hours at a time, Officer?'

Jacob ran a nervous hand over his cropped head and watched Amina go to her gramophone player. He wished desperately that he could step in and impose some calm, suggest some compromise. But that might overstep the bounds of his apparent role as manager of the café, and Officer Stewart had no idea that Jacob was in fact Amina's business partner. Coloureds and Indians simply were not permitted to co-own businesses together, but a helpful lawyer had assisted them in drawing up a secret power of attorney for Jacob, and the partnership was now widely acknowledged, yet closely guarded, by those around them.

Amina was kneeling down, her back to the policeman, sorting through a short stack of records. Stewart placed his peaked cap firmly back on his head and walked over to the back booth where he stood looking down at the occupants.

'Passes,' he said, holding out his hand. Doris and Jim looked instinctively to Amina.

'You know they have passes,' she said.

'I want to see them. Now.'

Jim took his from his back pocket. The cover was creased and worn from use and, even when unfolded, had a permanent curve in it from being sat upon often. Stewart turned it in his hands and glanced down at the cook.

'This is only a travel permit.'

'Yessir.'

'Where's your pass?'

'I don't have a pass, Sir, I'm Coloured.'

Stewart examined the permit for confirmation of this fact.

'You're Coloured?'

'Yessir.'

'You look like a *kaffir* to me,' commented Stewart.

'They said I was Coloured. At the board. They classified me.'

Jacob had appeared at the policeman's side without giving anyone the impression that he had even moved, let alone hurried.

'His grandfather was White, Officer. A Dutch. Like my father.'

'Okay.' Stewart flipped the permit back on the table and turned, taking in the café with a glance.

'You understand what I'm trying to say, Jacob, *ja*? I'm not trying to be difficult. I'm doing my job.'

The crack of a gunshot electrified the room, the sheer volume of it freezing everyone for a split second before they all ducked.

Kneeling by the gramophone, Amina could see Officer Stewart huddled behind the counter and Jacob doubled over beside him. The windows still held a residual rattle, as though a train had just rushed through the café. Gingerly, Stewart drew his own gun, edging it over the counter as he slowly stood up. Amina rose with him. His partner was standing by the door, spinning a pistol on his middle finger.

'What the hell do you think you're doing?' Stewart asked.

The blond man grinned. 'My job,' he said. '*Ach*, what are you *talking* to these people for?'

He stopped the gun mid-spin and fired another shot into the ceiling. Some plaster dust pattered down, and a high-pitched echo sang in the room.

'This is what they understand,' he said. He grinned again, and looked at Amina.

'You keep serving *kaffirs*, we'll kill the lot of them. Then you'll have to find new staff.' He laughed.

'If you carry on like that,' Amina said, 'we won't need any. You're not exactly good for business.'

His face darkened, but before the first curses were out of his mouth, Stewart was pushing him out of the door, and towards the car.

Amina looked around for Doris, but the booth was clear – every one of her staff had retreated to the kitchen or to the scuffed plot of land outside the back door. Those customers who had been waiting for take-aways had already left. Others were laying money on tables. Even the sound of frying in the kitchen had ceased. When she looked at the door again to check that the police had really gone, she noticed that the glass in the framed photograph of her late grandmother, which hung above it, was broken, the familiar defiance in her grandmother's eyes distorted by a crack. That hurt her the most.

'Don't ever be a slave to anyone. I was, all my life, and it ruined me.' These had been Begum's final words to Amina Harjan. She had uttered them with a rasp of desperate conviction on a sunny Saturday morning in Bombay, while her granddaughter had sat by her sick bed and breathed in the scent of crushed cardamom pods that wafted up from the sweet-maker below. By nightfall she had been dead. Her passing had left her granddaughter floating in a strange pool of shock that slowed the energy trembling in her coltish limbs, and for the first time in her life, Amina had felt the weeks passing by without making any attempt to grasp them and make something of them. So when her father had once again raised his old wish of making a new life away from India, she had hardly noticed that the arrangements were already taking place. Mr Harjan had held an unspoken bond with his mother-in-law never to emigrate to South Africa, for she had been cast out of that country in disgrace forty years before, but that promise ceased to matter as soon as she was dead.

With too few men to steady the small but awkward corpse of her grandmother, the body had slid into its grave with unseemly haste, landing with a thud that made those at the graveside wince. The earth was quickly piled over her and Amina remembered being stunned by how quickly Begum had disappeared from the surface of the earth. She had been the only woman present; the others had gone back to the house after the funeral rites, as was the custom. Against her mother's wishes, she had insisted on accompanying the men to the burial, and she had prevailed, because her father had not had the energy to argue with his fiery daughter, nor the will to deprive her of a final goodbye to his mother-in-law.

Amina stared up at the broken glass of the frame now, and looked searchingly at Begum's face. She had to wait a long moment before meeting Jacob's look, and when she finally turned to him with a smile, he could not tell whether the brightness in her eyes was a sign of tears held back, or of anger.

'Are you sure you're okay?' she asked him.

'Oh yes,' he replied. 'I may be getting old, but I can still dive behind a counter when I have to.'

She laughed, as he knew she would, and without another word, they began to clear up.

Delhof – outside Pretoria

Miriam stood still, a long way off from the new house, her hand raised to her forehead, shielding her eyes. The house had been a farmhouse once and it was built long and low. Everything seemed low in this place – trees, hills, even the few buildings – low and flat and without colour, as though squashed down by the weight of the sky and its spreading blueness. The sun hit her hand with a red-hot force that burned straight through the clear, veined skin of her wrist, and when she shut her eyes tightly and briefly against it, the heat still glowed under her eyelids like coals.

She opened her eyes abruptly at the cry of her son's voice. She turned, and the boy and his sister swam into focus, small and bony, on the *stoep* of the house, dwarfed by the stacks of boxes and upturned furniture that surrounded them. She watched, frowning, as though trying to recall who they were, and he called to her again and again, his shrill high voice bouncing across to her on the shimmering waves of heat that quivered between them.

'What is it? What do you want?' she called back. She spoke in Gujerati, even though her husband had instructed her to speak to the children only in English or, when she had picked up enough of the language, in Afrikaans. But she was preoccupied, and Gujerati was the language that she had been raised with, the language that her own mother had also used to discipline her.

The boy fell silent at his mother's tone.

'Go in, I'm coming,' she called, and obediently they ran into the house. Her body was completely still, like that of a threatened animal straining to catch a single sound. When she breathed the hot dry air, she could smell a burnt dust smell that she knew would form a part of everything she inhaled from this time onwards; she could already sense the scent of it lying lightly on her skin. Only the soft folds of her cotton dress moved a little against the heat, and a slow trickle of sweat trailed steadily from her forehead and down over the high plane of her cheekbone. Her hand came up and swept it away impatiently. She couldn't comprehend this place where her husband had brought her. She knew that Springs was no more than half an hour away, when the weather and the roads were good, and that it was a pretty town, but here there was nothing, nothing at all. There were a couple of ramshackle houses perhaps half a mile away, but they looked as though they had not been lived in for years. On the far horizon there were a few buildings – she thought they must belong to the farmers who were to be the customers for her husband's shop – but other than that there was only a railroad track, here before her new house, laid strong and bare against the rusty earth, lying all alone in the vast landscape.

So much land – she had never seen so much land, just lying there, empty. What were they to do in it? How were they to live so isolated? After the crowded existence with their extended families in Pretoria, the paper-thin walls separating suffocating rooms always overflowing with neighbours and relatives? Miriam had not been unhappy to leave her brother-in-law's house, for she had been treated by her sister-in-law as little better than a servant. And this new business of Omar's was a fresh start: a shop that would supply everything that the local farmers could need. But she was afraid of the quiet loneliness of the countryside, and unsure of how to manage with only her taciturn husband for company.

She raised her hand again and this time used the back of her arm to wipe across her face and eyes. Then, clasping her arms protectively about her body, she walked back to her family.

Chapter Two

THE FIRST TIME that her father's mother saw Amina Harjan she nearly fainted. The elderly woman's arrival in South Africa from India had caused a commotion in the Harjan household which seemed to affect everyone except her only granddaughter. It would probably have made a difference to Amina too, were it not for the fact that she was simply not there, and could not be found. She was away 'working' for a few days she had said in the scrawled, barely legible note that she had left for her parents on their kitchen table, and since her family rarely knew the full nature or location of the various odd jobs that she took on from time to time, no one could find her. This was not usually a cause for much concern to her father, who, unlike every other man of his age and background, had let his daughter do very much as she pleased since they had arrived in Springs several years ago. Amina's mother was a meek, stunted woman, and her worry was silent, spoken only by the permanent lines between her eyebrows and on her small forehead. It was she who understood most the complications to their routine lives that her mother-in-law's impending arrival would bring, and she went to the unusual trouble of leaving her kitchen and asking for her daughter at the café in Pretoria, about an hour's drive from their family home in Springs. Jacob Williams offered Mrs Harjan some tea and listened to her politely, but explained that he had heard nothing of Amina for three days, because she had taken a taxi job, driving two people on the long journey from Johannesburg to Cape Town.

'She'll be back soon, lady,' he said, using the deferent form of address common to the Cape Coloured community. He smiled encouragingly at the worried mother. 'She always comes back soon. Always.'

Although she did arrive back soon, she did not arrive back in time, and so the old lady was picked up by her son alone; not the effusive, crowded family welcome that she had spent her long and often sickening voyage imagining. Mr Harjan was a worn, transparent-looking man, whose gaunt frame appeared almost emaciated in his baggy work clothes. He met the train slightly late and found his mother rooted to the end of the platform, surveying the dusty station and the milling Africans with distaste. He greeted her without much enthusiasm, as though he had just seen her the day before, and installing her in his rattling car, drove back to his house without expression, and with little awareness of his enormous mother's discomfort, as though he had just picked up a package of no consequence. Her repeated listing of her ailments passed over his head like a cloud of gnats, irritating, but of little ultimate concern.

During that first day, the old lady claimed her place in the household, effacing any remaining trace of her son and daughter-in-law's personalities, and firmly imposing her own. She sat in the small parlour, in her son's armchair, as if sitting in state, and began to receive all her family and neighbours – graciously, but not without ensuring they understood the favour she bestowed by meeting them. Her concern at the absence of her granddaughter had been considerable, but her enquiries as to her whereabouts were met with such vague uncertainty from the parents that she had contented herself with a short lecture and left it at that. Two days later, Amina arrived.

The old lady heard an engine cut out abruptly outside the front door and from her seat near the window, she pulled back the greying net curtain that hung limply over the pane and looked out. She could not make out much, but something made her stare hard at the girl who jumped down from the small pick-up truck that stood outside, and she watched as the mother hurried out of the back door, and whispered urgently to her daughter and gestured to the house. She saw Amina nod and smile and watched her unload something – it looked like bags of flour – from the car and hand them to the maid, Rosemary, who came out smiling to greet her. Amina then handed Mrs Harjan two dresses, holding them out against her mother, who folded them quickly over her arm. The old lady frowned – what did *she* need new dresses for? She sat back in her armchair, a frown of consternation upon her round face as Amina strode up to the house, and through the screen door. She walked in and her grandmother saw that she wore what appeared to be a pair of her father's old work trousers, some braces and a collarless shirt. She wore also a wide-brimmed hat, pushed back on her high forehead so that it held back most of the long, black curls that otherwise tended to fall about her face. She looked like one of the Boer farmers who came to her father's filling station to buy petrol for their trucks.

'God forgive us,' the old lady whispered to herself. The girl had never looked entirely demure or docile in India, but this was something else. The mask of horror hardened over her face, so that when Amina entered the room, tall and smiling, she stopped short, appalled at her grandmother's expression. She followed the woman's gaze and immediately understood, of course, that the offence lay in her clothing, her attitude, her way of carrying herself. Amina had spent the last six years of her life in this place living in accordance with her own wishes, and her parents seemed, if not understanding, then at least accepting of their only daughter's wish for freedom. They had been worn down over a period of years, their best efforts to contain Amina having come to nothing even when she was a child. As a toddler in India, her mother would lose her at least once or twice a day. The house would be searched, the maid and the nanny would be questioned, the small garden scoured, and eventually the child would be found, exploring some new place, smiling and nodding her curly head at the relieved women who surrounded her. Only one maid, a young bright girl of nineteen, who shimmered with as much energy as the toddler, could ever keep up with her. But she had only stayed with the Harjans for a year, before eloping with a neighbouring house-boy, and after that, no one could control Amina. She was not a naughty child – any sense of deviousness or guile was alien to her; but her energy and curiosity were insatiable, and her quiet parents seemed slowly to fade away under the questioning mind and irrepressible movement of their growing daughter.

'You should have been born a boy,' her mother had told her wearily, more than once, and this comment had puzzled the girl, and hurt her. She thought deeply about it, as she thought about everything. She liked to play sports with the boys at school, and she was good at her schoolwork – when it held her attention – and she wanted to work at a business or a trade when she grew up. Why were these attributes only fit for a boy? Finishing school in order to get married made no sense to her, nor did it hold much appeal, and as ingrained as it was into the consciousness of everyone around her, it was still almost beyond her comprehension. She felt at times that she was living in a different universe, breathing a different atmosphere from other people, and as she grew up she found her refuge in work and in books. She would do any odd jobs that she could find, though only within her parents' house – there was no scope for her to take on manual work elsewhere – and when the house and garden were in perfect condition, she read. Tattered old novels, poetry and biographies followed each other on a dancing course through her consciousness and imagination, and with each one her awareness of the world and its variety and breadth increased.

She had finally left school at the age of sixteen, because her father had decided to emigrate. For years, he had heard stories from other families of the great opportunities in South Africa, but even as he worked at a poor accounting job he despised, he dared not bring up the idea of moving there, not while his mother-in-law was alive. He knew well that she still carried the scars of her time there in the misshapen, bruised bones of her body, and the brutal, battered memories of her mind. Amina had learned much from Begum, most of it knowledge or advice that few other women of her grandmother's age had dared to even learn themselves, much less impart to an impressionable young girl. Her maternal grandmother spoke to her of pride, of self-reliance, and of courage. These were the things to cultivate, she had told her granddaughter, and not a slavish attitude to duties and traditions that were built on subservience and pain and fear.

Amina knew this advice to be good, for it appealed to her natural sense of integrity and justice, but her admiration was as yet abstract, for she had never experienced the horrors of which her grandmother spoke. So, a few months after Begum's death, when her father decided that they should leave for South Africa, Amina felt no particular excitement at the idea, nor was she unhappy. The misery that her grandmother had endured was something she respected, but Amina knew that she could not hate a whole country on someone else's behalf, even Begum's. At the age of seventeen, the distant future was no more than six months ahead, and in six months all she knew was that she would be halfway through an ocean voyage to Africa with her parents.

On the morning that they had docked she had stood almost alone on the upper deck at daybreak, and had watched the coastline rise up from nowhere, out of the ocean, as clean and as bright as the edges of a map, and she smiled to see it. She could make out little then except the golden rim of the beaches, but they seemed to be unending, and at once she had felt at home, released, able to breathe, and her innate confidence had combined with this immediate empathy for the country they were now approaching, and had given her a strength of purpose that nobody could contain. Her parents had very soon stopped trying. The cursory, half-hearted attempts they had made in India to try to make their daughter conform to accepted conventions fell away completely in South Africa. The family went directly from Durban to Pretoria, but they did not remain among their own people in the Asiatic Bazaar; instead they chose a house and a business – a garage and gas station – outside Pretoria, in Springs, where the pressures of conformity were largely removed from Amina's father. Her mother was thrown into a life harder than they had been used to in India. Her weekly housekeeping money had to be carefully counted now, and there were no live-in maids – only Rosemary, the daily help who would not always work as she should. And Amina, instead of helping her mother in the kitchen, usually ended up working with her father in the garage. Mrs Harjan could do nothing but watch worriedly as her daughter pumped gasoline, cleaned windshields and generally fell into her own life in this new place. This untried and often wild country fitted Amina like a well-cut suit of clothes, and it was this ease and confidence of hers, that had by now been built up over a period of years, that so disturbed the grandmother who now sat before her. Amina was entirely lacking in any semblance of the expected attributes of docility and of self-effacement – and although her grandmother understood none of this, and thought that it was the trousers and braces that appalled her, it was really her granddaughter's attitude and bearing that affronted her most.

The old lady did not actually faint, however. In fact, she recovered very quickly, with the main points of her lecture to her son and his wife (who was mostly to blame, she was sure) already taking shape in her head. Right at that moment, though, before she could say anything at all to Amina, the girl extricated herself. She was, by now, quite used to these kinds of reactions, particularly from her elders, and her methods of dealing with them had gradually eased from anger and self-defence, until they had reached the kind of polite removal that she now effected.

Amina took a step back, removed her hat, and welcomed her grandmother with a few formal and correct Gujerati words of greeting. Then her hat was back upon her head, and before the old lady could even respond, she was closing the screen door behind her.

'God forgive us,' her grandmother breathed again, as though exorcising a horrible spectre. She stood up uncertainly and moved as quickly as she was able to the curtain over the door. By the time she had pulled it aside and peered through the hazy glass, her granddaughter was gone, and all that remained of her was a set of tyre tracks and a whirl of dust that sat for a moment in the air and then fell slowly to the earth.

Delhof

During that first year in the countryside, when she lay in bed at night, Miriam's head would ache with the silence. It was so large, and it seemed to come sweeping down from the sky, like something cold and solid. Especially now, in the winter. No insects or crickets to scrape even a hollow hole in the wall of quiet. Then Miriam would close her eyes tightly and force herself to listen to Omar's breathing, to the deep, fierce sleep of the man lying beside her. The slow rasp, the sliding of a head on a pillow – in the long night she fell upon these sounds like a beggar on a shower of coins.

At five or five thirty she would rise from the bed, often awake before the early morning light or the insistent crow of the cockerel on the farm next to them. She had always woken early as a girl in India, but this pre-dawn habit had only formed after she had married and come to live with her in-laws in Pretoria. Although Omar's strong self-assurance meant that he generally took charge of his family, his brother Sadru was older, and so Farah, his wife, took precedence over Miriam in the subtle hierarchy of women in the house. Omar's sister would have been above them both, but she was slow-witted and sick, and Farah easily controlled her by slapping and hitting. Miriam disliked Farah's bossy attitude and lazy ways, but she had had no choice but to accept them and to make up for her *bahbhi*'s shortcomings by working even harder in the kitchen. Every morning she was forced out of bed at five o'clock to start preparing the dough for the breakfast *rotlis*. With a shake of her head Miriam put aside the recollection and slipped out of bed.

She had to make no effort to be quiet – she was naturally light in her movements. Anyway, it was time for her husband to get up, and he knew this, and slowly reconciled himself to the subtle shifts of his wife's movements through the room, out into the cold bathroom and back through the hallway again, when he would hear her stop at the door of the children's room, before she descended the stairs. In the early morning gloom of the kitchen, she could see that Robert, the boy whom Omar had hired to help in the shop, was already loading with coal the fire that would burn throughout the day in the stove. Robert looked around with a smile, the hessian sack of fuel still in his arms. It was mined nearby in Witbank and was plentiful and cheap. Miriam wished him 'Good morning' quietly, and not without some self-consciousness. She had been used to having help in her mother's house while she was growing up, but that had been somehow different. Omar's attitude to the Africans was always a little patronising, and often harsh. Giving sharp orders did not come naturally to Miriam, but he had told her to be firm with them, and she felt she must try.

The back door opened then and the night watchman came in. They had soon discovered that here in the country, just as in parts of Pretoria, a guard was necessary at night.

'The *kaffirs*,' Omar had said. 'They would steal anything.'

So each evening, just as the shop was closing for the night, John would arrive, tall, heavy, his close-shaved hair almost completely grey. She would see him approaching the shop twenty minutes before he actually arrived, having appeared over the horizon from some unknown place where she knew all the African people lived together. He would help Omar pull the display tables back into the shop from the porch, and his long, lean arms, though much older than her husband's, made lighter work of securing the various padlocks. He would nod with deference at Miriam, but he was always consistent in politely turning down her shy offers of a drink or some food, until she came to see that she should not ask any more. He would settle down for the night then in his chair, on the edge of the *stoep*, before an old corrugated-tin cylinder, in which several coals burned in an effort to stop him from freezing. Sometimes, if she was up late, sitting before the kitchen range sewing, Miriam would watch John as he paced before the window, and she would see the red of the coals, which hissed and spat now and then, especially if the wind blew. At intervals during the night, John would unwrap a cloth parcel, and take out a portion of *mealies*, the ground corn which she had found was as much a staple here as rice was back home. This he would turn slowly over the heat before eating it.

'How are you, John?' she asked.

'I am fine, madam, fine.' He watched Robert load the stove with the air of an interested uncle, and once he seemed satisfied that the boy was doing the job correctly, he turned to open the back door.

'I see you tonight, madam,' he said, and Miriam raised her hand goodbye.

Robert stirred at the coal for a moment more before shutting the heavy black door.

'Shall I fetch the flour, Madam?'

She turned to him. He was fifteen years old, with a slight limp from some accident in his early childhood – when she had asked him about it, she had not been able to understand much of his English, accented in a different way to hers, and the details had been lost to her. He was a little smaller in height than she and had very shiny white teeth. She nodded and watched from the corner of her eye as he bent to the sack and measured out two cupfuls, and she marvelled again at the fiercely tight curl of his hair and the deep coffee colour of his skin, such a different shade to the ink black of John's. She had never seen a black person in the first twenty years of her life.

'You must not be friendly with them,' her husband had told her. 'If they think you are soft, they will take advantage. Make them work. That is what they are there for.' She had listened, and had had a hundred questions about 'them' that she had not dared to ask her new husband, and so she had only nodded and agreed with him. Upstairs, she could hear the occasional creak of a floorboard and she knew that Omar was up, and that his unthinking, heavy steps would wake the children.

At least it was better than it had been in Pretoria. There had been no quietness there, early in the morning – or at anytime. At the very least, her *bhabhi* would be up with her, and the sound of her neighbours' talk and their children's wailing would penetrate the thin walls and come up from the streets outside. And then she had to feed and wash Omar's sister Jehan, whose manic chatter and laughing always seemed to begin before any of them had fully woken.

She took the flour from Robert gratefully. At the front door, the boy found the milk which Mr Morris, the Coloured farmer whose smallholding was nearest to them, left there each morning. It sat in the darkness of the early morning, foaming and still a little warm. Robert carried in the big urn, with small quick steps, struggling beneath its weight. The milk smelt fresh, not sour, like the stale bottles they had shared in Pretoria. One of Miriam's last tasks each night, after cooking, serving and clearing away the evening meal, after putting her children to bed, and after ironing Omar's shirts, had been to make Jehan drink a glass of milk. Her brother-in-law had asked her to do it, in his blundering, well-meaning way, for he believed it would settle his sister's mind before sleep, and his own wife rarely bothered to do as he wished. But Farah would always pour out the old dregs for Jehan, and Miriam had learned not to protest, or her own children would also be slipped the stale milk when she wasn't looking. The smell of that milk, in Jehan's darkened, stuffy room used to make Miriam feel sick. At those times, nauseous from lack of sleep and light-headed with hunger, she would remember what her mother had said when Miriam had been hesitant about Omar's proposal of marriage.

'His parents are dead,' she had told her. 'That will make your life easier, because no mother is ever happy with the girl her son marries. Go to South Africa with him and be thankful that no mother-in-law will ever make you work like a slave.'

No mother-in-law, perhaps, but Farah had worked hard at making her life miserable. At least John and Robert smiled at her now. Miriam watched the milk as it heated and recalled the time in Pretoria when no one had smiled at her for ten whole days.

Pretoria, September 1951

She had known it was ten days because she had been counting in her head. The last person to smile at her had been the *halal* butcher when she had gone to his shop the previous Thursday. She had been back since then and had hoped that the butcher would break the run of days that she had counted, but the man had been busy hacking at a fresh lamb carcass, and had barely acknowledged her.

Farah smiled now and then, but never, it seemed, with pure pleasure. There was inevitably some sense of superiority or a hint of triumph in her face whenever she smiled that made Miriam discount any show of teeth from her *bhabhi*.

'What are you doing with that meat? There won't be anything left.'

Farah's voice cut into her reverie and brought Miriam's attention back to the pile of cubed mutton that lay before her. With deft strokes and pokes of her knife, Miriam was cutting away the edges of fat and removing all traces of sinew.

'My husband likes the meat to be clean,' Miriam replied. She had been scolded the previous week for leaving too much fat on the pieces of lamb that went into the curry.

'My husband likes it clean!' mimicked Farah. 'Well, *my* husband likes to eat all the meat that he has paid for, and not to have it all cut up so there is nothing left.'

Miriam immediately put down her knife and began to pile the meat into a large bowl to be washed, before it was added to the onions that were already browning on the stove.

'Don't worry,' she said quietly. 'There will be enough for them.'

'Yes, but what about you and me?' asked her *bhabhi*.

Miriam rinsed the meat. She knew that Farah had never gone without her portion of anything and that if there were a shortage, it would be Miriam herself who missed out.

'Maybe,' Miriam said quietly, 'we should buy more meat and more flour for the *rotlis*...'

'We don't have money for anything more,' Farah said. 'It's amazing that I manage to put enough food on the table at all with what they give me.'

Miriam began to skin and chop the rotting tomatoes which Sadru brought back from the markets, and which were too soft for anything but cooking. She knew that Farah was lying and that she took part of each week's housekeeping money to buy clothes and trinkets for herself and her children, but there was no way for Miriam to protest. Omar had refused to give his wife their share of the money – it was Farah who ran the house, he told her, and he did not want to cause problems.

Later that evening, while the men sat down to eat together at the table, Miriam quickly rolled out balls of loose, elastic dough into perfect circles. She picked them up lightly, passing them back and forth between her open palms, and placed them onto the hot cast-iron pan. She waited patiently as they cooked, shifting from foot to foot to try to ease the pain behind her knees. She had been standing up since five thirty that morning. Only her few trips to the bathroom had given her a moment to sit down. She turned the *rotlis* now and then with fingertips that had long ago become accustomed to the heat of the stove's flames. As soon as brown patches began to form and spread across the surface, the bread was removed from the pan and the surface rubbed with butter. Whenever two or three were ready, she would carry them in, still hot, to the men, and to Farah, who had by now joined them.

'Come and eat,' Omar told her. Miriam nodded slightly, but before she could sit down, Jehan began calling out from her room. She screamed loudly, long delirious streams of words. The men looked up, but Farah continued eating.

'Have you fed her?' Omar asked. Miriam nodded, and went to see what hallucinations or dreams had disturbed her husband's elder sister.

Jehan was easily placated for once. Miriam stayed with her for ten minutes, stroking her forehead and murmuring vague replies to the nonsense that she spoke. When she returned to the kitchen, Farah had already placed the empty dishes in the sink for washing. The serving plates were empty, so Miriam stood at the pot, and wiped the remaining sauce from the sides with a cold *rotli* and ate. Once again, nobody had smiled at her; not Omar when he arrived home from work – not even Sadru, who had a kind streak beneath his large, uncouth exterior, and who was often the most deferent to her. She pressed the aching lower part of her back. She had carried her son too much today, but he had been scared of Farah's girl, older and tougher than he. She dreaded having to bring up Sam and Alisha amongst her sister-in-law's badly behaved children, but she saw little way out. She had learned, though, through listening to the talk of other women, and from Farah herself, that there were ways to stop becoming pregnant, at least for a while. Omar's demands on her had lessened as they both became more and more exhausted, but nevertheless she had been trying these since her second child had been born.

The following day, the oppressive atmosphere of the windowless bathroom was making Miriam feel nauseous again, as she moved over the floor with a scrubbing brush, her knees cold against the tiled floor. She worked quickly, and was almost at the door when it burst open, nearly hitting her in the face. She looked up. Farah's eyes were wide, and her hands clapped together as she spoke.

'They said we can go! To the Bazaar café. For lunch!'

'Both of us?' Miriam asked, hardly daring to believe that she could be included in such a piece of good luck.

'*All* of us,' Farah replied, rolling her eyes. 'They made me promise to take that lunatic. They want to give her an outing.' She turned to leave, stopping to glance back at Miriam once more.

'Hurry up!' she said. 'Go and get her ready. I want to change.'

While Miriam dressed Jehan, she sang her a tune, a Hindi song from a film that had been popular years ago in Bombay. She smiled when she was finished and Jehan laughed too, sensing a lightness of spirit that had not been felt in the house for months. For it was the first time since she had arrived in South Africa that Miriam would be eating a meal that she had not had a hand in preparing herself. She would be outside, without having to go shopping, or listen to the gossip of the women who were Farah's friends and neighbours. And she would finally see Amina Harjan, the subject of so much of that gossip, for herself.

Miriam knew of her, of course; everybody did. For despite her lack of conformity, she was still Indian, still a very young unmarried girl, and her seemingly unlimited freedom and lack of concern for propriety was of great concern to everyone in the Asiatic Bazaar. Her way of dressing, the fact that she had just opened up her own business ('with a Coloured man'), even Begum's photograph hanging proudly in the café – all these facts only fed the interest of those around her. They were appalled and horrified and shocked, but many began to patronise her café because they liked the food, they liked the atmosphere, and they liked the prices.

Miriam's general attitude to Amina that day was one of curiosity, with an underlying sense of disapproval. For Farah's friends came to the house at least twice a week to gossip. They would bring with them boxes of hard-skinned, green mangoes to cut up for pickles, or a week's worth of dry garlic bulbs for peeling, and over their work they would talk. Looking down at her own heap of peeled cloves, Miriam had seen only the smart flashing of ten or twelve blades in the still air around her as they chopped and scored, and she had listened as they had made thorough work of blaming Amina's dead grandmother for the sins of her granddaughter.

'She steered that girl wrong from the start. Taught her to be too proud and above herself. Where does it get you?'

'But Begum had a hard life...'

'If you mess with the blacks, you can expect a hard life...'

'She didn't even feel any shame. Imagine. No shame. And this girl is exactly the same. Her poor mother!'

Miriam finished dressing Jehan and together they waited for
Farah to appear. Her *bhabhi*, almost sick with the excitement of
eating out, had dressed as though for a wedding, in a fiercely pink
shalwaar kameez, while Miriam herself wore a simple printed skirt
and blouse. At first, Jehan could not be persuaded to come out of
her room, and chattered continuously while Farah shouted and
cajoled and finally slapped the girl to stop the flow of meaningless
talk. At the sting of the hand on her face, Jehan was silent
suddenly, and then she laughed, loud and long, as though sharing
a private joke with her attacker. This unexpected laughter had
long ago ceased to surprise Miriam, but its incongruous nature,
the way that it spilled out without reason or warning still chilled
her. She had heard it first on the night that she and Omar had
arrived in South Africa. She had entered her new brother-in-law's
house, nervous and shy, a little way behind her husband, with her
head down and her heart pounding, and she had found herself in
the middle of a screaming argument.

Two small children sat silent and scared on the floor beneath
the table, and watched as their parents, Miriam's new in-laws,
screamed at each other. Or rather, Omar's brother shouted – Farah
attacked pointedly and venomously with a sarcastic comment now
and then. Omar had turned and glanced at Miriam briefly, with
eyes filled with embarrassment, and then he had shouted to his
brother to be quiet, he was here, and what kind of a way was this
to behave? The room was silenced, and her new sister-in-law had
turned at once to look at Miriam, and at the same time she had
smiled, a sly smile of triumph directed at her silenced husband.
He was incensed and had shouted at her again, 'So you think this

is funny? Now you laugh at me?' Miriam had watched appalled from beneath lowered lids as he continued to shout, with a voice that kept catching, that nobody would ever laugh at him, he wouldn't allow it, there was nothing funny, nothing to laugh about, did she understand? And it was then Miriam had heard it first, that long, low laughter, maniacal and strange, issuing from a back room somewhere, with impeccable timing, in the middle of Sadru's warning speech.

It was her first introduction to Omar's elder sister, Jehan, the one whose inherent mental slowness had been partnered with a kind of madness after a bout of syphilis some years before. The word 'syphilis' was whispered with a significant nod by Farah, but the word and all its associations were alien to Miriam; she thought perhaps it was a peculiarly African disease, though she could not grasp how it was contracted, and she prayed privately that she would never catch it.

Holding Jehan between them, Miriam and Farah left the children with a neighbour, and then walked the several blocks to the café, beneath purple-blossomed jacaranda trees and past the leaning rows of houses, from whose windows a few people waved at them as they passed. Jehan waved back with much windmilling of her arms, chattering all the while, and Farah walked a few paces ahead of them, itching with irritation.

When they entered the café, they were supremely self-conscious, but few people seemed to show any particular interest in their arrival. Jacob Williams waited behind the counter for a few moments while the three women arranged themselves in one of the booths that ran along the walls. Then he walked slowly over to the table, one leg a little stiff from the arthritis that was slowly invading his body, and nodding politely, he placed down three menus.

'We have mutton stew today, and fresh *koeksisters*,' he said.

Jehan clapped her hands in approval. '*Koeksisters, koeksisters, koeksisters*,' she said.

'Shhh!' said Farah.

'What are *koeksisters*?' stumbled Miriam, half to Jacob, half to her *bhabhi*.

'Here, try for yourself,' said a voice by her side, and she looked up to see a long fork held before her. A small golden fried doughnut sprinkled with coconut was impaled upon it, and Amina Harjan held the other end.

'See if you like it,' she suggested again, and shyly, Miriam took the *koeksister* from the fork. Breaking it in two, she passed one piece to Jehan and placed the other in her mouth. The warm, sweet doughnut tasted ripely of yeast and melted away in Miriam's mouth.

'And?' asked Amina, smiling.

'It's delicious,' said Miriam.

'We'll have some,' said Farah.

'KOEKSISTERS!' screamed Jehan, and Miriam blushed crimson.

Everyone in the café, it seemed, had turned to look at their table. In the sudden silence, Jehan shouted out again, an unintelligible word this time, and from the table behind them came a snort of laughter, a derisive, mocking sound. Amina looked around and stood watching the occupants of the table for a long moment. When she finally asked Miriam and Farah what else

31

they might like to eat, she was still watching, and she turned away only to nod briefly to Jacob. He nodded back, and by the time Amina had walked back to the kitchen with the new lunch order, he had given those customers their bill, taken part of their money, and the people were leaving. That they had not yet finished their lunch seemed to be irrelevant, and Miriam marvelled at the power this young girl, younger even than she, seemed to wield over those around her.

The three women sat, without speaking, and waited for their food. Over the murmurs of the other diners, they could hear from the kitchen the sound of Amina's voice, and that of the cook, and the sizzle of hot oil, and then the bounce and scratch of a record being placed upon the old gramophone behind the counter. The straining strings started up, wavered, and then righted themselves to form the opening bars of 'Night and Day'. This was not a song Miriam had ever heard before. She listened to the radio often in the kitchen at home and she knew many of Cole Porter's and other American melodies by heart, though she could not really put a name to any of them. Miriam looked over at the record sleeve propped up on the counter. It was hard for her to make out the details from where she sat, but she could see the outline of a man's face. The cover was lifted away as she peered at it, and she realised that it was being brought towards her, under the arm of Jacob Williams. He stopped at the table and deposited a bowl of steaming mutton stew, a platter of baked pumpkin, and a plate of bread yellow with corn grains. Then he removed the record sleeve from under his arm and offered it to Miriam.

'Amina says you might be interested to see this, ma'am,' he said, and Miriam thanked him and took it. Farah stared and raised a questioning eyebrow.

'Why did he bring this?' she asked, putting a piece of bread before Jehan, who ate hungrily.

Miriam shrugged. 'I don't know. Maybe they saw I was looking at it.'

'Maybe she likes you,' she said, but without any kindness, and with a laugh that Miriam could not read. She ignored Farah and looked down at the record cover. It was, as she had thought, a portrait of Cole Porter. Miriam listened to the record as it skipped along. 'In the roaring traffic's boom, in the silence of my lonely room, I think of you, night and day...' Even that name, Cole Porter, seemed to be invested with such glamour, such a sense of the debonair. The picture was black and white and grainy, but there he sat, hair slicked back with Brylcreem, leaning in towards his piano, eyebrows raised at the camera, a slightly sardonic expression on his face.

When Miriam looked up, Farah was still watching her. But for once, Miriam did not care. Her ten days of counting, of watching for some sign of concern or pleasure or kindness, had finally been ended with the smile Amina Harjan had given her.

Chapter Three

T H E   L A S T   D A Y of each month was pay-day for the scores of Africans who worked on the farms that surrounded the shop, and the day that the overseers, or occasionally the owners themselves, would drive their workers to the shop, clutching their small amounts of tattered cash, so that they could buy whatever dry supplies and clothes they might need for the following month. They started to arrive early, usually just after Sam and Alisha had left on the bus for school in Springs, and it was always the busiest day of the month for the shop. As usual, they had all been preparing since very early that morning. There was plenty of fruit, enough bags of *mealies*, and the dark wooden counters were clear. Omar stood checking his stock and making the occasional scratch with his pencil on the pad of paper that lay next to the till. He looked up for his wife. Squinting through the sun that glanced off the window panes, he could see her outside, hanging washing out to dry.

Everything she was clipping to the line was white. He could see Sam's tiny vests and his own bright, white shirts, almost blue under the unrelenting light of the sun. He shut his eyes against the glow; and for a moment the shop ceased to exist. He was not here, out in the African wilderness; he was not the father of two small children; he was not a struggling shopkeeper; he was not married to a woman he hardly spoke to. In his mind, he was transported. He was in Bombay for a visit, young, eager, fresh from South Africa, feted by his uncle and aunt. He saw himself, as though he were watching a documentary film, standing out on his uncle's tiny balcony, smoking a cigarillo, and listening to an unknown girl chatting on the balcony above. His curiosity had risen so high that he had leaned forward and looked up. That had been his first glance of his future wife. Then, as now, she had been hanging out a basket of washing, a waving line of pure white against the white-washed walls and the sun-bleached sky. His eyes had swum with red outlines for a moment, and when he recovered he had to squint to see her. She had also been wearing white, as though she were part of the conspiracy of light that glowed against him. But she was attractive – he had seen more beautiful, more conventionally pretty girls, but this one was tall and lithe and laughing and he had liked her.

'Shall I make some tea?' Miriam asked, her voice small in the large, quiet space of the shop. He looked up and nodded, and she went into the kitchen. At the range, she stopped abruptly and gripped the cold edge of the stove, and waited while a surge of dizziness passed over her. She closed her eyes for a few moments, and then looked out through the window for the first trucks. There was no sign of them yet, but she could see Robert walking slowly towards the shop from the store room, carrying a huge squash in each arm. At the back door he bent very slowly at the knees, so that his bony legs almost buckled, and lowered the vegetables gently onto the ground. He had dropped one earlier, and Omar had shouted at him not to be so clumsy – who did he think would buy a bruised squash? Robert had not been able to think of anyone who would and had therefore accepted his admonishment with good grace, and now he carried the squashes with utmost care, cradling them in each of his thin sinewy arms as delicately as if they were chubby children. His boss shouted at him frequently and, although there were often times when he was sure he had not done the thing he had been accused of, he bore all the shouting in silence and apologised where necessary. It had never occurred to him that he might defend himself – it was not his place.

Anyway, no amount of shouting could make him unhappy to be working for these people. Although his wage was small, his mistress would often send him home with leftover food, or bits of material for his mother to use in sewing clothes, and she treated him well. She trusted him with the children. He knew about children – he himself was the second of seven surviving brothers and sisters. Robert's eldest brother was in Johannesburg, working in the mines. His family had celebrated when his brother had left for the city, for they were hungry for income, and Johannesburg was where the jobs were. But his brother lived in rough conditions, and worked in even worse ones. Robert had been there once to visit him, and had had to share with his brother a tiny bed in a concrete building that housed more than one hundred men. The beds were so crammed together that Robert felt the raw breath of the man in the next bunk upon his face for most of the night. His brother was thinner than he had been at home and his face was worn and creased with dust. He coughed almost all the time that he was awake. The mines were dark and cramped and the air was bad, his brother said, and the hours so very long. Robert had left after three days, sorrowful at having to leave his brother there, but unable to contain his own relief at the realisation that if that was how life was in the city, he would be happy to remain in the countryside.

The kettle began its high-pitched whine, and Miriam spooned two heaps of the crushed dried tea leaves into the pot, then carried a cup in to her husband.

'Thank you,' he said, but he did not look up.

For a short while they went about their little tasks and, though neither one spoke, Miriam sang softly to herself, a tune that had begun as an old standard but which was being improvised into something longer and sweeter. Omar glanced narrowly at her, being careful not to move his head, or she would see him and stop singing, assuming that she was irritating him. This singing of hers was another thing that he remembered from that balcony in Bombay. He frowned at himself. He was not a man given to sentimentality or nostalgia, but today these memories kept pushing back into his mind. He had gone out on the balcony on the second day to smoke and she had been above him again, singing quietly, unaware that below her someone was listening intently. With a sudden burst of decision, and with the soft tones of her voice still lingering in his head, he had gone back into the apartment and had demanded to know who that girl was.

His aunt had raised her eyes from her sewing. 'What girl?'

'The one that lives above us,' he had said. 'The one that sings and hangs the washing.'

His aunt had shaken her head. 'She is a very pretty girl. But she is not for you.'

He had waited, with impatience, for her to explain herself.

'Her family is very humble,' she had added at last.

'Humility is a good thing.'

'Very *poor*,' she had emphasised.

And Omar had waved his cigarillo dismissively. 'Are they our people?'

'Yes.'

'Then I want her.'

When eventually they heard the approaching rumble of the first truck, they looked up at each other and Miriam moved with the practice of routine out across the shop floor to prop open the door with a small bag of flour.

The truck was driven by Mr Wessels, the foreman of the Van Wingen farm, and he ground the pick-up slowly up the track to the shop. The back of the truck was fully weighed down by his workers. There were perhaps twenty or thirty men crowded onto the back – sitting piled high and hanging over each of the sides, draped over the back like banners, their bodies moving like fluid with the rough movements of the truck. They jumped off lightly when it stopped, a slow overflowing of bodies, mostly clad in worn trousers and shirts. Mr Wessels was already in the shop, shaking hands with Omar, tipping his hat to 'the missus', and telling them it was 'hot as the breath of hell out there', before handing over his own list of groceries to be boxed up. Miriam set to work on these, while the foreman bounded out to the porch and beckoned his men inside.

In they poured, moving slowly, filling every corner, while Robert watched them, a mixture of welcome and warning on his face. He had been told by Omar to watch carefully for anyone who might shop-lift, and he took his duty seriously. The men milled about the shop, selecting their purchases and then stepping up to the counter to have them rung up on the huge metal cash register. A few bought only cold drinks and sat outside on the steps, talking and watching the dust from the truck settle around them.

Omar spoke to Mr Wessels occasionally throughout, but rarely to any of the Africans, except to give a price or clarify a request, although few of the workers asked him anything – often they looked more easily to Miriam to help them. One asked the price of some cloth for a dress for his daughter. When she told him, he shook his head and said it was too much, and could she bring the price down? She lowered it by two pennies as she knew she could, but he held out his poor salary in one roughened hand, and asked her how could he pay so much? She looked at the money in his palm and could not answer him. Miriam glanced at Omar to ask if she might take the price lower, but he looked across at her as he rang up the till and shook his head. She looked helplessly to the man, but he too had seen her husband's response and was already gone.

Robert also helped serve behind the counter, and he chatted now and then with the workers, greeting one or two, and laughing. As she watched him, Miriam felt the prickle of a gaze upon her, and her eyes went to the front of the shop where one of the workers stood apart, drinking from a bottle of Coke and watching her. He looked her up and down, slowly, and she felt the tiny hairs on the back of her neck rise.

'Don't trust the *kaffirs*,' her *bhabhi* had once told her. 'They want only one thing – from their own women, and from white women and Indian women too. They do. And they are strong,' she had added. 'If they attack you, there is nothing you can do. And then there is the syphilis. And God knows what else.' It was only then that Miriam had her first inkling of what had caused her sister-in-law's illness. But when she had asked about Jehan, Farah just laughed and said that Omar and Sadru only preferred to think that Jehan had been raped.

'Your sister-in-law had a *boyfriend*,' Farah had laughed. 'Almost as retarded as she is, for god's sake, but he loved her.'

'Why didn't they get married?' Miriam had wanted to know.

'Because he was a *kaffir*,' Farah told her impatiently. 'He hung around for weeks, until the men in the family caught him and almost beat the life out of him. He had to stay away in the end.'

When she looked up again, the African worker was gone,

replaced in her mind by a brutal vision of kicking and beating, the cold imaginings which had come to her so often after hearing Farah's flippant story. Outside, Mr Wessels was shouting for everyone to get back on the truck. He spoke in English, for Afrikaans was the White language. Omar spoke it – he had learnt it at school here, but the Africans usually only knew enough to comprehend their masters and, if they worked domestically, their White mistresses. Mr Wessels moved among the men, grasping a stick in his hand which he never used, only leaned on, or twirled about, using it as a prop, rather as other men might keep their hands busy with a cigarette. He shooed the workers back onto the truck as though they were so many huge birds, and one by one, they arranged themselves into the back, the last few perched on the sharp edges, keeping alight with a practised sense of balance.

They were relieved when the last truckload had left, and it was still only one o'clock. This pay-day had fallen on a Wednesday, and that meant that they would receive a visit from the sons of their landlord. George and David Kaplan often stopped by the shop 'on their way through' to somewhere, for a pack of cigarettes, or some small item. But in addition they always came by on the last Wednesday afternoon of each month for a social visit that softened the collection of the rent money with talk of politics and weather, and often they brought their wives.

The two Mrs Kaplans held a fascination for Miriam that she could not explain. It seemed to her that they always floated into the shop, bringing with them the slow whisper of a chiffon dress, the soft pastel of their low-heeled pumps, a shimmer of blond hair and the lingering scent of expensive French perfume. Their voices were high and laughing, filled with delight at greeting Miriam, as though she were the one and only thing they could have wished to see upon entering the shop. While their husbands talked business with Omar around the table in the back room, the wives stayed in the shop with Miriam, sipping tea and chatting.

They arrived today at two o'clock, the usual hour, by which time Robert had helped Miriam to set the tea-tray with a fresh cloth, embroidered by her own hand, and three cups and saucers from their best set of dishes. The milk was poured into a china jug that had once belonged to Omar's mother, the white sugar was brought out to replace the everyday brown, and then a replica of the whole tray was set upon a white cloth on the back room table for the men, to whom Robert would serve tea, while Miriam took care of the wives herself. In the kitchen, Robert kept a careful eye on the sponge cakes that were rising gently in the great range oven.

The car pulled up smoothly, and all they had heard of its approach was the slow crunch of the dust and stones beneath the solid tyres – a delicate advance, far removed from the rumble and grind of the farmers' trucks. Miriam sipped from a glass of soda water, trying quickly to overcome the light-headedness and nausea that she had felt in passing waves throughout the day. She looked out at the car, long and black and gleaming. She had no idea what make of car it was – Omar had told her once, as they watched it pull away, but she had forgotten. It was beautiful, though, redolent of a world which Miriam could hardly fathom, and she could only imagine what it must be like to sit ensconced in that shiny casing, sinking into the leather seats, and listening to dance music on the little radio that was fitted into the wooden dashboard.

The men jumped out with alacrity, relieved to stretch their legs, and looked around smiling, content, shrugging on well-fitted jackets before they held open the back doors for the women. The driver remained in the car, with his shirt sleeves rolled up and the windows rolled down, where in due course he would receive his own mug of tea and slice of cake from Robert. The women alighted, stockinged legs emerging first, followed by the swirling dresses of light flowery prints, and Miriam felt nervous suddenly as she stood at the top of the porch steps with her husband. Omar had donned a tie for the occasion, because the Kaplan brothers always wore one. They called hello, and came bounding up the porch stairs, followed by their wives – well dressed, cologned and glamorous, like four players in a Hollywood musical.

They all shook hands and exchanged pleasantries about the weather, the drive, the shop. From habit, the men gravitated towards the back room, and Miriam watched her husband lead them through – he was tall, Omar, taller than either of the others, and his clothes, though not tailored like theirs, looked smart. She felt a brief flicker of pride, pride that he held his own amongst them, and then she turned her full attention to the ladies who rattled on, their conversation as light and frothy as a milkshake.

'And the children?' Martha Kaplan asked, as she sat down.

'How are your gorgeous children? Such beautiful eyes they have – and so well behaved.'

'They are fine, both fine,' said Miriam. 'Getting to be more of a handful every day.'

'How old are they now?'

'Sam is five and Alisha is nearly four.'

Martha Kaplan looked delighted. 'So she's here?' she asked, looking about, but Miriam shook her head.

'She goes with Sam to Springs. They have a playgroup attached to the school. It's good for her. I think she needs to see and do different things everyday. She is so curious; she's into everything.'

'Oh, I know, don't even talk to me about it!' This came from Joyce, always the more dramatic of the two.

Martha Kaplan looked at her sister-in-law, amused. 'Joyce, you know you dote on those children of yours.' She looked at Miriam. 'She can't wait to be occupied with them – I think she wakes up earlier than they do. I, on the other hand, am more than happy to let Jennifer dress them and feed them in the mornings – it's always such a rush before school. I'm not fit to be seen before noon most days.'

They continued in this way for some time, and Miriam looked with genuine interest at the photographs of their children which they produced from their handbags. They had, between them, three boys and a girl; the boys stood together, casual and blond and confident, laughing at the camera; the girl darker haired and pretty, posed in her school uniform.

'David Junior is the image of his father, I think,' said Martha. 'I know he's only ten, but he has such a grown-up air to him sometimes. This morning he came downstairs and asked me to dance with him...'

'They're taking lessons,' interjected Joyce.

'...and it reminded me exactly,' continued Martha, 'of when David first asked me to dance one night at a party. That was when he proposed to me.' She shook her head. 'Those were the days. Romance and love letters and excitement! It feels like another lifetime.'

Miriam smiled and busied herself refreshing the tea cups. Romance, love letters, excitement. She knew nothing of any of these things. Omar's proposal had been conveyed to her through her mother and grandfather and she had not had to make a choice, for they had already accepted on her behalf. Perplexed and worried, she had followed her family into the front room of his uncle's house, demure and well covered, and as she entered, Miriam had caught the faint remnants of his cigar smoke, and it had occurred to her at once that she had been aware of this smell for many weeks now, curling up from the balcony beneath. She had not, during all that time, comprehended it as a single, new aroma. Rather, she had been only dimly aware of it, and had accepted it as a new addition to the mingled, familiar scents of spice and sweat and heat. She had breathed it into her body, unwittingly accepting the insidious invasion of the curling smoke. Her eyes had remained downcast, as was expected of her, throughout the short interview that was held to begin the wedding arrangements, but as she had followed with her eyes the pattern of the brush strokes on the newly swept floor, she had tried to comfort herself with the idea that, because of the intrusion of his cigar smoke, she had actually known this man longer than she had realised and that this tall, handsome stranger, whose eyes she had never yet looked into, was therefore already somehow a part of her.

'Anyway, the romance is always the first thing to go,' sighed Martha. She handed the children's photographs to Miriam who smiled admiringly, although what occurred to her now was that Sam would never be able to be at school or even in the same part of a public park as these boys with blond hair. Had he ever even seen a blond-haired child, she wondered? She decided that he must have, in Springs, around town, but she couldn't be sure.

'Are you all right, dear?' asked Joyce Kaplan, and Miriam looked up and smiled.

'Will you have some more tea?' Miriam asked.

Her bouts of nausea were short, but were becoming more and more frequent as the afternoon wore on, and she felt herself begin to perspire slightly with the effort of entertaining. She felt that the women had been sitting there for an age, and took surreptitious, deep breaths to try to calm her stomach. When she felt almost certain that she could fight it no more, she heard the sound of the men's voices becoming more distinct – a loud laugh and some banter between the Kaplan brothers as they emerged with Omar from the other room.

'Come, my dears, we must be going. We have troubled these good people long enough,' said George Kaplan, extending his arm towards the ladies. They placed their cups carefully back on the tray, picked up their handbags, straightened their dresses – all the little movements required before a leave-taking.

'My dear – your cake...' commented George to Miriam. 'Out of this world, as always.'

'It was very nice, thank you,' added David, placing his hat upon his head.

She smiled, by way of accepting the compliment, and waited as the couples made their way to the door, chatting idly, winding down the visit, reluctant to leave and to be in the heat of the car. She felt her stomach turn once more and pursed her lips against the feeling. So slow the Kaplans were to get into their beautiful vehicle, so slowly the driver turned over the smooth engine. She stood there, fighting the rising bile in her stomach, and she waved as they pulled away, but as soon as they had stirred up enough dust clouds down the track, she turned and ran towards the outhouse, banging through the door and thrusting her aching head over the bowl. She vomited violently, but there was little in her stomach and she could produce nothing more than a few spits of saliva. She waited, leaning her hand against the wall for support. At the door, Omar was knocking tentatively.

'Are you all right?' he asked.

'Okay,' she called, her voice shaky. She waited to hear him go, but still he lingered outside the door. He had done the same thing on the voyage back to South Africa. Their honeymoon. Her sea-sickness had continued without respite for six days before a kind-mannered doctor, from the same area of Bombay as she, had offered her some tablets. These stemmed the sickness at once, but left her with an overwhelming desire to sleep and this sleep she soon learned to dread, for it came to her filled with looming nightmares and wild hallucinations.

She had hardly seen her new husband during that voyage, and it was then that she had first felt the loneliness grasp her; the consciousness that she was sailing away from her mother and her home and her country to live with this unknown man only added to the misery of her sickness. He lacked the instinctive care that might have reassured her, and after he had sat awkwardly with her during the first couple of days, he began to stay away, and his absence was a respite to her. Her joy at seeing land after the interminable ocean was made up mainly of relief – the view itself was obscured by low clouds and the crowds of people milling on the deck in anticipation of disembarking – but it was tinged also with excitement. For despite everything, she was young, and aware of the possibilities that lay before her. It was a new life in a new country – she had felt that she were wiped clean, that her life till now had been a specific, enclosed block, and that now she could start again, a different life in a different place.

He knocked once more. 'Are you all right?'

'I'm fine,' she repeated. 'Go back, the children are coming.'

She could hear the school bus nearing the shop. She stood shivering over the bowl for another minute or two, and passed a thin hand over her stomach. Straightening up, she felt better, and looked down at the slight swell of her abdomen. She held her hand there for a moment and then went back to the house to wash.

Walking back, she saw her children, just off the bus, their legs rushing them like small tumbleweeds up the porch stairs, and into the shop. She knew they would be looking for her and that they would be disconcerted to be greeted only by their father. A moment later, she heard a crashing of broken glass and she was inside the shop in a moment.

It was only an unlit paraffin lamp that the children had upset in their hurry and it lay by the door, the glass in splinters.

'Are you okay?' she asked them, but they didn't hear her, because they were standing, heads down, listening as Omar shouted at them. He asked them if they thought paraffin lamps grew on trees, and did they know how much they cost, and why were they always running everywhere, and didn't they look where they were going? Miriam listened quietly, as they did, and when it was over, she saw that they were on the verge of tears and she nodded at them to go upstairs, and then went behind the counter for the broom and dust pan and began to clear the broken glass. Omar paced irritably and watched her.

'Robert can do that,' he told her. She continued sweeping.

'What happened?' he asked, his tone short.

She looked up from where she worked, picking out the larger shards with her fingers.

'Out there.' He nodded towards the outhouse. 'Are you sick?'

'Yes,' she said.

He paused. 'What is it? Something you ate?'

She stood up, holding the full dust pan out in front of her. She didn't feel like telling him about the baby now. She knew he was irritable with himself for losing his temper with the children, but she was also tired. The day had been long, she had yet to prepare the dinner, and she still felt ill. She dropped the glass into an open wad of newspaper which she folded up and held for a moment in her hand.

'It was nothing,' she said, and she dropped the wrapped glass into the bin. Robert had appeared and was reaching for the broom. She pointed to where the lamp had fallen so that he could finish sweeping there while Omar stood behind the counter, frowning and restless. He wanted desperately to do or say something that would stop her being so cold towards him but he found he could not move, except to take out his cash books from beneath the counter, and he could not speak, except to ask her when dinner would be ready.

'Soon,' she said, turning away towards the kitchen. 'It will be ready soon.'

He nodded, and went into the back room to start balancing his books, turning his head just a moment too late to watch his wife's slim figure disappear into her kitchen.

Chapter Four

Springs, December 1952

AMINA'S GRANDMOTHER HAD had her first glimpse of her granddaughter on a Thursday afternoon, and by the time she had awoken on Friday morning it had become unmistakably clear to her that she had been sent from India to this horrible place by God's own will, and for one purpose only – to see her granddaughter safely married. Amina's appearance that day had conveyed to the old lady the worst possible impression. Her worn, practical clothes were not only irretrievably masculine, but they also made it evident that she worked for a living – at what, she wasn't yet sure, though she would make it her business to find out very soon. As if her clothes were not enough to cause offence, the confidence with which she walked into the house was unbecoming; her general attitude seemed to acknowledge that she was different from other people, but to say that she was somehow still very much at ease with herself. Something was very wrong, and the old woman had wasted little time in upbraiding her son, beginning that same evening at dinner, but his responses were slow and lacked the concern and urgency that she felt were warranted.

'What does she do all day?' the old lady asked, changing tack from the stream of chastisement, which seemed to be useless in producing any effect.

'She works,' said Mr Harjan listlessly, his spoon moving in a steady repetition from his plate to his mouth.

'I know she works,' snapped his mother, irritably. 'That much is obvious from her clothes. What kind of girl runs around in trousers all day? Doesn't she have any *shalwaar kameez*?'

'Yes,' offered Mrs Harjan, timidly. 'They are upstairs. But she never wears them.'

The old lady listened to the reply, but gave no indication of having done so to Amina's mother. She continued to look at her son, who continued to eat, an impassive look on his worn face.

'Where is she? Why isn't she at home? Where is she sleeping at night?'

Mr Harjan sighed. 'She works in Pretoria. It is too far for her to travel everyday. So she has a room there.'

Amina's grandmother put a dramatic hand to her chest as though to subdue the shock.

'Is she living with a good family at least?' she asked. Mr Harjan glanced at his wife for the first time that evening, and she nodded, very slightly, and then turned crimson when the old lady turned

to her suddenly, trying to catch what was occurring between
them.

'Yes,' lied Mr Harjan, looking down at his plate again. 'She's
with a good family,' and he thought briefly of the single room
built behind her café that Amina occupied most nights. He had
only seen it once, and her enthusiasm had been so infectious, and
her reasons so logical that it had not occurred to him to forbid
her from leaving his house without being married until he had
heard the disapproval of others in his community.

Several 'friends' had arrived in Springs, in a kind of organised
demonstration, to tell them that it would be an unheard of
scandal, even by Amina's standards, if their daughter should
think of starting a business with a Coloured man. Amina's father
had missed most of these friendly visits from his community
by pretending to be hard at work in his gas station, despite the
fact that only four or five customers ever stopped there during a
day. It was not his custom or his pleasure to listen to gossip or
instructions from people who were strangers to him, even if they
did share the same skin colour, or religion, or traditions.

And by this time, Amina was already used to living away from
home, and he did not have the strength, or the will, or even the
wish, deep down, to fight her. He thought of her business – it
was doing well, she said – and of Jacob Williams, a good man,
whom he liked.

He became aware again of his mother's voice, harping at him
on his left side and he looked at her, watched her round mouth
working hard, producing sounds that he did not even hear. He
wondered how his father, a mild, quiet man, who had died at the

age of fifty-three of a liver disease, had coped with the continual sound of her voice, complaining and gossiping day after day. He tried to remember the sound of his mother's laughter, tried to remember when he had ever heard her laugh, but he could not.

This girl, her only granddaughter, was obviously running wild in this wild country, the old lady told him, with occasional pointed looks at Amina's mother, and it was his responsibility to do something. He nodded wearily and hoped that she would not remember to ask again what it was that his daughter did for a living. That her granddaughter worked was bad enough, but the fact that she was running her own business with a Coloured man, and that her other odd jobs were mostly manual, would be too much for the old lady to cope with.

'We have to begin now,' she said decisively. 'She must get married.'

The idea of her only granddaughter's marriage had of course been at the back of her mind since the day of Amina's birth and had often taken more detailed shape in the form of her daydreams, in which she herself had played the starring role, accepting the congratulations, good wishes and general adulation of all her friends and family at the marvellous match she had managed to make for her granddaughter, while overcoming the handicap of her daughter-in-law's scandalous family history. Over the years, such dreams had provided her with an undemanding way to use up the long, hot afternoons at home in Bombay. But now the marriage had become an absolute necessity, a deliverance from evil, and it must occur soon if the girl was ever to be brought back to a decent way of living. It was clear that she had totally gone to seed since leaving India. Besides, twenty-two or twenty-three was more than long enough for a girl to be single. It was over-long in fact, but Amina still looked young, and could pass, she decided, for being nearer to twenty.

'She must get married,' she repeated. The two pallid faces of her son and daughter-in-law looked up at her. 'She must. And soon.'

Mrs Harjan murmured something about how it might be a good thing; perhaps Amina needed to settle down. She was tired of her mother-in-law's voice, and was beginning to feel eroded by the constant wash of arguments lapping inside her head.

'I'm glad you see sense,' nodded the old lady, to Mrs Harjan. 'You see,' she said, turning back to her son. 'We women understand these things. You should leave such matters to us.'

'I have. I have left my daughter's affairs to her.' It was his first strong sentence, and it spilt from him almost involuntarily, under the weight of a headache that seemed to him to be caused by the thumping echoes of all his mother's words trapped inside his brain.

The old lady seemed not to notice the irony that he had pointed out.

'That's different,' she said, as though the difference were so obvious she need never explain it.

It was not in her son to ask her how it was different, or to stand up to his mother for any more than the two seconds it had taken him to utter that sentence, so he merely watched and listened as his mother outlined her plan for Amina. The boy she had in mind was the son of the Ali family. The father had been her husband's friend back in India, before they had emigrated to South Africa fifteen years ago.

'They are in Pretoria, and the mother came to see me last week. We will have them to dinner,' stated the old lady.

The idea of people coming for dinner seemed to throw both her son and daughter-in-law off balance. Mrs Harjan had no idea how to cope with people for dinner – it had been so long since they had invited anyone. What to cook, what to wear, what to talk about? Mr Harjan was simply unhappy at the thought of strange people in his house, especially people who would be coming expressly to weigh himself and his wife up as prospective in-laws, and his daughter as a prospective wife. This last thought jolted him into speech.

'Amina will never come,' he said.

His mother stared as though he had suggested that the world might stop turning.

'It is not up to Amina,' she explained with impatience. 'She is your daughter and my granddaughter. It is her duty to be where we tell her. She will come,' she added, and sat back with a satisfied air, her plump hands folded on her lap. Mrs Harjan rose to clear the dishes. Her maid, Rosemary, gathered them from her in unenthusiastic silence and began to wash them at the sink.

Mr Harjan did not argue the point regarding his daughter any further. He knew she would not attend a dinner in order to be introduced to a suitable boy. He also knew that she did not seem to be in a hurry to get married and if he was completely honest with himself, this suited him very well. He was a man of routine, who disliked noise and disruption, and people outside his immediate family. That was one of the main reasons he had moved to Springs, rather than staying in Pretoria. Here there was no extended family, no helpful community of friends and neighbours always ready to drop in at the slightest excuse. There were other Indian families, but they were widely scattered, and they did not live on top of each other. He disliked anyone with whom he was uncomfortable, and he was comfortable with no one except his wife. Amina's marriage to anyone, however suitable, would mean an endless stream of visits from his son-in-law and his family. They would probably have several children, too, who would run riot through his house. No, he disliked the idea of his daughter's marriage much more than he disliked his community's disapproval, and Amina in her turn had long been grateful for her father's introverted habits and hatred of change, for it gave her an easier route to a freedom she would otherwise never have had.

Amina was surprised to get a telephone call at the café from her mother a few weeks later, and had immediately assumed that some emergency was at hand. The black telephone stood on a table in her parents' house like a squat little god, whose workings they could not begin to comprehend, and which they disturbed only on rare occasions. Amina listened carefully to her mother as she asked her to come to the house for dinner the following Sunday night.

'What is happening on Sunday?' she asked, puzzled.

There was a silence at the other end.

'Mum?'

'Nothing is happening, Amina,' her mother said. Amina held the receiver a small distance away from her ear, because her mother had a habit of shouting into it. Mrs Harjan had never had a telephone in India and could not overcome her certainty that the very words that she uttered had to make a long physical journey all the way down the wires to reach her daughter.

'Are you sure?' Amina asked, because even with her voice raised, Mrs Harjan did not speak with much conviction.

'Your grandmother wants to see you. You haven't spent much time with her, you know,' she added reproachfully. Amina sighed. She had little desire to see her grandmother at all, but she felt guilty.

'Okay, I'll be there. Maybe I'll come a bit early and help you,' she added.

'Good,' yelled her mother, relieved. There was a pause. 'We are having some people, you know. It is your grandmother's idea.'

'Okay. What shall I bring?'

'Nothing, nothing, you bring me too much already,' Mrs Harjan called. 'Your father is already wondering where all the *chapati* flour is coming from.'

Amina smiled into the receiver. 'So I'll see you on Sunday?'

'Yes. Amina?'

'Mum?'

There was a silence, and then a crackle on the line. 'Nothing,' said Mrs Harjan finally. 'See you on Sunday.'

Amina arrived for dinner half an hour late, which was not how the evening was supposed to have started. Her grandmother had spent the week nurturing a vision of her granddaughter carefully and demurely dressed in a *shalwaar kameez*, perhaps in a nice pastel shade of lavender or pink, helping her mother in the kitchen before coming out to receive their guests and meet their son. This vision had trickled down in a diluted form to Amina's mother, so that Mrs Harjan had spent two hours on Saturday afternoon with the old lady, picking out suitable outfits for Amina to wear at dinner. Amina's father had arrived back from work and had watched the two women in placid silence for a few moments before going back downstairs to read his newspaper, leaving them with a look that clearly expressed his belief that they had both gone mad.

The guests were already sipping at cold drinks in the living room when Amina finally arrived. Her grandmother was too angry with the girl to even look up when they heard the rumbling of the truck wheels and the slam of the door outside. They heard a snatch of a jazz tune being hummed in the hallway, and Mrs Harjan smiled faintly at her guests and hurried outside.

Amina greeted her with a smile and an apology for being late. She was dressed in her work clothes and her hair looked more tangled and curly than usual. She followed the line of her mother's gaze and touched her head.

'I got caught in that rainstorm this afternoon,' she said guiltily.

Mrs Harjan said nothing, but her eyes widened in panic.

'I just need to have a quick bath, Mum,' Amina said. 'I'm sorry I'm late,' she added, but there was no response – her mother seemed to be struck mute with distress.

'You'd better go back.' Amina nodded towards the living room, where she could hear her grandmother's voice giving an opinion about something. Mrs Harjan sighed quietly and turned away.

When Amina emerged from the bathroom, she was surprised to see her mother standing silently on the landing.

'Mum! You scared me,' Amina said. She walked past her mother and into her own room, without even noticing the pale pink outfit that Mrs Harjan held up in her hands.

'Amina,' said Mrs Harjan, following her in, and still holding the outfit aloft.

This time Amina saw it, but seemed not to make any connection between the flowing pink cloth and her own undressed body. An understanding slowly began to dawn and Amina backed away, with a disbelieving smile.

'No, no,' she said. 'I'm not going to wear that.'

'Please,' answered Mrs Harjan. 'To please your grandmother.'

'No.'

'She's *old*, Amina.'

Amina failed to see the correlation between her grandmother's age and her own style of dress, but she took the outfit from her mother and looked at it.

'Please,' said Mrs Harjan again, sensing an indecision on Amina's part.

Amina disliked wearing such clothes mainly because she was not comfortable in them, but as she looked from her mother's pleading eyes to the suit, she decided that she could put up with discomfort for one evening. To make herself feel better, she thought with relief of her own bed in her own room behind her café, where she would be in a few hours, when this evening was over. She smiled.

'Okay,' she said. 'I'll wear it. Go down, I'll come.'

Her grandmother was pleasantly surprised at the sight of the *shalwaar kameez* when Amina walked into the room. She was a tall, striking girl, who looked well in whatever she wore, and the old lady looked pointedly and with some pride at the parents of the boy. They, too, looked satisfied and not a little surprised at Amina's appearance. Her father merely seemed relieved that Amina had appeared at last, and without further ceremony told Mrs Harjan to start serving the food. This instruction provided Amina, who had said nothing since entering, with a welcome escape from the eyes in that room, and she followed her mother to the kitchen where she silently helped her to spoon various curries from steaming pots into serving dishes.

'You look nice,' offered Mrs Harjan as she handed Amina a full plate. She spoke nervously for she knew her daughter's silences and was afraid of them. Amina nodded, but still did not speak, for she was inwardly digesting the information that she had gathered from the one look she had taken around that room. She had entered and greeted her grandmother and had seen her pleasure at the outfit – that had not surprised her. The triumphant look that her grandmother had given their guests had not escaped her either, however, and when she saw their son, a youth of about her age whom she remembered vaguely from some community gathering a few years ago, sitting stiffly in his best suit and tie, regarding her as though she were a piece of porcelain to be evaluated, she realised that she had been set up to meet a suitable boy.

'Amina...' her mother began, but Amina had already gone into the next room with two filled dishes which she placed on the carefully laid table. She was angry – with her grandmother, whose idea this undoubtedly was; with her parents for allowing her to attend this dinner without warning; and with herself for not realising this possibility much earlier. She paused by the table, listening to her grandmother's voice in the other room, asking the boy a long stream of questions. He answered firmly and with a deep, commanding voice. Amina was not a person who enjoyed anger, nor did she ever hold onto it for very long – she had always had the ability to see a whole series of alternatives to whatever situation she might be in, a quality that made it difficult for her to find anything too upsetting for long. Now as she stood by the table and listened, she knew that nothing fundamental in her life would ever change unless she wanted it to; her financial independence and her own self-confidence had seen to that, so what was the use, she decided, in being angry? Her mother's collusion bothered her still, but as her glance wandered over the table she noticed that, as careful as her mother had tried to be in her place settings, she had reversed the knives and forks, placing them on the wrong sides of each plate. Amina smiled to herself and moved around the table, switching each set of cutlery, before she returned to the kitchen to collect more of the food.

By the end of the main course, the boy had still only regarded Amina furtively, but now he was made bolder by her open gaze, and he relaxed enough to venture a few words in her direction. At the start of the meal he had made a move to take off his jacket, and had stopped, feeling obliged to keep it on. Amina had caught him in mid-decision, and she had nodded briefly, a nod of empathy, underlaid with permission, and he had stared at her, surprised, and then he had removed the jacket and hung it over the back of his chair.

He looked better without the ill-fitting coat – his shirt was clean and ironed, and showed broad, well-filled shoulders. He was not bad-looking, Amina decided. A strong chin and broad forehead. He did not seem to her to be particularly intelligent, however, and when he did manage to speak, he deferred to his parents on all matters. These observations were made to fill up her time, for she was not expected to speak unless spoken to, and she was spoken to very little, for her grandmother soon realised that the less that was said about Amina's daily life the better. The old lady could not draw attention to Amina's accomplishments in cookery or cleaning or needlework, as she did not seem to have any. Her 'work' – and here the old woman remembered that she was still not sure what her granddaughter did for a living, and made a mental note to ask her son later – was not a subject to be brought up before prospective in-laws. It was unseemly and in any event, irrelevant, since after she was married she would no longer be running around working. She thought it prudent to point this out in her own rambling way to the boy and his family.

'I think young girls are just as happy to stay at home these days as they were when I was married. I don't know why people say they are too modern. They may go out and want to see things for themselves for a while, but I think our girls always find it better to stay at home in the end.'

Amina coughed, while the visiting parents looked surprised, and the boy's mother leaned forward to examine Amina as though her interest had suddenly been caught.

'Doesn't Amina work any more then?' she asked Mrs Harjan.

Amina looked with interest from the visitors to her mother, as though waiting for the next line of dialogue in a bad play. Mrs Harjan stuttered something inaudible, and shrank back in her chair until her mother-in-law took over.

'Of course, she works now and then,' her grandmother said smoothly. 'But she is with a very good family.'

Confusion settled over everyone at the table. 'A family?' asked the boy. 'What about the caf...'

'Why isn't anybody eating?' called Mr Harjan. He had not actually noticed whether anyone was eating or not, but could not face a scene at the table with his mother, before these people, about Amina's work. He shot a warning glance to his daughter, but for once she seemed in no mood to stand up for herself. Mr Harjan was relieved and yet found himself frowning, hardly recognising his daughter in the young woman who sat low in her seat, with a look of resignation about her face.

'Amina,' he said sharply. 'Give your Uncle some more rice.'

Amina sat up at once and carefully held the serving plate for the guests. Mr Harjan continued to talk loudly, dominating the conversation with details of his garage, and asking them about their business (a clothing shop) until at last the subject of his daughter seemed to have been left behind.

In the meantime, Amina's mind wandered far and wide. She stifled a yawn and suddenly realised that a question had been asked and still hung in the air, unanswered. She looked up to find that everyone was looking at her. She took in all the faces at the table, and then fixed her gaze on the boy.

'Did you ask me something?' she said.

A look of mild panic crossed his face. 'No,' he said, hesitantly. 'That is . . . my mother was asking how many children you would like.'

Amina looked at him blankly.

'I mean . . . do you want a large family?' he asked, blushing, but determined to finish his attempt at conversation.

'I don't know,' she replied. 'I haven't thought about it much, but perhaps two or three children would be nice. If I were going to have them. But I think that would be something to decide with your husband, wouldn't it?'

'Yes, I suppose,' said the boy, smiling. 'Do you want only boys?' he asked, pleased to be able to talk with her at last.

'Why do you assume I would want boys at all?' she asked him, and his eyes widened in surprise and he looked down at his plate, embarrassed. The old lady moved swiftly in.

'What rubbish!' she told Amina. 'Everybody wants a boy first. Everybody.'

Amina glanced at her mother, who had never given birth to a boy, and saw her shrinking in her seat again.

'I am not everybody,' Amina told her grandmother in a clear voice. 'I am not everybody, and I wouldn't care if I had a boy or a girl as long as the child was healthy and happy. Anything else does not matter.'

This drew an audible breath of disapproval from Mrs Ali, who exchanged knowing glances with her husband.

'I think she's right,' volunteered the boy, breaking the silence.

'I think it's time we were leaving,' said his father at once. 'I have to work very early tomorrow.'

'But you haven't had any sweets yet,' said Mrs Harjan desperately, rising from the table. Amina rose with her and helped her clear away the plates.

In the kitchen, Mrs Harjan plaintively asked her daughter what she thought she was doing, and began to plead with her to behave well and not to embarrass them.

'Mum...'

'Please, Amina.'

'Mum, I'm just trying to explain. Don't you see?' She took hold of her mother's arm and turned the reluctant woman towards her.

'Did you really think I would marry this boy?' Amina asked slowly. She held onto her mother's shoulder and looked into her eyes for some sign of understanding, but when her mother finally looked up, all that Amina saw there was a cold bitterness.

'My mother ruined you,' Mrs Harjan said, in a whisper that was almost a hiss. Amina took a step back under the unaccustomed hatred of her mother's look.

'She ruined *my* life by what she did,' continued Mrs Harjan. 'I grew up as an outcast that nobody wanted...'

'My father wanted you...'

'I was *lucky*,' she spat, as though this luck were something she took no joy in. 'And now she is ruining you, even from beyond the grave, and she is ruining me all over again. How can I look those people in the face? Her talk of bravery and being smart and looking after yourself. She has made you into what you are, and you are...'

'I like what I am,' said Amina.

The sentence was spoken with such conviction that Mrs Harjan was left silenced. Amina had interrupted instinctively, not wanting to hear her mother's evaluation of her. She watched her for a moment, her face drawn into a frown of sorrow and puzzlement. She was hurt by her mother's words and appalled by the depth of her resentment towards Begum.

'Did you really think I would marry this boy?' Amina said again, but this time her tone held no plea for understanding, and in her own ears, her voice sounded harsh.

But Mrs Harjan had collapsed into herself again under the clear light of her daughter's gaze. She held out a plate of Indian sweetmeats, gaudily coloured and decorated, and she met Amina's eyes for only a second before she looked down again.

'Your grandmother thinks you should marry whoever she chooses,' she said. Amina closed her eyes for a moment, then took hold of the plate and went back inside.

Chapter Five

Delhof, April 1953

OMAR WAITED IN silence in the kitchen, at the foot of the stairs, straining to hear any sound from the room above. It had been two hours since he had heard anything of the women who had taken over the upstairs of his house. He held his breath, listening hard, and almost at once there came the scraping of a chair on the floorboards above, and the click of a door handle. Hastily he moved away, through the kitchen and into the shop.

When Mrs Benjamin appeared in the doorway, she found him poring over his cash books, with a pencil in his hand and a frown of concentration on his face, as though he were in the middle of some particularly difficult calculations.

'Hello, Mister Husband,' she called to him in her sing-song

accent. He glanced up with a calculated look of surprise, and waited to hear what she had to say. Mrs Benjamin was a stout, old Coloured woman, renowned in this part of the country as a midwife. She was the aunt of Mr Morris, the farmer who was their nearest neighbour, whose eggs and milk Omar sold in the shop. So when Miriam, six months into her third pregnancy, had tentatively sent word via Mr Morris's housekeeper that she would like a good midwife, Mrs Benjamin had appeared at her door and assured her that when her time came, she would be there to assist. Omar had driven over to Mr Morris's place at dawn that morning to ask for her, because his wife had been awake and in some pain for much of the night. Mrs Benjamin had arrived an hour later with a smile and a covered basket containing what looked to Omar like various home-made medicines and oils. Farah had come to the house soon afterwards, bearing a plate of biryani and a weary expression, in order to play the part of the solicitous sister-in-law.

'How is the father-to-be?' Mrs Benjamin enquired jovially.

'Fine.' Omar frowned slightly. This joking familiarity of Mrs Benjamin's disconcerted him.

'Why don't you go on up and say hello to your Missus?' she suggested.

'Is she all right?' asked Omar, suspicious.

'She's tip-top. But you should say hello. Keep her spirits up. Send your sister-in-law down to me, and we'll make everyone some tea.'

Omar nodded, secretly comforted by the detailed instructions, and closed the cash book which he now realised lay opened before him upside down. He followed the midwife into the kitchen, where she was already filling the kettle, but before he reached the stairs the old lady called him back.

'Here,' she said, and when he turned all he could see was her ample backside, because her head was peering into his ice box. She straightened up, and held out a bottle of Coke.

'Take this to your young lady,' she said. 'The sugar will give her energy.'

He nodded again and took the drink, feeling on his sweaty hands the cold beads of water that coated the bottle, and he walked slowly up the stairs. He was not eager to go to his wife's room, partly because he wished to avoid Farah but mostly because he did not know what to say to Miriam when she was in pain.

Omar knocked at the door and waited – it opened to reveal his sister-in-law's sardonic face. He was immediately irritated and walked into the room purposefully, pausing at his wife's bedside. She was well covered up, in anticipation of his visit, and she only smiled when he asked her how she was.

'Sit down,' Farah suggested, her hand on the back of the chair. Omar ignored her and remained standing. Miriam looked pale, her hair damp with sweat and her eyes dark with circles. He looked at her, helpless and distant, and his eyes wandered to the window.

'Mrs Benjamin is making tea,' he offered, finally. He looked at Farah, remembering his instructions. 'She said you should go and help her,' he added.

'Oh, did she?'

'Yes.'

'How hard is it to make tea?' Farah grumbled, but she moved reluctantly to the door. She did not close it fully behind her, and neither Omar nor Miriam said a word until they heard her descend, and caught the sharp tones of her voice echoing with Mrs Benjamin's downstairs in the kitchen.

With some relief, Omar remembered the Coke bottle that he still held in his hand. He offered it to his wife.

'Here. Mrs Benjamin says it will give you energy.'

'Thank you,' Miriam said. 'Can you open it for me?'

He took back the bottle and prised off the cap, and Miriam shifted upwards in the bed so that she could take a sip. She winced with sudden pain.

'Shall I call her?' asked Omar, alarmed.

'No, no. It's fine.'

They waited together in silence for a while.

'Mrs Benjamin thinks it will be a boy,' Miriam told him.

'Good. How does she know?'

'From the shape of my stomach.'

Omar smiled slightly and shook his head at the foolishness of women, and Miriam laughed.

'You want a boy, don't you?' she asked him.

'Yes, but... I'll just wait and see. I don't believe in these things... Old wives' tales,' he said.

'Sit down,' offered Miriam, for when he was pleasant like this she liked to talk with him. He hesitated, though, and moved back a step.

'I have to go back to the shop,' he said and she nodded, disappointed.

He opened the door just in time for Mrs Benjamin, who announced her arrival with a lilting call on the landing.

'Coming in, coming in!' she shouted. She was breathing heavily from the exertion of the stairs, and handed the tea tray to Omar with relief. He placed it down, then excused himself. Mrs Benjamin looked unhappy that Mister Husband was leaving so soon, but his mind appeared to be made up, and he disappeared back down the stairs, closing the door behind him.

'He is a strange one, your hubby,' Mrs Benjamin told her patient. She picked up the tea-pot and swirled the steaming liquid around. 'Doesn't have much time for a chat, does he?'

'No,' replied Miriam. 'He doesn't have much time for a chat.'

The mere idea of her husband chatting almost brought a smile to her lips. But in truth, she was depressed, and disappointed that he had not stayed with her a while. The shop was all he ever thought about.

'Shame, it doesn't matter,' said Mrs Benjamin cheerfully. 'He's a busy man, and running a business and all – he has a lot on his mind. And anyway, men are like that.' Miriam nodded and then gasped with pain. Mrs Benjamin took a peek beneath the sheets, checked her watch, and squeezed Miriam's hand.

'It'll be over soon,' she said. 'In the meantime, have some tea.'

Omar went directly to the doorway that led into the shop, to check for customers.

'There's nobody there,' Farah informed him from the kitchen. 'I don't know who you think is going to come flooding in to buy groceries at this time of the day.' She glanced from the window at the empty landscape beyond the shop. 'Or at any time,' she added, with distaste.

She turned to offer him tea, but her tone had needled him and he had already gone into the shop and busied himself so that he would not have to see her in Miriam's kitchen. Within a few minutes, though, she followed him in and came directly to where he stood behind the counter. He looked at her, surprised. She deposited a cup of grey-looking tea beside him, and then touched his shirt.

'You have a button missing,' she said, and looked up into his face, her fingertip resting on the tiny piece of thread that frayed out from the shirt. She looked around.

'Where is the boy?' she asked.

'Robert?'

'Of course.'

He almost lied and told her that he was working outside and might come in at any moment, but she seemed to have immobilised him with that one brazen touch of her finger.

'He's gone to visit his family. Until tomorrow.'

This finger, this touch of his shirt was a liberty his own sister would not have taken and Omar found that he could not move. They faced each other for a long moment, like silent adversaries, but she did not remove her hand, only let it travel slowly down the thin material.

'I should check the others,' she said, watching his eyes carefully, and he looked down and waited while her finger paused at each button in turn, her touch becoming firmer and bolder with each stop. He closed his eyes and tried to think of his wife, but she appeared to him now in his mind as a stranger, someone whose features he could conjure up in a moment, but whose thoughts were a mystery to him. He had never known how to speak to her, how to hold a conversation with her – or with any woman. He was not a good listener by nature, even with other men, nor had he been brought up to regard a woman as a real companion of any kind.

Farah's hand was at his belt now, and he breathed in sharply and turned away from the smell of her perfume, applied with too-liberal a hand that morning.

'What are you doing?' he asked her, his tone bad-tempered.

She gave a slight, mocking sound. 'Has it been so long that you don't know any more?'

He pulled away slightly, made stronger by her sarcasm, which was a grating reminder of all that he disliked about her; but she stepped towards him again, her hands moving downwards.

'I don't suppose she lets you touch her when she's pregnant, does she?' Farah asked.

Omar said nothing.

'It's difficult anyway when a woman is that size.' She took hold of his hand, put it around her waist and leaned against him, and he closed his eyes so that he couldn't see her. He could see nothing, could only feel the plumpness of her breasts pushing against him.

'Has it been a long time?' she asked again, and again he would not answer, but was stunned at her boldness. He was no longer angry, but his mouth was dry and he felt dizzy. He frowned, and drew her to him with the hand that was imprisoned behind her, and pulled her roughly into the back room.

*

Farah was gone by the time the children arrived back from school. Omar had not been able to bear the sight of her after a while and had made her leave, but even now there seemed to be no escape. Her too-sweet perfume lingered about him, on his clothes, on his skin, and he went upstairs to try to wash off whatever he could of the smell. He did not think about what he had done, nor did he think about the date he had made with her for the following Tuesday, when he would be due to drive into Pretoria for business anyway. He did not think about his brother, working away from home as a fruit trader in Johannesburg all week; but the thought of his own wife pushed into his mind, for he could hear her in the bedroom, struggling hard with the delivery. He reasoned to himself that it would be a relief for Miriam if he took his sexual requirements elsewhere for, although she never protested, she rarely seemed welcoming of his advances any more, or satisfied by them, and he knew he was usually too quick for her. He did not know what to do to please her, and it was not a topic they could ever discuss. His sister-in-law seemed only too happy with him, though, and it felt reassuring to be wanted by someone, even Farah. He splashed off the remains of the coaltar soap with lukewarm water and went back down to the shop.

He had forgotten about his children coming home from school. As he entered the shop, they were running up the stairs of the *stoep*, racing each other. They stopped dead at the entrance, their wide brown eyes scanning the room for their mother. When their search was unsuccessful, their gazes reverted to him, and he watched them also and wondered inwardly what he would do with them until their bedtime. They seemed reluctant to enter into the room where there was only this familiar but unknown man awaiting them.

'Do you live here?' he asked, after a moment.

Sam and Alisha looked at each other as if conferring.

'Yes,' said Alisha, finally, for though she was the younger, she was also the bolder of the two. Both children giggled.

'Then you should come in,' said Omar, as though they were guests who had arrived for tea.

He turned and went into the kitchen, and the children followed him. He looked around, trying to remember whether they ate when they came home, or what it was that they did. As he strode about, looking at the bread from that morning's breakfast, and opening the saucepan of food Farah had left, an idea occurred to him. He turned to the children, who were watching his movements with some interest.

'Homework,' he said, with an air of slight triumph. 'That's what you do when you come home, isn't it?'

Sam nodded.

'Good,' said Omar, more to himself than to them, and he picked up the plates that had remained on the table since breakfast, and placed them in the sink, where Robert would wash them when he returned the next day. He disliked mess, it disoriented him, and he wrapped up the bread in waxed paper, and straightened the bench. He then pointed at it and the children sat down, reluctantly taking their books from their satchels. Once they were sitting down, Alisha spoke.

'I don't have any homework.'

'Why not?'

'I'm only four,' she informed him. 'You don't get homework until big school.'

'Oh.'

Alisha regarded her father, and seemed to feel some pity for his confusion.

'I can make a picture,' she offered. 'With my crayons.'

Omar looked pleased. 'Good,' he said, and he waited while they arranged themselves at the end of the kitchen table.

'Where's Mummy?' his son asked, and Omar stared at him. He had not anticipated this most obvious of questions and he was unsure of how to answer.

'She's upstairs,' he said, a moment before they heard Miriam shout in pain. The children looked at him, fearful. Sam began to cry. Omar stared at them, uncertain of what to do.

'What are you crying for?' he asked his son finally. He was answered by a continued sobbing and he saw his daughter's mouth begin to tremble.

'She's fine,' he said, desperately. 'Your mother is fine. She's having the baby, that's all.'

The crying stopped, to be replaced with wonderment at this unexpected development.

'Why is the baby hurting Mummy?' asked Alisha. Omar sighed, and sat down at the table. He passed his hands through his hair and thought hard.

'It's not hurting her,' he said, talking firmly over the sounds emanating from upstairs. 'It's just that having the baby is a bit difficult. It won't be long. You'll see.'

Sam watched his father closely. 'Is that how Mummy felt when she had me?'

Omar nodded, and the child's eyes began to fill up again.

'No!' he said, back-pedalling as quickly as he could. 'I mean, it was difficult for your mother, but she didn't mind, because she had you – and Alisha – afterwards.'

'How small was I, Daddy?'

The word 'Daddy' seemed to surprise Omar for a moment – it had been a long time since he had heard it. It had been a long time since he had spoken to either of his children except to give them an order. He looked at his daughter, with her short hair and huge dark eyes and button nose. That was his wife's child, he thought to himself – the resemblance was astounding. He held his hands about a foot apart.

'You were about this big,' he said. 'With the smallest toes in the world.'

This made the children laugh, and Sam wanted to know who had been bigger as a new-born. Omar had no idea, but he told the boy that he had been the bigger, and that that was because he was a boy and because he would grow up tall and strong.

'So will I,' said Alisha and Omar looked at her, surprised at the feisty tone of his daughter's words.

There was a thumping above them as Mrs Benjamin began her descent.

'Hello, Mister Husband!' she called as soon as the family were in sight. She gazed with great satisfaction at the three of them sitting around the table. 'Or should I say, Mister Father!'

Omar stood up and the old lady nodded. 'Yes, it's all over, everything's fine, they're both tip-top.'

'Is it a boy?' he asked.

'What a question!' Mrs Benjamin exclaimed, glancing at Alisha. Omar looked down at his feet.

'It's a beautiful, healthy girl,' she told him, and he nodded and looked to his children, but they offered no support; they only looked back, waiting for some sign from him. He turned back to Mrs Benjamin, forced a smile, and tried to mutter something approving, before she told him to go upstairs and see his wife.

Chapter Six

Delhof, May 1953

THEY ROSE EARLIER than usual on the first Sunday in May, to journey to Pretoria for lunch with Omar's family. During the previous week, Miriam had found out that Rehmat, Omar's other sister, was due to arrive back in South Africa. Since her marriage, she had heard nothing of Rehmat from her husband; all her information had been gleaned from the slim shards of gossip passed to her secretly by Farah. In fact, Miriam had almost forgotten that Rehmat had ever existed at all, which was a state of affairs her husband seemed to prefer. Unexpectedly, however, Omar had received a short letter from Paris, a slim airmail missive that had stood out from the sturdy brown envelopes of their usual mail like a delicate blue flower. Miriam had admired the exotic stamps and the words 'Par Avion' that were stamped across the paper, and had pictured the letter being written with a silver fountain pen upon a polished wooden bureau in a tasteful French salon so very far away. She had looked to Omar for an explanation, but he had only frowned as he ripped open the letter, and had frowned harder after reading the meagre lines. It was only three days later that he told her that his sister Rehmat would be arriving in Pretoria that weekend.

This lunch was to welcome her, but it was not to be a large, extended affair; there was to be no showing off, or overt demonstrations of devotion for the benefit of friends and neighbours. It would be only the brothers and their wives, and Jehan in her back room. Still, considering that her in-laws all seemed to spend their lives pretending that she did not exist, Miriam was amazed that any effort was being made at all in Rehmat's honour, but she was curious to meet her other sister-in-law. She had seen her picture once. It was a photograph that stood on a chipped coffee table in Sadru's house, on a hand-crocheted doily that was yellowed from the shafts of sunlight that had fallen onto it every day over the past two decades. The picture was fading too, and had two illegible words scrawled in one corner – a date and a place perhaps. Omar, Sadru and Rehmat were standing against a car, squinting into the sun. Omar was smiling, his arms crossed as he leaned back – he must have been about nineteen, and Rehmat was watching him, laughing, her face in profile showing the planes of angular cheekbones and a straight, pointed nose. Miriam had looked at that picture so often, for there were many aspects that drew her to it – the feeling of the sun on those young, laughing people, or perhaps her husband's relaxed attitude, so alien to her.

She did not dare to question Omar too much, but she did venture to ask about Rehmat one night as they lay in the cool darkness of their bedroom waiting for sleep. She had paused to see if he would reply, but he said nothing for a few moments; then he simply stated that Rehmat had always refused to take on her responsibilities, that she had driven their mother to her grave with her strange notions and continually spoken back to their father. She had felt their father's belt more than the rest of them put together – but what did she expect when she read so many smart books and then thought that she was smarter than everyone else?

'Where has she been for so long?' asked Miriam. This was the longest paragraph her husband had spoken to her for some time, and she liked it, this possibility of conversation. Carefully, as though trying to grasp a small but slippery fish, Miriam asked her quiet questions.

'Europe. France.' He turned over, so that his back was to her.

'Paris,' Miriam had said softly, almost involuntarily, and he had turned to frown at her.

'Yes. How do you know?'

'Farah told me.'

He had not replied, only muttered something unintelligible and had turned again and tried to sleep.

'She went there with her husband?'

Omar turned again and viewed his wife over his shoulder, as though she were a stranger.

'She went to get married.'

'A professor?' said Miriam.

'Yes.' His tone was abrupt and there was a short silence before he spoke again. 'He had an offer of a job there. In Paris.'

Miriam opened her mouth to form another question – about the circumstances of their departure – but Omar looked cold now, and angry, as though he were daring her to continue this conversation which was obviously distasteful to him. Miriam looked into his eyes for the briefest of moments before she lowered her head down onto her pillow and closed her eyes.

So this Sunday morning they dressed early, and the children waited in a state of anxious anticipation, except for the baby who slept peacefully after her early morning feed. Their excitement slowly seeped away when they realised that they would be forced to wait through three hours while the shop was open. They were always open on a Sunday morning, and nobody's arrival from the shores of Europe was going to change that.

Miriam opened the shop alone, except for John, who stopped before leaving to help her with the padlocks, and she waited in the quiet for any sign of a customer, before she moved back to the kitchen, where the children sat toying with their bowls of porridge. She shook her head at them.

'Eat, now,' she said. 'I can't sit here waiting for you, I have to mind the shop. Eat up, Sam.'

'Why can't Robert mind the shop?' asked Alisha.

'Because he goes home on Sunday,' said Miriam, irritably. 'You know that.' The children looked down at their plates.

'When are we going to see Aunty Rehmat?' asked Alisha.

'We're going soon,' Miriam replied. 'But not if you don't finish your food.' It was an idle threat, and the mother and the children both knew it.

'I'm not hungry,' ventured Sam.

'Eat,' said Miriam, and she turned and went back into the shop.

She waited, knowing that at the very least, Christina from Mr Weston's farm would probably come by for a can of peas, or a piece of dress material or some such thing. She always shopped for the household on a Friday, but she inevitably forgot something. The clock ticked slowly above her, and Miriam glanced up at the ceiling where her husband's steps made a muffled noise in the bathroom. He was taking an unusually long time to get ready today, and Miriam smiled to herself, then walked to the open door and went out to the *stoep*. The sun was sweet on her face, and warm for the time of year, with a cool breath of wind which moved through the grass and trees now and then, lifting her hair as it went. Somewhere birds were singing, but when she looked up at the trees she could not see them. Walking back inside she called to her children, asking them had they eaten, were they getting ready? She heard them scrape their chairs, then she heard the clatter of heels and the echo of giggles as they flew up the stairs. They ran straight into their father. He made a sound of surprise to have his children crash into his legs, and then he told them to hurry up – even though, Miriam thought to herself, they would not leave for another two hours.

Omar walked into the shop dressed in a stiff white shirt and his best tie, his face carefully shaven, his hair trimmed and neatly combed. He always looked smart, but there was an air of effort about him today, made more apparent by his deliberately careless manner as he walked about the shop, and the way that he managed not to look his wife in the eye.

Not one single customer arrived in the following two hours. As soon as the clock struck the hour, Miriam put baby Salma into her carrycot and ushered the children into the car, around which they had been playing for the last hour. As he started the engine Omar looked at his wife, his glance moving over her dress and hair for a moment, and he nodded, very slightly and to himself. Then he turned and surveyed his children, who looked back with their liquid black eyes. 'They look nice. Did you bath them?' he said.

'Yes. They are wearing their best things,' she added, and he nodded again.

'Good,' he said. 'Very good.'

When Sadru's house came into view at last, Miriam was astonished at the noise around them. There were people everywhere, out in their yards, walking along the dusty streets, lingering with bottles of soda beneath the gnarled jacaranda trees, visiting neighbours. Children shouted and shrieked, playing in the road. She understood for the first time that she really had become used to life in Delhof, in the countryside. Now it was the quiet humming of the grassland and farmland that seemed the natural state to her, not this bustle and activity, which she had barely noticed when she lived here. After her neat, wooden-framed home, the ramshackle series of houses, whose roofs sloped at odd angles, looked stifling to her. Walls of corrugated iron leaned lazily onto brown brick ones. Groups of men looked up as they drove by, slack-jawed, momentarily curious.

Miriam turned and looked at Sam and Alisha, sitting mute as waxworks in the back seat, having been forbidden to speak for the last half hour by their father, who peered tensely from the windscreen as they slowed to a halt before his brother's house. The children had been arguing and had become boisterous with the baby, stroking her head and moving her arms, causing her to wake and start crying. Now Sam's eyes were filled with tears, but Alisha refused to acknowledge her mother's look, staring steadfastly from the window, her little arms crossed defiantly over her chest.

'Come on,' Omar said, and he waited outside, straightening his tie as the children struggled with the door handles. Once they had all emerged, he took the baby's cot in one hand, put the other on his son's shoulder, and led them all into the house.

At first glance, everything seemed to be as it always had been – Farah was in the kitchen, out of sight, but still somehow managing to emanate waves of discontent at having to cook even greater quantities than normal. Her children were running around upstairs, providing a background of shrieks and laughter. Only the sight of Jehan sitting in the living room was unusual. She was dozing in a chair, having been put into her best dress. Her hair had been washed too, Miriam noted, although no one had bothered to dry it. Omar's brother walked over to the door to greet them, his frame tall and lumbering, his face smiling and harassed at the same time. He shook his brother's hand nervously, pinched the new baby's cheeks, and greeted Miriam with a gentleness that she appreciated, knowing that it did not come readily to his heavy body. He tousled Sam's hair and in a smooth, swooping movement bent and picked up Alisha and tossed her up into the air like a bag of sugar. The child laughed hysterically and Miriam smiled as she watched, but her heart had skipped a beat, and it was only when her little girl was back on the ground that she relaxed again.

'Farah!' Sadru called, ushering them to seats. Farah made no reply but they all knew that she had heard and would emerge when it suited her. Miriam guided her children towards the stairs, telling them to go up and play with their cousins. Alisha and Sam looked at her plaintively, as though willing her to reprieve them from this inevitable ritual, but she looked sternly at them and made them go. Then she went towards the kitchen to help her *bhabhi* with the food, but her brother-in-law stopped her, insisting that she sit. Omar ignored the chair that was offered to him, and paced up and down.

'So, how's business? How's tricks?' asked Sadru, settling back into his armchair, from one arm of which tufts of stuffing protruded.

Omar looked towards the stairs. The noise upstairs had suddenly ceased.

'It's fine. Everything's fine, *bhai*,' Miriam volunteered. Omar spun around.

'Where is she?'

'Who?'

'Your sister.'

Even Sadru had to smile at this.

'She's coming. She's not here,' he added, following the impatient darting of Omar's eyes. '*Our* sister went to meet her husband at his hotel.'

'That's a stupid thing to do,' Omar said. Miriam watched her husband. He looked angry and somehow helpless. 'Are they trying to get caught? I can't even believe they came back here together.'

'His father is dying...' said Sadru, unhappily.

Omar turned away. 'So what? He'll be dead in a week, and they'll be in jail. Do you think the police care who's dying?'

Miriam looked at Sadru in the silence that followed. She had learned from Farah some time ago that Rehmat's husband was white, and that this was the root of her family's displeasure, but the realisation that since the 1948 laws Rehmat's marriage would also be illegal only occurred to her now.

'Which hotel is her husband at?' she asked finally, to break the silence.

'The Royal, if you can believe it.'

This information came from Farah, who walked out of the kitchen adjusting her dress.

'Who do they think they are?' She looked directly, almost accusingly at Omar, and with surprise, Miriam caught the way that Omar looked back at her, holding her glance with a casual intimacy that she herself had rarely experienced with him. She looked back to Farah, but by this time her *bhabhi* was continuing the story of Rehmat's arrival and her unrelenting tone of sarcasm had caused both men to look at the floor, as though not seeing her might somehow block out her voice as well.

*

Fifteen minutes later there came a knock at the door, and they all looked at each other until Sadru got up at last to open it. Omar also rose suddenly and stood awkwardly, waiting. The couple that was revealed as the door opened stood smiling expectantly on the threshold. The woman wore a pale pink skirt suit that covered most of her long legs but only by emphasising them. Her hair was fashionably swept back from a high forehead before curling down over her ears, and she wore lipstick that was several shades too evident for it to be at all acceptable in the conservative and predominantly Muslim Asiatic Bazaar. Her husband stood behind her, little more than a silhouette at present, but an impossibly sophisticated one, smartly suited, his hat worn at a rakish angle, his hands in his pockets. Miriam could hear that the noise in the street had died down, as though people outside had stopped to watch. She saw the woman walk in, kissing first one of her brothers, then the other, and she saw the good-looking man with the neatly slicked hair follow her, shaking hands and smiling. She realised that the very sight of a man following a woman into a room, rather than leading the way, was alien to her. Who were these people? Was it possible that this woman, who seemed to have walked straight off a movie set, was actually related to her in-laws? And to her? Rehmat was hugging Jehan now, and then she went to Farah, who accepted her kiss with as much deference as Miriam could have imagined her capable of, as though she too were swept away by this vision. And finally Rehmat stood before her, smiling and holding out a hand that wore the most intricately worked, delicate ring that Miriam had ever seen.

'And so, is this my new sister-in-law?'
'This is Miriam,' said Omar.

All four children were stunned by the arrival of this new aunt. They had come racing down the stairs only to stop abruptly at the bottom, bumping into each other and forming a tangled knot of wide eyes and awkward limbs. They examined Aunty Rehmat and her husband from a safe distance; and after each of them had come forward under duress to be introduced and kiss the goddess-like creature, they ran back to the banisters and sat crouched on the stairs. Only Alisha ventured to stay nearby, and Rehmat touched the child's head and praised her beautiful eyes ('you must have your mother's good looks,' she said) and then she laughed, embarrassed at such an awed reaction from the children. Their quiet did not last long, however – as soon as they saw that the new lady was talking and joking with their parents, they understood she might actually be one of them. When Rehmat's husband James took some French centimes from his jacket pocket and proceeded to make them disappear, they moved closer still, until they were right next to him, where he could reach down to pull the missing coins from Sam's ears and Alisha's nose.

Miriam was aware of very little of the opening conversation – she felt a wave of relief when drinks were offered and Omar looked at her to go and get them. She followed Farah into the kitchen where they poured Coke and passion fruit juice into the best, gold-rimmed glasses, and Miriam looked at her *bhabhi* for some recognition of the wonder of this new sister, but Farah banged down the glasses irritably without uttering a word.

'They are so nice,' whispered Miriam.

'Yes,' Farah replied flatly, and picking up the tray, she went back into the living room.

When the time came to serve lunch, Rehmat followed Miriam into the kitchen to help bring in the food. They carried in bowls of aromatic lamb curry and rice, and plates of golden fried samosas while Farah followed at last with her centrepiece platter of chicken biryani. Sadru had started eating before the women had even sat down, and he met Omar's look of annoyance with surprise. 'Eat,' he told him. 'Aren't you hungry?'

Although Farah was generally acknowledged to be a good cook, people expressed this opinion with a strange and almost imperceptible sense of hesitancy. It wasn't that her food was not always delicious. It was just that she seemed to prepare it under a glowering cloud of discontent at having to be in the kitchen at all, and this infected those around her with a sense of guilt at having to consume what she had produced. Sadru always consumed his meals at high speed, as though he were afraid the food might escape from his plate if he left it there for too long, but others, including Miriam, tended to eat with care, lifting the steaming morsels gingerly to their mouths, as though the fragrant scents might somehow be hiding within them the poisonous fumes of Farah's frustration.

Rehmat, Miriam noted with frequent furtive glances, was tall and light-skinned like Omar and bore an extraordinary resemblance to her brother.

'You could think that you and my husband were twins,' said

Miriam, so quietly that she went almost unheard. It was the first sentence she had ventured to say directly to her sister-in-law. Rehmat caught the words and smiled across the table at her.

'We are,' said Rehmat, arching an eyebrow at Omar. 'We are twins.'

Miriam gave a gasp of surprise and looked at her husband. Rehmat laughed, throwing back her head so that the thin string of gold that circled her long neck caught the light and shone in the room. She held out a hand and covered Miriam's with it briefly, as though to reassure her that she was telling the truth. Omar merely gave a short movement of his head, not even a full nod, but an acknowledgement nonetheless.

'Do you know then, each of you, what the other is thinking?' asked Miriam, conscious suddenly of the manicured hand on hers. Farah snorted at the question, and Rehmat shot her a look.

'Unfortunately, no. We're not that close – for twins, I mean. My brother was always too quiet for me to read his thoughts. You probably know him a thousand times better than I.'

Farah snorted again, and something in the sound made everyone stop and look. Omar stared at Farah angrily, and Miriam felt suddenly sick, as though she had been hit in the stomach. She glanced at Rehmat, as though the sight of her might somehow lift the feeling, but it only intensified it, because Rehmat's eyes were moving wordlessly from Omar to Farah, as though she were trying to gauge something between them. Something between them, Miriam thought again to herself. Only Sadru seemed oblivious to any change. James cleared his throat:

'Well, it's good to be back. And here with my wife's family.'

'We were sorry to hear of your father's illness,' Miriam said.

'Thank you. Rehmat finally met him, and he finally gave us his blessing. Seven years after disowning me. I imagine death gives you a different perspective on what's important.' He smiled at Miriam and took a drink from his glass of juice. 'And now we're here, eating with all of you. There was a time when that seemed impossible.'

'It was impossible,' commented Rehmat. Omar shifted in his chair, and looked at no one.

'It's funny,' James continued. 'I always told Rehmat that in the end my colour and hers just wouldn't matter.'

'It matters now more than ever,' Omar said tersely. 'My father may be dead, but the South African government is much worse.'

'What would happen if you got caught?' Miriam asked.

'People like that don't win, Miriam.' James met her enquiring look with a clear gaze. Before Omar could formulate a retort, Rehmat turned to Miriam and asked that she tell her about her life at Delhof and the shop. Was it very quiet and lonely, or did she like it? Miriam spoke a little, reddening under the weight of Rehmat's kind glance, and then she fell silent, waiting for a moment when she might ask her new sister-in-law about life in Paris.

'You must come and visit us there,' Rehmat told her. 'It is so beautiful – the streets are all cobblestoned, and the buildings... they are like nothing I had ever seen before.'

'I would love to see it,' Miriam replied.

With an abrupt scrape of his chair, Omar stood up from the table and paced about, his lips pursed together, followed by

Sadru, who appeared relieved to be able to sink back into his armchair. Miriam continued to talk with Rehmat, her shyness slowly lifting, while Farah met her glamorous sister-in-law's attempts at conversation with an undertone of sarcasm. Sadru alone seemed to be enjoying himself, explaining all the details of his fruit and vegetable business to James, who listened with great politeness, his head leaning towards Sadru, while his eyes darted towards his wife. Rehmat smiled at him from the table, where she stacked the dirty plates.

Between them the three women cleared the table, while their husbands waited for tea. Rehmat was the first to return to the living room, ushered out of the kitchen by Miriam. She looked at her brother.

'Do you want your tea now, or can we have it later?' she asked him.

'I don't mind.'

'Because I thought we could go for a quick walk. Around the old neighbourhood,' she said, glancing from the grime-streaked window. 'Is the Bazaar Café still around?'

Omar nodded. 'It's not owned by the Patels any more.'

'No? Who owns it?'

'The Harjan girl. And a Coloured man. Williams.'

Rehmat looked blank.

'You wouldn't remember her,' Omar told her. 'Her parents are in Springs. Anyway, she is only a girl. I don't think they came till after you left.' His voice was hard, and Rehmat wondered if she imagined the subtle emphasis on the last words he had spoken.

'No, I don't remember,' she said. 'It's been a very long time.

Another lifetime. Everything always changes,' she added, lightly. 'Maybe we can go anyway and have a look around.'

Omar nodded his agreement and waited while his sister moved back to the kitchen, emerging at last with Miriam, insisting that she come with them. She wanted, she said, to get to know her sister-in-law a little better. Omar was relieved that Farah had not managed to include herself in this outing. He smiled for the first time that afternoon, and conscious of James' quiet presence, held open the door for the two women. As they left, Rehmat turned and glanced back, blinking, and for a moment she saw that room as it had been on the day she had left, nearly eight years ago. It had been her father's house that she had left then; their mother having died some years before while they were all still in their early teens. She had been a grown woman when she had left that day, but she had been treated like a wayward child. She had emerged from her family home with heavy bruises leaching out across her arms and legs, bruises that her father had given her the night before with the rough side of his belt, for he had finally heard the rumours about James and herself.

Rehmat had known then that her father would marry her off at once, probably to a cousin, or some other relative that she hardly knew, and so she had left silently in the early hours of a chilly April morning, and she had never been able to return. She could still recall the shock of the cool morning air on her reddened skin as she crept out, and the weak sun that had looked so welcoming that she had managed without too much effort to hold back her tears. James had been waiting for her and had taken her away to Cape Town and then on to Europe. They had needed to get out of reach of the group of thugs, all of them her relatives, that had spread out at once across Pretoria, trying to locate her by means of rumours, sightings and whispers. James's rooms at the university had been broken into and searched by men carrying knives and sticks. If she had been found within a day, she would have been dragged home alive but beaten. After two or three days, they might have simply brought her home dead, for by then it would have been too late to pretend that she had never left; the damage to her reputation would already have been done. On the boat out of Cape Town she had had plenty of time to consider this, and to wonder whether her own brothers and father had been amongst those searching for her.

'Come on.' Rehmat jumped slightly at Omar's voice. When she looked at him she saw the even features of her mother, the same features she saw in herself each day when she looked in the mirror, and the sight relieved her in some way. Silently, she turned to follow her brother and sister-in-law along the street, towards the café.

Chapter Seven

REHMAT SMILED TO see Amina walking around the café with a quiet air of ownership.

'Is that the Harjan girl?' she asked Omar.

'Yes.'

'My God, you're right. She is young. And she owns the place?'

Omar nodded.

'She must have been just a girl when she started,' Rehmat added, her tone full of admiration.

'She's still a girl,' said Omar, but Rehmat ignored him.

'Good for her. Imagine running a business at her age.' She noted the filled booths and the heaped plates moving back and forth across the room. 'A good business, too.'

'Sunday is always their busiest day,' said Omar.

Rehmat rolled her eyes. 'That's my brother,' she said. 'Heaven forbid he should actually give credit where it's due.'

Miriam smiled a little, but inwardly, she was amazed at the way in which Rehmat spoke to Omar. For the first time, it made her imagine her husband as a little boy, as one of a pair of twins. She had always considered him, as he considered himself, the most intelligent, the most reliable in the family – the one whose decisions were law. Now this twin sister of his arrived with a spark of energy and wit and life, and made him seem no more than average.

'It's good to see people doing well,' said Rehmat.

'Yes,' said Miriam. Omar looked at her with a frown, but she hardly noticed, for she was watching Amina at work on the other side of the room. It had been some time since Miriam had seen her, and Amina looked different somehow, older perhaps, and more serious than she had remembered.

A waitress appeared at their table and left them with a set of menus.

'Her family had a big scandal here years ago,' said Omar.

'Who?'

'Amina Harjan.'

'What do you mean?' Rehmat looked irritable at Omar's vague tone.

'Have you ever seen one of our girls with such curly hair?' he asked.

Rehmat looked hard at him from over the top of her menu.

'Are you saying she's part black?' she asked, under her breath.

Omar shrugged. 'So they say. From her mother's side.'

He leaned forward in his seat and looked up at the wall above the front door. His sister and Miriam twisted to follow his look, and they saw a faded picture, carefully mounted and framed, of a young woman dressed in a *shalwaar kameez*. The setting of the photograph suggested that she was in India, and beside her stood a little girl with cropped curly hair, solemn and sad, barely looking into the camera lens at all. The woman – the child's mother, Miriam presumed – had no such compunction, and stared at those who passed by her photograph with an air that was almost defiant. She was very beautiful and her figure was slender, but she did not stand up straight; she leaned on a chair back with one hand, the other arm held protectively round the little girl.

'Who is that?' asked Miriam.

'Amina Harjan's grandmother. Begum, her name was. And the child is Amina's mother. Look at her. Doesn't she look half...? Don't you remember the story?'

'No,' said Rehmat, studying her menu.

'She messed around. With the Africans. And she got caught out.' He shrugged.

Rehmat snapped the menu shut irritably. 'And now, God knows how many years later, this is supposed to matter?'

Miriam found herself stifling a smile.

'After all,' Rehmat continued. 'I suppose most white people in the world – maybe even some of James's family – will sit there like you, all self-righteous, and tell me that my children – *your* nephews and nieces – are half Indian.'

'It's not the same thing.'

'It's exactly the same thing.'

'You don't have any children...'

'But I will,' she declared, emphasising each word. 'But I will. And in this place, in this horrible country, they will never be accepted as people, only as a mixture of colours.' She sighed and watched Amina as she walked about the back of the café, talking to the cooks and tasting something that had just come out of the oven.

'How can she live in this country? How can *you* stay in this place?' she asked her brother, accusingly.

'I was born here,' he said simply. 'Africa is my home.'

'I feel at home here,' said Amina Harjan, quietly and with certainty, as though the truth of the words were somehow self-evident. She was standing now by Omar's table and talking to Rehmat. She had looked over and nodded at them from afar, and her curly head had done a double take at the sight of Rehmat sitting there, poised and confident and well dressed, such an anomaly in this community of Indians. Before long she had quietly steered their waitress to another table and had come over herself to take their order.

'Why? How can you stand it?' Rehmat was asking her.

'Stand what? I love it – I love the country, the space. I don't know, I just feel at home here. It's not like India.'

'Yes it is,' replied Rehmat, shaking her head. 'It is exactly like a mini India. Our people come here but live the same way – keep their women inside, keep their children inside. And God help anyone who tries to fight it.'

'God helps me to fight it,' smiled Amina. 'I don't stay inside. And I think you probably fought it too.'

Rehmat smiled, but her eyes were sad as she looked at Amina. 'I did. I fought it so hard that I had to leave.'

Miriam watched them both and then glanced at Omar. He was looking at his sister as though she were a stranger. Abruptly, he stood up and walked over to the counter. Amina turned to follow his movement and, when she saw him talking to Jacob, she turned her attention to Miriam fully for the first time.

'Hello,' she said.

'Hello.'

'Do you still like *koeksisters*?'

'You remembered,' Miriam answered. 'Yes, I do.'

'And have you had any since that were better?' Amina asked.

Miriam smiled. 'No. Never.'

'Good. I'll send some in a few minutes, they're just frying now.'

'You don't have to ...' But Amina had passed over Miriam's polite protests, and was already talking about something else.

In a few moments, Jacob was by her side.

'Amina, this gentleman is looking for someone to build him a vegetable garden. You want it? Or do you know someone who could do it?'

The women looked around to see Omar standing awkwardly at the counter, where Jacob had left him. Slowly, he walked back to the table.

'You need a job done,' Amina said to him, more as a statement of fact than an enquiry.

'Yes.'

'What is it?'

'I want a vegetable garden at the back of my house. Behind the shop,' he said, putting his hands in his pockets. 'Do you know someone?'

'I can do it.'

The response seemed to unsettle Omar. 'It's heavy work,' he said. 'Hard work. The ground needs clearing; there are deep roots everywhere. And I want a big space. I want to grow enough to sell, not just to eat.'

'Okay,' Amina said.

'I need a big area cleared and made ready for planting,' he repeated.

Amina smiled, a disarming, charming smile that showed her white, even teeth. 'Listen – you are the one paying for the work. If you want me to do it, I can do it.'

Omar rubbed his forehead. 'When could you start?'

'Whenever you want. How much are you paying?'

Omar hesitated. 'Twenty shillings. There shouldn't be more than two days work there.'

Rehmat gasped at the poor offer and stared at her brother. 'Omar!' she said.

'What?' he asked, defensively. 'If I had a *kaffir* doing the work I would pay him less.' Miriam blushed crimson, and Rehmat shook her head.

'Two days of my time, or an African's time, is worth five pounds,' Amina replied. 'And it will be ready in two days. And I'll be able to give you some cuttings from my own yard.'

Everyone waited in silence. 'Four,' Omar said finally.

Amina looked at him and smiled. 'Okay, four. I'll see you on Tuesday?'

'I come to Pretoria on Tuesdays. Can you get to the shop before I leave?'

Amina stopped a waitress and relieved her of the plate of hot *koeksisters* that she was carrying. She deposited the plate in the centre of the table, but towards Miriam.

'What time do you leave?' she asked Omar.

'Seven, seven thirty.'

'Good. I'll be there between six thirty and seven,' she said.

'Do you know where it is?' he asked.

'Delhof? More or less. Don't worry, I'll find it. It was a pleasure meeting you,' she said to Rehmat. 'Are you here for a while?'

'Just ten days, then we go to Nairobi. My husband is lecturing there.'

'Too bad,' said Amina. 'I hope you like South Africa a little better by the time you leave.'

'I like the country fine,' said Rehmat dryly. 'It's the people that bother me.'

Amina nodded thoughtfully, and Miriam noticed her eyes flicker upward and rest for a moment on the photograph of her grandmother.

'You are not the first one to feel that way,' she told Rehmat, looking back at her again. 'I'll let you have your tea. And I'll see you on Tuesday,' she said to Omar, and although she spoke these last deferent words to her husband, Miriam noticed with a sense of nervousness that Amina was looking at her.

Chapter Eight

'THAT GIRL IS late,' Omar stated gruffly, walking away from the window with his jacket in his hand. 'I told her six-thirty. Where is she?'

Miriam did not look up from the table, where she was simultaneously preparing the children's lunch and trying to coax Alisha into finishing her porridge. She was tired – the baby had been up three times during the night – and the children seemed to be bursting with energy this morning.

'You told her six thirty or seven,' she replied.

'It's quarter to seven now. I have to go to Pretoria today.'

'I know,' she said, a little too quickly and curtly, and she knew at once that he was angry at her tone. Her head throbbed as she lowered it again and went on with her preparations.

Miriam spread a thin layer of fig jam onto two warm chapatis, wrapped them in greaseproof paper and placed them into two small brown paper bags. Her husband still watched from the window, and stood up straighter when he heard the rumble of a truck coming up the track. The children welcomed the diversion from their breakfast and ran to look outside, while their father went through to the shop.

'Come here,' Miriam told the children. While Sam obeyed, albeit reluctantly, Alisha remained rooted to the spot, watching fascinated from the window as Amina Harjan stepped out of the truck and came walking up the *stoep* stairs. Miriam continued to fuss around the children, but as she did so she listened to hear what was going on just outside, and when she raised her eyes to glance through the door that led to the shop, she smiled to see Amina shaking Omar's hand, as though she were a farmer or someone here on business. Her husband, she noticed, looked surprised. She listened as Omar explained the area that needed to be worked on, and then they came into the kitchen, to go through to the back where the vegetable garden was going to be.

Miriam did not look up at either of them, but felt very conscious of her own movements and the sound of her voice speaking to her children. She combed their hair and tried to hasten them outside.

'Hello,' said Amina, and Miriam looked up and nodded.

Amina greeted the children as well, pausing to touch their heads affectionately, and then she followed Omar through the back door and they were lost to sight as he hurried ahead to finish giving his instructions.

'Mummy, why is she wearing trousers?' asked Alisha.

'She works outside. She dresses for her work.'

'I want to wear trousers to work when I grow up,' the little girl announced.

'It depends what work you do,' Miriam said, fighting against the headache that thumped in her temples. 'If you study hard and become a nurse or a secretary, you must wear a skirt.'

Robert put his head through the door.

'The bus is coming, madam.'

Miriam hurried the children through the front door and together they walked down the track to meet the bus as it made its slow passage up the dust road.

'Mummy?' said Sam, looking up at her, wide-eyed.

'Yes?'

'When will Salma come with us to school?'

Miriam smiled. 'Not for a long time. Maybe five years.'

'Five *years*,' repeated Alisha, appalled. 'I'll be...' She stopped to count, and Miriam looked down at her face, intent and serious. 'I'll be *ten*, Mummy.'

'I know,' replied Miriam. 'You'll be a big girl. Go on now, get to school.'

They ran forward to the bus, which wheezed to a stop before the house, and Alisha turned and shouted to her mother:

'But I'm a big girl now, Mummy.'

Miriam laughed. 'Yes, I know,' she said, but her reply was lost in the noise of the doors closing and the ancient gears being engaged. She waved at her children as they were carried away from her, and waited until the last edges of dust raised by the bus were beginning to settle. Only then did she turn and go back to the shop.

Omar was waiting inside, impatient. He gestured up to the ceiling.

'The child hasn't stopped crying. Where have you been?'

'Putting the children on the bus,' she said, going to the stairs.

'I'm going now,' he called after her.

His voice was angry, almost petulant, as though he were willing her to give him some attention also, to repeat the routine she had just followed with the children. She stopped on the stairs and considered, listening to the baby crying. Then she turned and came back into the shop, where she stood at the door and watched her husband get into the car and drive away. He waved as he left, a short unsmiling gesture, and she raised her hand in response, automatically and without much feeling. Then she went upstairs to see to the baby, pausing only to look out from the back window, and to instruct Robert to take a mug of tea and some bread to the young lady who was working outside.

Miriam waited. She moved up and down behind the shop counter, her hands passing in quick movements over the polished wood, neatening a display here, straightening a tin there. Her eyes flickered at irregular intervals to the clock above the door, and between these glances she walked up and down, making a game of seeing how long she could wait before looking again. The time dripped by, until the awaited chime of midday caught her between glances.

She looked up once more at the clock, to confirm the news she had heard. Then she removed her apron, folded it, and laid it carefully on the counter. She smoothed back her hair and listened to her steps echo beneath her as she walked into the cold-tiled kitchen. At the stove, she lifted the lid on a large pot of potato curry and stirred at the mixture. A few threads of steam snaked up, bringing with them a delicious scent, and she smiled. Onto one of their large, heavy plates she spooned a generous portion – the size she would normally give her husband – and taking up two *rotlis* from that morning's stack, she went out of the back door.

Amina was nowhere to be seen. Miriam peered hard through the sun, over towards the place where she had been working – a large square of earth was already turned over and hoed, standing out in that landscape as a place that was being carefully tamed.

She looked about her, puzzled, and then realised that she had not been able to see the girl because she was lying down. Under the grudging shade of the only tree nearby, Amina was lying on the grass, sleeping. Her legs were stretched out, her ankles crossed; the fine stripes of her cotton shirt lay in soft folds over her body. The top two buttons of her shirt were open, showing the long line of her tanned throat and neck. Her hat was pulled down over her eyes and nose, leaving only the delicate bow of her mouth exposed, slightly open, and set in a half-smile.

Miriam halted and watched her for a moment – counted in her head the measured rise and fall of Amina's breaths. She tried to decide whether or not to wake the girl, and glanced up at the branches above them, intently, so that the deep green of the leaves and the brilliant cornflower blue of the sky became welded into a dizzying glare of colour.

When she finally turned her face away, her eyes swarmed with red images, the sun lurking behind her irises still, so that she looked before her without seeing anything. When the hot blindness left her, she began to see that Amina was now awake, and that she was sitting on the grass cross-legged, her hat pushed back upon her curly hair, and she was smiling at Miriam, a smile that was polite from the mouth, but laughingly amused from her eyes.

'I brought you some food,' Miriam said, holding out the plate. The girl jumped up, losing her hat in the movement and, wiping her hands on her trousers, she came to where Miriam was standing. She took the proffered plate and thanked her.

'This is a lot of food,' she said.

'Working outside can make a person hungry,' replied Miriam.

'Oh, I won't have any trouble eating it all,' said Amina. She smiled. 'It smells delicious. I wish I could cook so well.'

'Cooking is nothing,' said Miriam, avoiding the compliment. 'All women can do it.'

'I can't, believe me.'

'But you run a café.'

She waved a hand. 'All Jacob's recipes.'

'Then you should learn.'

'So my mother tells me.'

'Your mother is right,' said Miriam firmly. 'What will you do when you get married?'

Amina shrugged and smiled, and held Miriam's gaze for a moment.

'I don't know. I'll have to find a man who can cook,' she said, and Miriam felt again the laughing eyes, and felt the colour burning in her face, suddenly and unexpectedly.

'I'll bring you a cold drink,' she said, and started back to the shop.

Amina called after her that a cold drink would be nice, then sat down against the tree and began to eat.

It took a few minutes for Miriam to return with the drink, and Amina was halfway through her meal when an opened bottle of soda was handed to her from above.

'Thank you,' she said, making a polite gesture, as though toasting Miriam before she put the bottle to her lips and drank a long draught. She had to catch her breath when she stopped, and she looked up at Miriam, standing above her.

'Have you eaten?'

'Not yet.'

'Why don't you join me?'

Self-conscious, Miriam wondered what she could possibly talk about to someone like Amina, if they were to sit down and eat together.

'You don't like me do you?' Amina said, looking down.

'No, I like you very much...' said Miriam, startled.

'Do you?'

'Yes. It's just that... I feel you must find me boring. You run a business and do so many things, and I am just a housewife and mother.'

Amina shook her head. 'There's no such thing as "just a housewife". It's hard work. And anyway, don't you have feelings and thoughts and ideas and wishes just like everyone else?'

Miriam watched the girl, overwhelmed by her simple question. It seemed to her to acknowledge something which no one had ever before noticed. She stood there, lost in thought, her dark eyes frowning.

'What are you thinking?' Amina asked, her face turned up, a hand against her forehead to shield her eyes from the sun.

'Nothing...'

Amina waited.

'I was thinking that you were the first person to smile at me in ten days, once,' Miriam said.

'I don't understand.'

'In Pretoria. The first time I came to your café. With my sisters-in-law.'

'I remember it well.'

'Nobody had smiled at me for over a week before that,' continued Miriam. 'I had been counting the days.' She smiled wryly, an acknowledgement of the absurdity of counting such a thing. 'And then in the café, you offered me that *koeksister*. And you smiled at me.'

'What a strange thing to remember. Why didn't anyone smile at you for so long?'

Miriam shrugged. 'I don't know. That's the way they are, I suppose, my in-laws.'

'And your husband too?'

Miriam nodded, a barely perceptible movement, and then frowned as if berating herself for disloyalty. She turned to go back to the house.

'Can I bring you anything else?' Miriam asked.

'No, thank you.' Amina hesitated, uncertain whether to try to keep Miriam engaged in conversation. But Miriam herself stopped almost as soon as she had turned away and spoke:

'You know you said you couldn't cook?'

Amina nodded.

'It doesn't matter, really. There are more important things in life.' And before she had even finished the sentence, Miriam was walking back to the shop.

Amina drank the last of her soda, and watched Miriam walk lightly up the porch steps. She ate the remainder of her meal quickly and alone, and then she rested for a minute, before she stood up and walked back to where her tools lay in the hot grass, humming under her breath as she went.

At half-past three the school bus lumbered back up the road, stopping about twenty yards from the shop. The rusty hinges of the doors whined open and the two children spilled out. Miriam watched them from the window of the kitchen as she kneaded the dough for the *rotlis*, a half-smile on her lips. They ran towards the house – they ran everywhere, were incapable of walking slowly, and Miriam tried to recall Bombay, and the apartment blocks, and tried to remember whether she too had run all the time as a child. She could hear their high, laughing voices as they raced each other up the porch steps and into the kitchen. They both spoke together, loudly and quickly, and Miriam could understand neither of them, but leaned to kiss them both, her floured hands held away from them, above their heads.

'Is the lady still here?' asked Alisha and Miriam nodded. Before she could tell them not to disturb Amina, they were out of the kitchen. Miriam went to the window and looked out to where Amina worked, hatless now in the late afternoon heat. The children raced around the corner of the building like a pair of tiny greyhounds and then stopped abruptly when they caught sight of her. They stood at a safe distance, suddenly shy, until Amina turned and saw them, and beckoned to them to come over. Miriam watched Amina kneel down to talk to them, gesturing to the plot of land, evidently explaining what she was doing. After a few minutes, Miriam came away from the window, washed her hands and took a bottle of Coke from the deep red refrigerator in the back. She called to her son, and he came to her, breathless with excitement:

'Mummy, the lady says there is going to be a storm!'

Miriam looked up at the lowering sky, and the solid grey clouds and handed her son the Coke to deliver to Amina. Longingly, he looked at the cold, beaded bottle, and Miriam, although she knew Omar would disapprove, went back to the fridge and took out two more bottles which she gave to the delighted child for himself and his sister.

By the time Amina had finished for the day, it was almost dark outside, and the rain had just begun to fall. She felt the first drops hit her face as she looked up to the sky, and she wiped them gratefully across her warm forehead, for the humidity had become almost unbearable during the course of the afternoon. She had worked until she could hardly see what she was doing. Miriam had glanced out once or twice during the early evening, and had seen the girl working away, her shirt clinging to her back and ribs from the rising heat. The children had done their homework and were finishing their supper when Amina came to the back door and knocked. Opening the door, Miriam found a slim leather-bound book held out before her.

'What is this?' she asked.

'Poetry. I've finished it for now. You can have it if you like.'

Miriam was curious and touched the book but did not take it until Amina pushed it into her hand.

'I can't take it . . .'

'Why? Don't you like reading?'

Miriam looked up and smiled, her eyes alight, and Amina watched her intently. It was as though a spark had been struck.

'I love reading. I used to,' Miriam added, less confidently. 'I used to read a lot.'

She remembered suddenly a small battered box of childhood books that she had brought with her from Bombay, an extra box that she should not really have dragged across the ocean, but which she had found it a comfort to keep with her. She had last seen it in her in-laws' house in Pretoria, but in those days there had been no time between cooking, cleaning and children to even open it. She wondered what had happened to the books; whether they had come with them to Delhof when they moved.

Amina leaned against the door frame. 'Take it,' she said, of the book. 'I have plenty.'

'You do? Where do you get them?'

'Here and there.'

'Stop and have some food,' Miriam offered. 'You must be hungry.'

Amina shook her head. 'Thank you, but I should go to my

parents' house for dinner. It's been a while since I've seen them.' She glanced at her watch, a large, brass-coloured face that clung to a worn, soft leather strap. It made her wrist look thin and frail, and Miriam was surprised for a moment that these same hands were taming such a large patch of ground outside.

'I'd better go. Thank you for the lunch and drinks,' Amina said as she moved away.

'You're welcome. Thank you for the book.'

'I'll see you tomorrow?' Amina asked.

'Yes,' said Miriam. 'See you tomorrow.'

Thirty minutes after Amina had left, there was a knock at the front door of the shop. Miriam looked out from the bathroom window, where she stood holding a jug of water suspended above her eldest child, but she could see nothing. The rain formed a low hum in the background, and she hushed the boy and watched intently as the water ran in slow rivulets over his shoulders, snaking past his sharp shoulder blades and over the thin muscles of his back. The knock came again. She wrapped a rough towel around the child and told him to dry himself, and she ran down the stairs, calling to John as she went.

'Madam, it is a lady,' he called through the window to her, smiling so she should know not to be alarmed. She could see Amina out there with him on the porch, her hat in her hands, her hair damp. The girl took a step back as Miriam opened up the shop door.

'My tyre had a puncture,' she said. 'I tried changing it, but the spare one also...'

'It's okay, come in,' said Miriam, standing aside and ushering the girl in.

'I would have walked, but it's not safe, really, and I'm not as reckless as some people think,' Amina added.

'Good,' was all Miriam said. She was struggling with the last padlock, and Amina bent and closed her hand over Miriam's to help her click the metal into place.

'Thank you,' said Miriam, watching the long fingers that lay over hers.

'You're welcome.' With a smile, Amina cleared her throat then looked away and walked across to the window where she watched John settle back down in his wicker chair and hold out his hands to the warm coals before him.

'If you're going to stay you should come upstairs with me now.'

Amina nodded, but made no move to follow Miriam.

'Where is your husband?' she asked. 'Isn't he back yet?'

'He usually finishes late on a Tuesday. Usually he stays over at my *bhabhi's* . . .' she caught herself. 'At his brother's place, I mean.'

'Oh.' The drive back from Pretoria was not an arduously long one long one and Amina knew that Omar's habit made no sense unless he was up to something, but she was relieved to find him elsewhere tonight.

'I'll give you something to eat.'

'Please don't worry about me,' Amina replied. 'I'm not hungry.'

'But you've been working outside all day. Do you mean you don't like my cooking?' Miriam asked, smiling slightly.

'I thought that was already agreed. That was the finest potato curry I've ever tasted. Though I wouldn't admit that to my mother.'

'Then let's see what you think of this *daal*,' said Miriam from where she stood at the stove, and she handed Amina a bowl of fragrant lentils that were still warm from the supper she had eaten with the children. Amina took it gratefully, and started to eat.

'Thank you,' she said.

Miriam watched her for a moment. 'I'm going to put the children to bed. Come up when you are finished.'

Amina nodded. 'This is delicious, Miriam,' she said, and Miriam had to cover the smile that came to her lips when she heard her name pronounced aloud. It was a rare sound, for Robert and the children never used her name, and Omar's terse conversation consisted mainly of 'yes' and 'no'.

'You're welcome,' she replied, and turned and went quickly up the stairs.

By the time Amina had eaten, rinsed her plate, and come tentatively upstairs, Miriam had soothed the baby to sleep, and had both children in their beds. The girl waited awkwardly on the landing, until Alisha heard her quiet steps and said something to her mother.

'We are in here,' called Miriam. 'Come inside.'

Amina came into the room, but hovered by the door. The children lay side by side in their tiny beds, watching her, wide eyed. She smiled at them.

'Are you ready to sleep?' she asked them.

Alisha shook her head emphatically. 'We don't want to sleep.'

'Mummy do we have to sleep?' piped Sam, taking his cue.

'Yes.'

'Why?'

'Because I said so.'

Miriam watched them struggle, knowing they would not answer back, and yet they both lay there galvanised with a sudden energy, with the excitement of an unknown stranger in their usually routine household. Their small limbs wriggled with energy, and Miriam smiled.

'I will read you one story...' she said, and the children nodded, happy to have achieved some kind of respite. 'And then you must sleep. Okay?'

'Okay.'

Amina cleared her throat. 'Is there somewhere I can wash?' she asked.

Miriam pointed the way to the bathroom. 'There is still some hot water in the tank,' she said, and she heard an acknowledgement from her guest before the bathroom door closed, and she picked up a book and began the story.

It took no longer than ten minutes, and the children enjoyed it as though they had never heard it before, and laughed when Miriam did the different voices for each character, and waited breathlessly for the happy ending which they must have known would come. When she got up to tuck them in and kiss them goodnight, they protested again, but with a defeated air, as though they understood that it must come to nothing, and she leaned to kiss her son and stroke his head, and then went to her daughter.

The little girl flung her arms around her mother's neck and told her that she didn't like it when she made her voice low like the storybook villains.

'Like this?' said Miriam, in the same voice.

The child squealed and grabbed hold of her mother more tightly, and Miriam laughed, tousling the girl's hair, and tickling her chest, booming in the same voice. The girl laughed hard from being tickled and Sam laughed to see them both struggling with each other, until finally Miriam pulled away and stood up, smoothing back her hair.

'Sleep now,' she said, still smiling, and without waiting for further protests she turned out their oil lamp. Closing the door, she stepped out into the hallway and bumped straight into Amina. The girl was waiting in the half-gloom, her shirt-tails hanging over her trousers, her face scrubbed and the ends of her wild curly hair wet. A fresh, clean scent lingered in the hallway, one that Miriam had noticed earlier in the day, and that she now recognised was somehow peculiar to Amina.

'I'm sorry,' she said, touching Miriam's arm to reassure her. 'I finished, and I didn't want to disturb you while you were with the children...'

'I forgot for a moment that you were here...'

'Are you sure it is all right for me to stay?' Amina asked.

'Of course. Do you want a night-dress?'

Amina shook her head. 'No, this is a clean shirt. I always keep one in the car. I like to be prepared...' She was smiling, that same disconcerting half-smile.

'For what?'

'For anything,' said Amina.

She followed Miriam to the end of the hallway, and they turned into the room next door to the one she shared with Omar. It was small, with a gently sloping ceiling which ran under the eaves of the house. A narrow, low bed lay beneath the slope, and there was nothing else in the room but two upturned orange crates, upon which Miriam's sewing lay, together with two half rolls of striped material.

'Is this okay?' Miriam asked.

'It's fine,' said Amina. 'At least I can start very early tomorrow. If the rain lets up. Perhaps I can even finish the garden. If I have one more full day...'

'Don't worry, it will get done. My husband is impatient, but I can see how hard you are working.'

Amina made no reply but went to the tiny window over the foot of the bed and looked out at the railroad tracks that ran in converging lines into the distance.

'How many trains are there every day?'

'Past the shop?'

'Yes.'

'One.'

Amina laughed, and then remembered the sleeping children and stifled the noise.

'One?' she repeated. 'Must be quite an event when that train shows up,' she smiled.

'It is,' replied Miriam. 'The children get very excited when it comes, and they are home.' She covered a smile guiltily. 'They run out and stand there and wave as it passes.'

'There are passengers?'

'No, it is a goods train…' They looked at each other and laughed out loud. Amina looked again from the window, her eyes fixed on the tracks, hesitant.

'You have very good children,' she said finally.

'Thank you.'

Quickly, Miriam left the room, returning in a few moments with a pink towel which she placed on the end of the bed.

'I mean, it is very nice to see how you are with your children,' Amina added. She ran a long finger over the tiled sill. When she turned back, Miriam was looking at her questioningly, a frown shading her face.

'I couldn't help overhearing…' Amina paused, embarrassed to admit that she had heard them. 'I mean, it was so nice, the way you are close with your daughter.'

The frown remained, and Amina sensed disapproval and coolness. She shrugged, more to herself than to anyone, and turned back to the window.

'Anyway, I liked that you are affectionate with her. I'm sorry I saw,' she added abruptly.

Miriam ignored the apology, but kept herself busy, tidying up the sewing things that lay on the crates, and then turning back the bed, concentrating on the cool feel of the sheets and the rough hair of the heavy blanket.

'My mother never hugged me,' she said simply, without looking up and Amina turned around.

'No?'

'No,' said Miriam, her face reddening. 'She never gave us much affection. I got used to it, but I didn't want my children to feel the same.'

'My mother can be cold too,' said Amina.

'My mother wasn't cold,' said Miriam, defensively.

'No, I didn't mean...' Amina ran a hand tiredly over her forehead. 'That was clumsy of me,' she said. 'I didn't mean to say that your mother was cold.'

She gazed from the window again and sighed. 'It's raining,' she said quietly. 'It'll be good for the soil.'

For a long time after she had seen everyone to their beds, Miriam lay under her own sheets and watched the ceiling. She had the double mattress to herself, but remained on her own side, not used to spreading herself out, or taking more room than she needed. Expansiveness did not come naturally to her, in her movements, her speech, her thoughts. She listened, relieved at the rain tonight, at its breaking of that silence outside which she was now so used to. It drummed hard and hollow on the roof, like the hooves of a thousand distant horses, and she listened, and heard the steady pouring as it ran off the eaves, and the splashing as it hit the sodden ground beneath. So many sounds that same water was responsible for, such a variety of noise. She closed her eyes and listened again, wondering about her husband, what he was doing, and if he was happier now to be away from home for a night.

These trips to Pretoria had become more and more frequent in the last few months, and almost every week he stayed a night there, something he had never done before. She tried not to think about it too much, but she knew that his night visits must coincide with the times that Sadru worked away from home, haggling in the vegetable markets. And then there were moments when she carried the laundry downstairs for washing, and she would turn her face away from a sudden smell of stale, familiar sweet perfume that rose from his shirt. Blinking hard, she pushed the idea from her head, and smiled to think of her daughter hugging her, and then she almost laughed aloud when she remembered Amina's face as they thought of the children waving at the freight train. She strained to hear if the baby was awake, but the rain drowned out all noise for the moment, and she was grateful for it. She turned on her side and the repetitive rush of the water lulled her gently to sleep.

Chapter Nine

MIRIAM FELT THAT she had been sleeping for only a few moments when she awoke and lay wide-eyed in her bed, straining to make out what it was that had roused her. The silence, perhaps? The rain had ceased; there was no longer any trace of it in the quiet that reigned. She sat up and listened for the baby, but there was no sound from the children.

Wide awake now, she lay in her bed for ten minutes more before she got up and slipped quietly down the stairs to the kitchen. She felt like some tea, but the stove was barely warm. She pulled a chair close to it, lit an oil lamp, and opened the book that Amina had given her. The pages fell open at a poem by John Keats. Miriam had seen nothing of his before and began reading slowly, pausing to savour each word, as though she were tentatively tasting a new kind of food, one that was unfamiliar but exquisite:

'My heart aches and a drowsy numbness pains my sense...'

Within moments she felt someone watching her. Instinctively she looked at the window, but John was pacing at the other end of the *stoep*; there was something else out there, though. She peered into the glass and saw a woman, insubstantial, suspended in the pane, and it took her a moment to realise that it was Amina's reflection. Miriam turned her head and saw the girl standing at the foot of the stairs.

'You scared me!' Miriam said.

'Sorry. I heard you come downstairs, and I just thought I'd check everything was okay.'

Miriam pulled out another chair. 'Everything is fine.'

'Do you often have trouble sleeping?' Amina asked.

'No,' replied Miriam. 'I woke up when the rain stopped, I think.' She turned the oil lamp up further but the warm light could not illuminate much more than the small circle in which they stood, leaving the rest of the kitchen in a cold, blue darkness.

'Me too. But I don't feel sleepy any more.'

'Good, then we can talk. I can ask you things.' Miriam put the sentence out into the cool air before she lost her nerve.

Amina sat down, a half-smile on her face. 'What do you want to ask me?'

'So much. About your business, about your life.'

'What about your life?' Amina asked her.

'It's not as interesting as yours.'

'It is to me,' the girl replied. 'I already know all about my life.' She held her hands out to the poor warmth of the stove. 'When did you come to South Africa?'

Miriam shut the poetry book and studied the cover.

'Just approximately,' added Amina, encouragingly.

'It would have been 1946. Just after I got married.'

Amina nodded. 'Me too. January.'

'June,' said Miriam.

'So you saw the Indian Congress protests?' Amina asked, excited. 'Yes, did you?'

'I was there. Protesting the Ghetto Bill. I'd sneaked off with some friends. My mother thought we were visiting their aunt in Durban. She never even read the newspaper, or she would have known.' She sat back and smiled. 'It was an incredible time. My God, I was seventeen. A new country, a new world, and these terrible new laws – I thought we could overthrow the government in two weeks. I sat there every night, with the rest of the crowd, and wished they would choose me next to occupy that piece of land.'

'Umbilo Road,' said Miriam. 'I just stood and watched. I didn't even know the significance of what was happening. It was our first evening off the boat from India. I was so tired and homesick and it seemed very frightening to me. That the government had just decided to take back land from people just because they were Indian and not White. And then all the police. The guns.' She shook her head. 'I couldn't imagine why my husband had brought me to such a place.'

'I suppose it was frightening, but I was young and it seemed exciting too. It's only now, years later, that I look back and realise how much worse things have become.' Amina sighed slightly. 'Are your parents still in India?'

'My mother is. My father died when I was a girl.'

'Were you close to him?'

Miriam's face darkened. 'Yes. More than with my mother anyway. He was a good man. He made sure I had a good education, even though we were not a very well-to-do family. He always said that girls should learn as well as boys, so as to be able to teach their own children. I appreciated that – my mother alone would not have done it.' She turned the book over in her hands.

'Do you miss India?' Amina asked.

'Not any more. I used to. I felt very alone and isolated when we came here.'

'Delhof is a small place,' Amina commented, but Miriam shook her head.

'Even before Delhof. Even when we lived in Pretoria with my in-laws.'

'That was when we met first, when you came to the café that day.'

'Exactly. Even then, I felt lonely. There was no one to talk to and everything was new to me. My husband was always out working and anyway, he does not like to talk much.'

'Your *bhabhi*?'

Miriam shook her head.

'So who do you talk to now?' Amina asked.

Miriam laughed. 'I talk to you.'

'Tonight, maybe!' said Amina, smiling. 'But otherwise?'

'My husband is around the shop all day. And my children are here too. Anyway,' Miriam said, shifting a little in her seat, 'it's different now. I'm used to it. I like it here. What about you?' she asked quickly.

'I love it here,' said Amina. 'I left school when I was sixteen, and soon after that we came to Springs. My mother was born in South Africa, actually, but her mother brought her back to India when she was a baby.'

Miriam looked surprised. 'So you have more family here?'

'Probably,' replied Amina. 'But we don't see them. Nor do they want to see us.'

'Why not?'

Amina looked at Miriam carefully. 'My grandmother, Begum, was sent back to India to her family. They disowned her and my mother. You must have heard somebody's version of it.'

Miriam hesitated. 'I saw your grandmother's picture in the café... I mean, there's always the gossip, but I don't like to hear it...'

Amina looked to the stove, as Miriam watched her. Was she looking for a way out of the conversation?

'Would you like some tea?' Miriam asked.

Amina nodded, reaching for the matches. Miriam moved to get up but a touch of Amina's hand on her own stopped her. Her voice was soft and serious in the darkness.

'No, I'll make the tea. I'll make the tea for you. For Miriam, who is always making the tea for everyone else.' She struck the match, a dramatic hiss and burst of light in the dark. Leaning down she applied it to the back of the stove. 'Tell me, who looks after you, Miriam?'

Miriam's head spun with the intimacy of the question, with its pure, direct pertinence. Disconcerted, her mind reeling, she looked down at her hands, still gripping the book of poems.

Nothing could induce her to look up until she had recovered herself, at least a little. Beside her, the sound of Amina's step, the grating noise of the kettle being placed on the iron stove top, the scrape of the chair as Amina sat down again – these were her focus. And then, the house was silent, except for the slow internal creaks of its wooden frame, and the occasional clink of an unseen pipe. She knew Amina was watching her.

'I'd like to tell you about my grandmother,' Amina said gently. 'I think you'd understand why she is so important to me.'

'Is she still alive?' Miriam asked, able to glance up now.

Amina shook her head. 'She died when I was sixteen. Cancer. She was tough about it though. She was already used to terrible pain, all through her life, in her back and legs, so when the cancer came, she didn't even complain.'

'In the photo she seemed to be leaning on a chair,' Miriam said. 'Did she have back problems?'

'Not till she was nineteen,' Amina replied.

'What happened then?'

'The beatings.'

'Beatings?' Miriam shook her head. 'But why?'

Amina passed her hands over her eyes. 'I'll tell you,' she said. 'I'll tell you the story the way my grandmother told it to me when I was fifteen years old. And it begins with the beatings.'

*

Pretoria, 1892

Begum had ceased to feel anything at all after the eleventh or twelfth blow to her back. She lay sprawled on the floor, her body flat against the flagstones, where she had fallen after her knees had buckled finally against the cracks of the birch wood. After a while, all she could feel was the coldness of the stones against her stomach, which was pressed against them, exposed, her long blouse having ridden up at some point during the violence that had preceded this whipping.

Eventually she realised that she could not hear anything either, except that, when her mind drifted from the pain that shocked her body in a steady rhythm of beating, she could hear a gushing, liquid sound – but one that came from inside her head. She couldn't hear their curses any more; that much at least was a blessing. The words that had come from the mouths of her mother-in-law and her family had shocked her even more than the first blow they had cracked against the thin bones of her back as she turned away from them to attend to her new-born daughter. Slut, slut, whore, bitch, they had chanted as they moved in on her, taunting and angry. She had watched their gaping mouths forming the words and seen the glint of her mother-in-law's gold fillings, and had moved back open-mouthed and frightened, her hands spread before her to protect her new baby.

It was the child that had started all the problems. She had given birth two weeks before in the upstairs room, with her mother-in-law and an African midwife in attendance. Neither had seemed much interested in the birth, and they had sat near her bed, their bodies listless in the humid evening, watching her as though she were a particularly unexciting exhibit in the zoo. Pushing and straining in the heat of the October night, she was only four hours into her labour when she had unexpectedly felt the slide of the baby's head at the neck of her womb. The midwife had disappeared from her view, had pushed Begum's knees farther apart, and seemed alert for the first time. She had pushed again, hard, an almighty effort that had almost made her pass out. When she had recovered she could hear the bawling of her new baby and she had seen the two women leaning over the child and looking. Her mother-in-law had frowned and left the room without a word, and she knew then that she had had a girl. She herself was happy. A girl was what she had wanted, and she lay there catching breaths and waiting, listening while the African woman wiped the child off with an old piece of sheet, and then she took into her hands the baby that was offered to her. The little girl was quiet now, and wrinkled, and her eyes were wide and dark with long lashes, like her mother's. It was only later, when the afterbirth was washed fully from the child that Begum noticed the hair, dark and thick and curly. In a family of Indians, all of whom had thick, but irretrievably straight hair, a child with curly hair was an oddity. Begum's stomach had turned when she noticed this, and she held the baby closer to her for a few minutes, her eyes closed, refusing to think about what the reason for this curly hair might be. Then, with sudden resolution, she had held the baby away from her and examined her carefully. The baby's complexion seemed dark, too, darker than her own or her husband's. One of the main reasons that Begum had married so well at the age of fifteen before being sent to South Africa with her new husband was that her skin was fair. A prized asset, to look so white. A good thing to pass on to one's children. She was nineteen now, and had produced her second child. The first-born had been a son, and they had all been happy about that. But her husband disliked the idea of daughters and had told her early on that he wished to have only boys. It was a good sign to have boys, and he was working here in a new country and he needed help from his children in the future. She had nodded to his beard – so as to be respectful she very rarely looked him directly in the eyes – and she wondered privately what she could possibly do to arrange such a thing. Her mother-in-law had prayed over her swollen stomach during both pregnancies, but it seemed that the second time, the heavens had not been listening.

With gentle fingers, she touched her daughter's curls and began to cry silently. She had buried away this possibility nine months ago, when it had happened. She had buried it so deeply that in her mind it was almost as though it had not occurred; it had become to her a terrible story that she might have heard in relation to a stranger. But she knew that she had changed, or rather that she had been altered by the incident. She had become nervous all the time, more afraid of the dark and of being outside, even during the day. She even had nightmares sometimes; they were unclear and relived nothing obvious, but sometimes when she woke from them, intermingled with the taste of relief in her mouth was the acrid, sweet taste of that rough skin against her gums. He had pressed the heel of his hand hard into her mouth so she would not scream, and then he had pulled up her clothing with quick, violent movements. He had been working in the yards of her husband's new warehouse, picking up the huge crates of hardware and loading them with his trolley, and sometimes he helped with painting and cleaning and other odd jobs. That was all she knew, for she had never noticed this African employee of her husband's more than any of the others, until he was suddenly there upon her in the corner of the deserted warehouse, with his muscled arm against her ribs and throat so that she could hardly breathe. She had felt him fumbling with his trousers and then pushing into her. He need not have even bothered to cover her mouth – she was too shocked to speak, to say a word. Her struggling body was pressed back against something – piles of sacking she had thought afterwards – and her limbs strained uselessly under his weight.

She had cried continuously afterwards, not hysterical, but helpless. There was nothing she could do, and no one she could tell. Even if they believed she had been raped, she would be worthless to her husband now, a damaged thing, and she would be sent back to India. Perhaps they would want to keep her son as well. She could not speak of it, and so she spent the night blocking the thing that had happened from her mind, and wondering if there was some way she could ask her husband to fire the African. As it turned out, she did not have to – the next day he did not come to work, or the day after, and after five days her husband hired another man, cursing under his breath the unreliability of *kaffirs*.

As her young, coltish body began to fill out again, she worked hard to keep the rape and the possible consequences from entering her mind. But now she sat in her bedroom with a child that did not look like her husband, and she rocked herself back and forth, and pulled at the baby's hair with gentle fingers praying that they would not notice.

They did notice, within the space of a fortnight. Her confinement was over, and she was up and around in the kitchen when she heard her husband and brothers upstairs, talking together in undertones, and she knew instinctively that she was the subject of their discussion. They said nothing to her that night, and although her husband hit her once, he did not directly accuse her of anything. But the accusations came quickly the following day and she defended herself as best she could; she swore to them that two of her grandparents had had curly hair, that the child was his, how else could it be? They did not listen, only cursed her and told her she would have to go back to her own family and then the beating began

So it was that she came to be lying face down on the floor of the kitchen, with the pain of the sticks no longer felt. She rolled her eyes, looking up at the wall before her, and then she used them to look down at the stone floor beneath her, simply to feel that some parts of her body were still within her own control, even if it were only her eyeballs. She felt her mouth opening, and words coming out, a weak protest perhaps, a pleading to stop, and then she felt a wave of tension leave her body and she realised, helplessly, but with some relief, that she was about to pass out.

When she had stopped moving altogether, they stopped hitting and looked at the inert girl lying on the floor and thought for the first time that they might have in fact killed her.

'She's strong,' said her mother-in-law, spitting onto the floor. 'She will get up.'

They all accepted this remark as a kind of absolution, and they left the kitchen, passing her husband, who came in from the dining room where he had been sitting, motionless, for the last twenty minutes. He looked down at his wife's beaten body. She was only nineteen years old, and now more than ever looked like a child, curled motionless on the floor. He made a half-hearted gesture to the young maid, who acknowledged him with a slight nod, waiting while he followed his family back out.

Once they were alone, the maid knelt beside the girl and tentatively touched her forehead. She could hear her mistress breathing still, and was relieved. She did not know what to do – calling a doctor without the permission of her master was out of the question – so she just knelt there and waited, stroking the head of the injured woman and murmuring softly into her ear.

Four weeks later, Begum sat on the edge of the bed, with some difficulty because of the pain in her back and ribs, and regarded her suitcase without much feeling. She had always known that her personal possessions were few, but she was still shocked that everything that could rightfully be considered her own after four years in South Africa could fit easily into one medium-sized case. Her children, thank God, were hers. For them she had fought tooth and nail in the last month, while her husband's family had refused and then argued and then bargained with her. She had watched them make her travel arrangements back to India, had watched them pack up her things, and she had become almost deranged from fatigue and from the unending pain in her back and stomach. She wondered continually what parts of her body they had broken with their sticks, and whether she would ever be free of the throbbing pain that consumed her nights and days. Through it all, however, she had fought against them and she had sworn on her own mother's life that she would not leave if she were not allowed to take her children with her. They offered her the curly-haired girl at once – it was only her son that they wanted – but she refused to leave him, and would not listen to their shouts and arguments that she had no right to refuse. She continued to resist, until her mother-in-law gave in to her one day with surprising grace, confirming that she could take both of her children, but stipulating that she must go back to India without further delay or further demands. She agreed, relieved at the outcome, for she knew that she had no real rights under the religious laws that governed her marriage, and she had prayed hard that night for the first time in two years, a prayer of thanks to God for letting her keep her children.

For a few brief seconds as she stood on the platform, she was swallowed up by a blast of steam issuing from the train behind her. She was blinded, surrounded by the billowing shrouds of white, and she held on a little more tightly to her son's tiny hand. She carried the baby in a large cloth that they had wrapped around her back. The added weight upon her only increased her pain, and so she had gone to board the train to Durban as soon as it had arrived, but her husband and his family had held her back.

'There is no need to hurry,' he had told her in Gujerati. 'You will have a long enough time sitting on that train.'

So she waited with them in silence, watching people milling about, and she tried hard not to cry. She was still in shock at the difference that six weeks had made to her life. In that time she had given birth to another child, had been beaten senseless by her in-laws and was being sent home in disgrace to her family in India. She no longer had a husband, or a home. She was nineteen years old, and all acceptable avenues to a normal, respectable life were now closed to her forever. She did not even know that her father would allow her back into his house after what had happened. Perhaps she would be made to marry an older man; a widower perhaps, or a poor farmer who couldn't afford anyone else. She had shuddered at this possibility and cried herself to sleep at night, but now as she stood on the platform, surrounded by these people, she felt very little. Mostly, she felt a desire to get onto the train and sit down, to try to relieve some of the pain that coursed in thick, winding streams through her body.

The little boy began to cry and, with some effort, she picked him up, pressing his hot, salty cheeks to hers. Finally, the warning whistle sounded, and she looked expectantly towards her husband. He nodded and picked up her case, walking towards the back of the train, where he found an empty carriage, with the sides open to the summer weather. He climbed aboard and deposited the case, and then came back out and stood aside from the door for Begum to enter. He watched her from outside as she settled the children, looking only at his son, and he gave her no word of farewell.

'Hold him out so I can kiss him,' was all he said and she looked up in surprise at this and tried to look into his face, but his eyes were cast down. He is sad to lose the boy, she thought, and though she blamed him for his choice in sending her away, the unusual tenderness of his request made her feel sorry for him. So he has feelings after all, she thought, and she nodded to him, and laid the baby down on the seat, and then took her son in her arms and stood with him at the side of the train. The boy was calmer now, and smiled down with questioning brown eyes at the family he was leaving. Begum's head was hidden in the darkness of the carriage, and her husband could not see her smile as the train began to sway as a preliminary to setting off. She looked down at them, at her mother-in-law, the two youngest sons, each bearded, and their wives regarding her from beneath covered heads. These people who had been her family, and whom she had hardly known. She would not be sorry to leave them, but her husband? She could not comprehend how easily it was that this man who was supposed to be tied to her for a lifetime was now lost to her forever. She watched him with sadness, and something almost like pity, for he was sending her away for something that was not her fault, and he was doing so even though she knew he cared for her in his own way.

The train began to move, edging slowly down the track, and she held up the boy's hand so that he should wave to them. They walked down the platform with her, alongside the train, until it began to pick up speed, the wheels turning with a slow, inexorable movement. Her husband still walked alongside them, and began to run a little now in order to keep up, and he shouted to her again to hold the boy down so he could kiss him goodbye. She leaned forward and held the child out, and his father's hands reached up to touch him, she thought, to caress his son, but the big hands were grasped suddenly around the child's waist. She pulled back, not understanding what it was he was trying to do, but she was already leaning too far forward and his strong hands gripping and pulling at her son were unbalancing her more, and the train was quickening over the track, and she could not hold on to the boy, try as she might to cling on to his clothes. She could hardly conceive what had happened when she looked at her hands and they were empty. She stared back at the group that stood together, triumphant on the platform, her son in their midst in her husband's arms. She stared as they passed away into the distance, as she lost sight of their faces, until they were only tiny figures on the platform.

The figures did not linger for very long in the station, but moved hurriedly to return home, because they, and everyone else who remained in the station could hear the screams of the woman on board the train even after it was long out of sight.

Delhof

'I didn't mean to make you cry,' said Amina. Miriam looked up, wiping her eyes.

'I can't imagine losing a child like that. She must have wanted to die...'

Amina sighed. 'I think a part of her did die that day. It made her hate everything that had led to it. For as long as I can remember, she was always warning me about the dangers of losing yourself in a marriage, or being ruled by family.'

'Is that why you haven't got married yet?'

Amina smiled, but her eyes held no trace of teasing or amusement as they looked into Miriam's. 'No,' she said. 'That's not the reason at all.'

Miriam looked down, and her glance fell on Amina's watch. 'It's two o'clock,' she said. 'We should both try to get some sleep.'

The sound of the baby's cry pierced the quiet darkness and they both looked up. Quickly, Miriam pushed back her chair and hurried to the stairs.

'Miriam...' Amina said. Miriam turned, one hand on the banister and waited. The girl looked thin and frail sitting there in the kitchen in her tiny pool of light, and Miriam felt bad. She had been relieved to hear the baby, for it had provided her with an easy escape from the tumult that Amina was stirring in her mind and heart with her stories and her very presence in the house.

She took a step back towards the girl and looked at her kindly. 'What is it?' she asked.

Amina studied her hands for a second and then looked up and shook her head. 'Nothing,' she said. 'You'd better go, the baby needs you.'

Chapter Ten

Delhof

MIRIAM WAS AWAKENED the following morning by the unfamiliar brilliance of the sun beneath her curtains. She sat up and squinted at the window, her thoughts still heavy with sleep. Something felt very wrong. She could not remember ever having woken up in this house when the sun was already so high. She looked at the clock that sat on Omar's side of the bed. Seven o'clock.

She got up swiftly and pulled on her robe, running to the children's rooms to wake them, for they had only half an hour before the school bus would arrive. Bursting into their room, she found herself entreating two empty beds to wake up. She whirled around, thinking that they might be behind her, playing hide and seek, but this morning, neither child jumped out, giggling and excited.

She went next door and checked the crib. Her baby at least was still there, sleeping. She could see an empty bottle beside her, and knew that Robert must have fed her in the early hours. How had she slept through that? Across the hallway, the door to Amina's room stood wide open and the bed was neatly made up. Miriam peered out of the tiny window. Her children were outside by the vegetable patch, fully dressed, and Amina Harjan was kneeling down in the soil, showing them something.

After a hurried detour to wash, Miriam rushed downstairs, and went straight to the back door.

'Sam! Alisha!' she called. She waited on the threshold, impatient. Within moments, the children came running.

'What are you doing?' she asked, knowing that she had nothing to be angry about, but somehow disconcerted by the change to her usual routine. The children looked at her with wide eyes, similarly confused by the tone of the question, pitched somewhere between curiosity and anger.

'Nothing,' said Sam.

'Something!' corrected Alisha. 'Amina was showing us the garden, Mummy. Do you know in a month we will have vegetables there?'

'*Aunty* Amina,' Miriam told them. 'You call her Aunty. She is much older than you.'

'I'm twenty-four,' said Amina, approaching the back door. 'Not an old lady yet.'

Miriam smiled, a little embarrassed, and ushered the children into the kitchen.

'I like to make sure they are respectful to their elders,' she said as she set the milk to boil. 'They'll be late for the bus,' she continued, but Amina was still lingering at the back door and did not hear. Miriam beckoned her in.

'Come and have some breakfast with us,' she said, and Amina kicked off her boots and came inside.

'Thank you.'

'They are going to be late for school,' repeated Miriam. 'I haven't even made their sandwiches yet.'

'I'll help you,' said Amina. 'Where's the bread?'

Miriam seemed unconvinced, but nodded to the covered loaf on the table, then opened a drawer and handed Amina a bread knife. She took it and balanced it on the tip of her finger. When the children laughed she looked up as though she had forgotten their existence altogether.

'What are you having for breakfast?' she asked.

'Porridge,' they answered.

'Are you going to eat it straight off the table?'

They shook their heads.

'Then,' she said, slicing into the loaf. 'Why don't you help your mother and get the bowls and spoons ready?'

They both ran for the crockery and within moments had set four places at the table. Miriam stirred the porridge and turned once to glance at Amina. She was focused on cutting the bread, but saw the movement of Miriam's head from the corner of her eye and looked up.

'I never imagined I'd be so domesticated,' she said, and laughed.

Miriam hesitated and then spoke. 'I never imagined anything else.' she said.

'Mummy, the milk!' Alisha shouted, and Miriam looked down, startled to find the pan seething with bubbles. Before she could even think, she felt Amina's hand by her own, closing around the handle of the saucepan and dragging it from the heat.

Amina smiled at Sam and Alisha. 'Another breakfast saved.' She turned to Miriam. 'I don't know what to put in their sandwiches. Why don't you make them, while I give them the porridge?'

They changed places and Miriam worked quickly, speaking little, content to observe as Amina spooned out the children's breakfast, chatting and joking with them as she did so. It was a new experience for Miriam, this help in the kitchen, this fun over breakfast, this care for her children from someone other than herself, and she liked it.

Amina ate with the children, by way of encouragement, and they had almost finished when Robert came in from the shop to announce that the bus was coming. He laughed when Amina jumped up and ordered the children into a short line behind her. She stood with the solemn rigidity of a toy soldier, waiting while Miriam gave each child a satchel and lunch bag, and then she began a stiff march through the kitchen and the shop, with Sam and Alisha following in step behind her. They marched all the way out to the porch and down the front steps, where she turned and saluted them with great seriousness. Giggling, they saluted back and ran down to the bus.

'Mummy?' shouted Alisha, from the door of the bus. Miriam came out onto the steps.

'Yes, sweetheart?'

'Can Amina...can Aunty Amina live with us all the time?'

Miriam glanced sideways to the girl who stood behind her, but Amina kept her amused gaze fixed upon the children. The women waited in silence at the foot of the porch steps, watching until the bus was out of sight and all that remained was the vast plain before them, that huge stretch of land that Miriam had once dreaded, but had now become so accustomed to.

'Would you like some more breakfast?' she asked. 'It's our turn to eat now.'

Amina turned and watched her intently, as though she were weighing up an offer of much greater importance than porridge, and once again, Miriam had to look away from the searching eyes.

'I think I'd better be getting back to work.'

'Are you sure? We have fresh eggs delivered on a Wednesday.' Omar allowed her eight eggs each week for cooking and baking.

Amina smiled at Miriam's persistence.

'Eggs?' she said. 'Well, that's different.'

In the kitchen, Miriam set a heavy black pan to heat while Amina stood nearby, covertly watching. As soon as the oil was hot, three eggs were cracked into the pan, where they spread out and lay sizzling and spitting. Miriam dragged the pan slightly away from the heat and watched them as they cooked.

'I didn't sleep for a long time after hearing your grandmother's story,' she said.

'I'm sorry,' Amina replied.

'Don't be. I appreciate it very much that you told me. It can't have been the easiest thing for you.'

She sprinkled salt, pepper and a little cumin powder over each egg and then turned them over with an easy motion, holding each yolk intact. She slid two eggs onto a plate for Amina, and the remaining egg onto another for herself. On the table between them she placed a dish of *rotlis*.

'You know,' Amina said when they sat down, 'every now and then, when I think back to my grandmother, I understand her story a little better because of what I have learnt or seen as I get older.'

'What do you mean?'

'Yesterday, for example. For the first time, I really felt it inside, the agony of how it must feel to lose your own child. So brutally. Maybe it was seeing you with Sam and Alisha, or maybe it was just that I told it out loud to you, but it meant a little more to me last night than ever before.'

Miriam broke off a piece of bread. 'I'm glad you told me.'

'So am I. Anyway,' said Amina, 'family history or not, I am glad we came back here. It was the best thing that could have happened to me.'

'Why?'

Amina laughed. 'Can you imagine me being able to start my own business – so easily anyway – in India?'

'It's unlikely,' Miriam admitted. 'But then, it's unlikely here. But you still managed it.'

'Yes. It was Jacob who had the idea and he put up most of the money. I met him when I was working at the house of one of his relatives. His nephew, I think.'

'What work were you doing?'

'Painting. Window frames and things.'

Miriam smiled. 'Is there anything you don't do?'

'Very little,' smiled Amina. 'That's why I'm such a good source of gossip. Anyway, Jacob helped me more than he realised. He ignored all the criticism we got early on and he trusted me; he gave me a chance that no one else would have given me.'

'You like your work?' Miriam asked.

'I love it.'

'Don't you ever think of getting married and having a family instead?'

Amina wiped a piece of bread over the yolk that spilled across her plate. 'It's that word "instead" that I don't like. That I don't understand. *Won't* understand, some of my family would say. Why can't a woman do both – if she wants to, that is?' She looked up at Miriam, waiting.

'I...I don't know,' Miriam replied. 'No reason, I suppose. It's not usual, is it?'

'No, but neither am I,' said Amina, smiling. 'And neither are you. And neither is any human being. People should look at themselves, how they feel, how they think, and then do what is right for them. Most men do that. Your husband didn't stop working when he married you did he?'

'No. But someone has to earn a living.'

'Why not you?'

'Because he has always worked.'

'Why haven't you?'

'Because it wasn't expected.'

'Why not?'

Miriam smiled this time. 'Because I am a woman? You have got me with your logical argument, Amina. There is no way out for me.'

'There is a way out. You could argue against me for hours if you really believe that the old, traditional ways are right. But you don't,' Amina told her. 'You don't believe it, you believe *me* deep down, and *that's* why you like my logical argument.'

'Perhaps.' Miriam was looking down at her hands.

'You don't like to commit yourself to anything without thinking it over a lot first, do you?' Amina noted. Now that she had finished her meal, she gave her full attention to watching Miriam.

'Is that a bad thing?'

'Not at all. I am much too impulsive myself, and I always admire patience and thoughtfulness in other people. I need someone with those qualities with me, to keep me balanced.' For some reason, Amina's dark eyes made Miriam look away again.

'Like Jacob,' Amina continued, with a half-smile. 'He stops me from ruining the business with my crazy ideas.'

'More eggs?' Miriam asked, half standing.

'No, thank you.' The girl remained seated for a moment, wishing to continue the conversation, but Miriam seemed restless, or perhaps nervous. Amina politely looked at her watch and exclaimed at the time.

'That garden will be growing weeds if I leave it much longer,' she said, picking up the plates. 'I better get to work. Thanks for the breakfast.'

'It's nothing,' Miriam replied reaching to take the dishes from her.

'I'll wash them,' Amina said. 'It's the least I can do after you cooked.'

'No, no. It will take me two minutes. Come on. You have a garden to make.'

Amina yielded the plates and went to the back door. As she stepped out, she pushed her worn felt hat back upon her curls.

'What time does your husband get home?'

'He should be here any minute.'

'Oh.' She sounded disappointed, Miriam thought. 'Well, thanks for the breakfast. And for the conversation,' she added, glancing at Miriam from beneath the brim of her hat. 'I hope I didn't worry you with my strange ideas.'

Miriam shook her head. 'You don't worry me. You make me think. And that's a good thing, isn't it?'

Amina grinned at her. 'That depends on who you ask,' she said, as she walked away. She raised a hand as she reached her new patch of garden. 'I'll show you where I've planted everything later,' she called, and Miriam nodded and stood watching for just a few moments as Amina rolled up her sleeves and set to work once more.

Chapter Eleven

FOR THE LAST week, Miriam had not been able to tell exactly what day it was. The days seemed to have lost their particular ability to change mechanically from one to another, and now, for her, they just drifted sinuously together with nothing to differentiate them at all, not even the passing of a whole night. She had long ago become accustomed to routine, to a life where each day often differed little from the one that had gone before, but this was something new, a mass of time that sat heavily upon her, and that had somehow welded itself unevenly into an unmarked stretch of consciousness. She remembered little bits of the routine that had carried her through those long reaches of hours – she recalled feeding the baby, again and again, and cooking dinners and opening the shop and re-stacking some shelves. At one point, she had dropped a saucepan of food that she had just cooked. It had hardly even startled her. She had merely waited for the noise of the falling pan to stop echoing in the kitchen, and had then looked at the spilled food as though it belonged nowhere else but on the floor. Robert had cleaned up the splattered mess, watching her with flickering, concerned eyes, while she had gone upstairs to see to the crying baby.

She was tired. She felt exhausted – she had hardly slept for five nights. She blamed the baby, but the child had cried only once in the middle of each night. Whenever she got up to feed or change her, though, she remained away from her own bed for a whole hour, sometimes two, standing at the window, holding the slumbering child and rubbing her back soothingly. Miriam had no wish to return to the sleeping man in her bed, or to fall into sleep herself, because her dreams were filled with him – with images of him and of Farah, together. Her sister-in-law was always laughing in those dreams, loudly and without joy, and the noise had woken Miriam each time, leaving her forehead damp with sweat and her pulse racing unevenly.

Her day-time thoughts formed a whirling sequence in her head that gave her no peace. She thought about Rehmat and James, and the way they had chosen to live and she wondered if, in the same circumstances, if the option had even occurred to her, she would have fought convention and run away as Rehmat had done. She considered Sam and Alisha, how their lives might turn out, and her thoughts wandered to her mother in Bombay, who had never seen her grandchildren. The letters between them were more and more occasional; usually delayed and often lost. She reflected on Amina Harjan for a long while, and stared now and then at the new vegetable patch that lay outside the confines of the shop, neatly hoed and planted. Although Amina had been at the shop for only two days, Miriam had missed the girl's presence during the past week and had found her dormant loneliness acutely sharpened. When she returned to her bed, it was to lie motionless on her back, her features as still as those on a death mask, listening as she once had during her first months here, for any sign of life in the vastness outside, for any sound to come and distract her from the voices that were crowding in her mind.

For relief she had begun to read through the book of poetry that Amina had left with her that day. It was all love poetry and this, combined with the memory of Amina's eyes watching her, had caused a flicker of nervousness in Miriam. Something about these poems disturbed her; some twisting image of a rose or a breaking heart would wind its way into her restless dreams, and she would awaken unrefreshed and saddened. There were certain lines that she had read over so frequently that they were imprinted forever upon her mind, and those words would shock her sometimes during those days by appearing to her with a clarity that was strange, but somehow appealing, as though they were words she had thought of herself and was laying at the feet of some lover as yet unknown.

At three o'clock that afternoon Omar went upstairs to get his jacket for a trip to a wholesaler in Springs. Miriam picked up the broom and waited for him to come back down again. Within a few moments he appeared in the doorway, straightening his lapels.

'I won't be long,' he said, and she nodded and walked with him to the *stoep* and watched him as he got into the car. He wound down the window and leaned out and she stepped forward to listen.

'Rehmat's going back tomorrow,' he said. 'We should drive over in the morning and say goodbye.' He started the car.

'What about the shop?'

'Robert can mind it.'

'Okay.'

Pretoria. A glimmer of change to break the monotonous days. Miriam returned to the shop and began brushing the floor, her mind on tomorrow's trip and on Rehmat. As she worked, she recited under her breath the parts of the poems that she knew, the beats of the verse forming a rhythm for her work, and she watched the knots and the grain of the floorboards appear and disappear beneath the bristles as she moved the brush back and forth in swift, even strokes.

She saw their feet first, as she swept towards the open door. Big, black boots, the tops shiny, the edges laced with red dust from the road. Like the falling pot of food, it was a surprise but she was not visibly startled. She looked up slowly and saw two pairs of legs, encased in blue uniform trousers; then belts, holsters, batons, epaulettes, and two pairs of eyes – one brown, that watched her flatly from above a beard, and one intently blue. She took a step back and watched as the two policemen entered the shop. The blue-eyed one touched his cap.

'Afternoon,' he said, pleasantly.

'Afternoon,' she replied and waited there, still holding the broom. The other man began walking around the shop, browsing casually through the counter displays as though picking through items at a sale. She parted her lips to ask what she could get for them, but closed them again, knowing instinctively that they were not here as customers.

'I'm Officer De Witt. This is Officer Stewart. We need to ask you some questions, *ja?*' He had blond hair, the policeman that addressed her, and he smiled when he talked.

'My husband is out – he just left…maybe you saw him,' she said, and then she realised that she had not heard the police car coming up the track.

The men glanced at each other. '*Ja*, we must have just missed him. It doesn't matter, though. It's not him we came to see.'

Miriam looked at Robert, who had appeared at the foot of the stairs. There was a raw fear in his eyes, in the set of his thin arms and legs, that seemed to be preventing him from entering the shop. Miriam felt his terror infect her at once. She beckoned to him and he walked in with reluctance, waiting beside her, eyes cast downwards. Neither officer gave any sign that they had noticed him come in.

'Would you like some tea. A drink?' she asked, in barely a whisper. Her eyes moved down to the baton that hung at the policeman's side. Behind it, she realised, was a gun. She swallowed.

'*Ja*,' he said, looking at his colleague, eyebrows raised. 'A Coke would be nice.'

She nodded to Robert who returned in a moment with two bottles and glasses. Miriam said nothing, but gripped the broom handle as though it alone were supporting her.

'A good shop you have here.'

'Yes. Thank you.'

De Witt tilted back his head and took a long drink from his Coke bottle. Miriam watched the liquid passing in gulps down the taut outline of his throat. He gave a satisfied sigh as he brought the bottle down, and wiped the corner of his mouth with the knuckles of his hand.

'Who are your main customers?' he asked.

'I suppose the farmers, mostly.' Miriam cleared her throat, which was tense and hoarse. 'There are many farms around here.'

The man nodded, but looked vaguely bored. 'That's interesting. Don't you find it too quiet?'

'No, sir. I am used to it now.'

'So you like it here?'

'Yes, sir.'

'Is your sister-in-law here?'

Miriam felt her heart jump. 'My brother-in-law and his wife live in Pretoria,' she replied, as casually as she could.

The officer laughed, showing even white teeth, then shook his head and put his hands firmly on the counter, so that he was leaning in towards her. Despite herself, she took a step back.

'There is nothing to be afraid of,' he said. He looked over at Stewart, who had circled the whole shop and now stood before Miriam, by his partner's side, his fingers pulling absently at his beard.

'Let me make things clear,' said De Witt, smiling. 'We are looking for James Winston and Mrs Rehmat Winston.' He put a sarcastic emphasis on the word 'Missus' and looked towards the stairs.

'And we have very good reason to believe they are staying with you. With her brother.'

'They aren't staying here,' said Miriam, and she winced as she saw the officer smile, broadly this time.

'Oh. But you know where they are staying.'

Miriam said nothing and looked down.

The men nodded at each other and walked towards the back of the shop.

'Where are you going?' asked Miriam.

'Upstairs. To take a look,' replied De Witt. 'I think they are here.'

The last sentence was directed at his partner, and Miriam watched helplessly as they ran up her stairs two at a time. She listened to the rubbery squeak of their boots, and then to the footsteps above, creaking into the bedrooms. At once, she remembered the baby, sleeping up there, and she ran up the stairs and into Salma's room. The men had not been in there yet, and she looked down at the child, her soft cheek pushed up against the pillow, her tiny chest rising and falling in the yellow sleepsuit that had once been Alisha's. Miriam's hands held tightly to the edge of the crib and she watched her baby and listened hard as they strode about her bedroom next door, opening closets, scraping the bed back across the floor. She heard the drawers being opened and closed one by one, and she felt a rising anger that they were seeing and touching her things.

She picked up the sleeping child and followed them into the children's room, greeting them with a look of defiance. The handsome face of the blond, blue-eyed officer watched her for a moment, but his smile was gone. Stewart paid no attention to her, only dropped to his knees to look under the children's beds, and then he looked into the old wooden wardrobe that stood in the corner. There were notches cut into it at about waist height, and he stopped and touched them.

'What are these?' he asked. It was the first time he had spoken since they had arrived.

'The children measure their height,' she said, and turned away. The baby shifted but did not awaken and De Witt stopped to look at her.

'A beautiful baby,' he said. She waited for him to move away, but instead he reached out a large hand to touch the baby's head. Miriam made an abrupt movement away from him and he turned and looked up at her for a long moment, as though gauging her response. He took a step towards her.

'Listen,' he said. 'You could be in a lot of trouble if you help them. Tell me where they are, and we won't need to bother you again.'

'What have they done?' she asked, so quietly that the policeman had to listen hard to hear her.

'What have they done?' he repeated. He looked incredulous. 'Is that what you asked? What have they *done*? They have broken the law. There is a law against mixed race marriages.' He explained this slowly and not without some sarcasm, as though the concept might be too much for Miriam to grasp.

'The Prohibition of Mixed Marriages Act. 1949,' he continued, his voice official. 'We are trying to make sure people know we mean business. That the law is not there to be ignored. You understand?' he asked.

Miriam said nothing.

The policeman sighed and stood back. He walked about the room. Then he looked at his watch as though calculating something.

'What time do your children come home from school?'

Miriam felt her stomach drop. De Witt looked again at his watch. 'I mean, it should be some time soon, *ja*?' He looked at his partner with an air of innocent inquiry. 'Maybe we should just hang on and have a chat with the kids?'

'*Ja*, why not?' said Stewart. He leaned against the wall, as though settling himself for a wait. They all stood silently, and listened to the breathing of the baby. Miriam shook her head, and the policeman gave her a querying look.

'Don't question my children. Please.'

'But we have to. You're not helping us.' He watched her, casually scratching his ear with his little finger.

'You will leave my children alone,' she said finally, her voice unnaturally high. 'Please,' she added, suddenly conscious that she was talking back to a policeman.

'That's up to you.'

They waited, watching Miriam, whose gaze went from the floor to the baby, until De Witt spoke again.

'Are they at your brother-in-law's in Pretoria?'

Miriam said nothing.

'Just give me a yes or no. Is that where they are? You don't have to say anything. Just nod.'

Miriam shook her head. 'I don't know where they are. How do you expect my children to know... they don't even know who she is.'

'Then you won't mind us asking them.'

The tone was nasty and heavily caustic, and it shook Miriam into the kind of alert wakefulness that she had not felt in days. She felt her uncertainty, her wavering fear dissipate and she decided then, without qualms, that she would not answer these men and that she would find another way to get rid of them before they got to her children.

'No,' she said firmly, looking the officer directly in the eyes for the first time. 'I don't mind.'

Swiftly, she walked out of the room and downstairs. She heard them follow a few seconds later. She held the baby close to her chest and stood behind the counter. De Witt followed her there without any hesitation, walking straight to her, quickly, his face hard and set like a mask, and she backed away beneath his stare.

'Where are they?' he demanded, still advancing upon her.

'I don't know.'

She moved backwards, clutching the child who was now beginning to cry and De Witt matched her steps, following her down the length of the counter.

She stopped, terrified, with a bump that startled her like a gunshot. A display cabinet stood heavily behind her and she was trapped between it and policeman. He smiled tiredly and leaned forward, one muscular arm placed on either side of her head, his solid palms pressed flat against the cabinet. The baby cried, and she hugged the tiny body closer to her neck. His blue eyes were no more than two inches from her wide brown ones, and she turned her head away. She watched his forearms, forming a barrier on either side of her, saw the muscles taut beneath the tanned skin and the raised blond hairs that covered them. He spoke harshly and very quickly:

'Are they in Pretoria?'

'No.'

'Then where are they?'

'I don't know.'

'Where are they?' he shouted.

'I don't know.'

'WHERE ARE THEY?' he yelled, and she felt droplets of his saliva spray onto her face.

Miriam said nothing. Her eyes were tightly shut and the baby was screaming. The policeman moved his reddened face even closer, so that when she breathed she was forced to inhale his own hot breath.

'Do you *really* want me to ask your kids?'

She opened her eyes, moving the baby up and down in a poor effort to soothe it, and watched his red, violent face and his cold eyes only inches away from hers. She imagined that face close to her daughter's, but she felt no real sense of fear now, only a disgust and loathing for this boorish man before her. She looked directly into his blue eyes, noticing the thin red veins that crept out from his irises, and then she spoke:

'You'll never find them.' Her tone was firm but quiet. 'Just leave us alone now.'

The policeman's eyes grew wider – he looked stunned. From the corner of her eye, and with relief, Miriam saw his partner step forward and place a restraining hand on his shoulder. De Witt paused a moment, his arms still up against the wall, trapping Miriam and the baby, and then stepped back and turned and walked out to the kitchen. His partner waited in silence. There was no sound for a few moments, but then came a crash of furniture that made Miriam jump. She paced up and down, rubbing the baby's back, listening to the din that now issued in a continuous stream from her kitchen. Plates were being thrown – it sounded like every last one of them was being smashed – and she heard four loud thumps that she thought must be chairs being kicked over. A clatter of metal followed, and she knew her saucepans of freshly made food were now lying on the floor.

With as little warning as they had begun, the noises stopped. In the profound quiet that followed, a tap was turned on in the kitchen and Miriam listened as she fought to control her sobs. She heard the water drumming on her iron sink, and when De Witt returned his face was damp, and his blond hair darker now that it was wet, and he looked calmer. Stewart had waited without speaking, or even moving, except for the chewing motion of his jaw, but he looked up now.

'You'll never find them,' Miriam repeated, softly, and De Witt ignored her, although she knew he had heard by the tensing of the muscles in his neck.

*

Miriam recognised the low throb of the bus before they did but she made no sign, only prayed for some miracle to keep her children away from the shop; but the moment they caught the diesel shudder of the engine, the two men raised their heads in unison, like coyotes scenting a corpse. De Witt even managed a smile.

'Home from school!' he said, cheerfully. 'How nice.'

'I won't let you talk to them,' said Miriam, her voice rising.

'Don't panic, lady. You don't have anything to do with it. We're going to take them with us and talk to them at the station.'

'You can't take them...'

Stewart turned to her.

'We can,' he informed her. 'They may be holding valuable information about someone who is wilfully breaking the law.'

'No!' She ran forward, still holding the baby, but a firm hand grabbed her shoulder and pushed her back with no more effort than if it had been swatting a fly. The men walked out to the porch where they stood waiting for the children. They came tumbling off the bus as they always did, running up towards the shop, but they saw the policemen as they reached the porch steps and they stopped, looking up at them expectantly.

'Hello,' Stewart said to them.

'Where's my mummy?' demanded Alisha, regarding them with much suspicion.

'No manners. Just like her bloody mother,' muttered De Witt, under his breath. He turned and called to Miriam over his shoulder. She came out and beckoned to her children to come in. They ran up the porch steps, but could not find a way past the huge legs of the policemen that blocked the doorway to the shop.

'Let them in please,' Miriam said.

There was no reply, except that each man took hold of one child, De Witt grabbing Sam and swinging him up over his shoulder.

'Ever been to a police station, young man?' he asked. Miriam watched her son, saw the mixture of fear and uncertainty in his eyes, saw the man's smiling white teeth in her son's face. In the meantime, Stewart was pushing her daughter towards the car.

'Mummy,' Alisha cried, tears in her voice. 'Mummy, come with us. Where are we going, Mummy?'

Robert appeared at last and took the baby and Miriam started down the steps but De Witt pushed her back.

'We'll bring them back later, or tomorrow. Whenever we get time.'

Sam was also crying now as the car door slammed on his sister who stared tearfully out, shouting for her mother to come and help her.

'Stop it,' Miriam said. 'Stop it, please! I'll tell you where they are, I'll tell you everything, just bring them back. Please, bring them back.'

De Witt almost threw Sam into the back of the car.

'Shut up!' he screamed. 'You want me to whip you?' His hand went threateningly to his belt. The crying stopped.

Stewart was looking at Miriam.

'I'll tell you,' she said, holding his glance. 'Please. Give me back my children. Please.'

Stewart turned and spoke to his partner. She could not hear the low undertones of his voice, but she heard De Witt's reply.

'She's lying, the bitch! Anyway, we'll teach her a lesson. Come on.'

Now Stewart's voice raised. 'How much more time do you want to waste? Let's hear what she has to say.' He opened the car door and motioned the children out, but held them firmly before him.

'Don't move,' he said, looking at Miriam. 'So where are they?' he asked.

Miriam could not speak.

He grasped Alisha's arm harder.

'They're in Pretoria,' she called out.

'You know if you are lying to us, I'll beat you and your children and the baby?' De Witt said evenly.

'Yes, I know.'

'Where? At a hotel?'

Miriam shook her head and felt tears escaping from her eyes. 'At my brother-in-law's. In Boom Street.'

He watched her closely. 'Are you *sure*?'

'Yes, I'm sure,' she said, her eyes fixed on her children. Stewart examined Miriam closely for a few moments more then turned and nodded to De Witt.

'Dammit, I should have known...' shouted De Witt.

'How would we know?' asked Stewart, frowning. 'That bitch of all people should have been telling the truth.'

Miriam listened, confused, waiting for them to release the children.

De Witt kicked the porch post with his boot, leaving a splintered crack in the wood. He glowered at his partner, but Stewart was looking at Miriam.

'Thank you, ma'am,' he said. 'You've been very helpful.' He touched his cap, the epitome of good manners now, and then he stood aside, allowing the children to escape. They ran into her arms where she held them briefly before pulling them into the shop. Robert stood holding the baby.

'See if they've gone,' she said. The boy went to the window and peered out. The car had all but disappeared, leaving a faint stir of dust behind it.

'They are gone, madam,' he said.

Miriam moved straight through the shop and back out onto the porch.

'Where are you going, Madam?' asked Robert, alarmed. She was moving now as she hadn't moved in days, quickly and with purpose. She ran down the porch steps, stopping only to call to him to give the children something to eat and to lock the doors. She ran, stumbling in her slippers, through the grass, ignoring the pathway because that was a longer route to the Weston farm and the nearest telephone, and as she went she felt the tears falling and her heart crashing in her chest, and she hoped that Rehmat would not hate her for what she had done.

Chapter Twelve

'YOU SENT US on a wild goose chase,' said Officer De Witt. There was an air of permanence about his stance, feet apart and firm, arms crossed, and he made sure to carefully enunciate each word that he spoke. Farah swallowed hard. As her husband had discovered very soon after he had married her, she was a woman capable of responding to anyone's bad mood with one of her own that was ten times worse, but she instinctively understood that she had met her match with the policeman who stood before her. He was tall and blond and good-looking, or so she had once thought – but there was nothing pleasant or flirtatious in his face or tone now.

Farah turned away.

'What did she tell you?' she asked.

'The truth,' he replied, with irony. 'I trust her more than I trust you. She may be a *plas-jappe*, living out there in the sticks, but that kind doesn't even *know* how to lie. She *told* me that bitch was here. All along she was here.'

'She *told* you?'

'*Ja.*'

Farah was surprised at Miriam. She had expected her to be more honourable for Rehmat's sake – she was the type. Her surprise evaporated, however, under the pressure of the problem she was now facing. She had no idea where Rehmat was at this moment, and now she was in trouble with the very people she had been trying to assist. She considered her options and, in accordance with her usual custom, decided that aggression might help her more than submissive compliance.

'She was here,' she said, turning defiantly to the two men. 'So what? What did you want me to do? Tell you right there and then, when you came the first time?'

'That's exactly what you were supposed to do,' De Witt said. 'You called us here, remember?'

'In front of my husband? He was standing right next to me. He would have killed me. Was I supposed to tell you while *she* could hear me? Hiding upstairs? It's your fault, you should have looked harder. What kind of state police don't even search the house properly?'

In the next moment she was aware of nothing but a searing pain as her arm was gripped and twisted. De Witt held her look until her eyes dropped to the ground.

'Where is she now?'

'I don't know. I've been out shopping all afternoon.' She indicated the sacks of groceries that lay scattered on the floor. 'She wasn't here when I got back.'

'And if the *plas-jappe* warned her, she won't be back at all.' De Witt dropped her arm and pushed her away. He looked at his partner.

'Check upstairs,' he said.

Amina Harjan was in the small, plainly furnished room she kept behind the café. She was lying on her bed, positioned directly before the orange glow cast by the setting sun, and she was sleeping. It was her habit to take a nap on afternoons when business was quiet in the café, and more so on the weekend, when she kept the place open for business well into the night and long after Jacob had finished for the day. That was why Jacob politely asked the breathless woman who ran wildly into the café to come back a little later if she must see Miss Harjan, as Miss Harjan could not be disturbed. He had not known quite what to do though, when the woman had watched him as though his speech were incomprehensible to her and had then run past him towards Amina's room.

The hasty knock on the door roused Amina, but she thought she must be dreaming still when she saw Rehmat's face leaning over her as she lay there in her bed.

'Can you help me?' Rehmat asked, her face drawn and pale.

Amina rubbed a hand over her eyes, and pushed back her mass of curly hair. She smiled at Rehmat, appearing to find nothing incongruous in the situation.

'What is it you need?'

'They know where I am and they are coming after me.'

Amina's smile disappeared as she watched Rehmat's eyes fill with tears. 'The police?' she asked.

'Yes.'

'When?'

'They could arrive at any moment. They're bound to search the whole area and people must have seen me...'

'Don't say a word,' said Amina. 'And don't cry.'

Rehmat hardly saw the girl leave her bed, but she felt herself moving, propelled by a guiding hand on her arm, and moments later she heard a door click behind her and she was plunged into darkness.

Officer De Witt left Farah with a narrow glance and strode into the kitchen. He squinted against the light of the setting sun that spread in through the high windows and skylight. The room was small and held few potential hiding places. He opened a few cupboards half-heartedly and then turned and glimpsed the narrow passage that led to Jehan's room. Farah called after him as he walked along it.

'Don't wake her,' she said, but he was already gone, and she finished her sentence muttering discontentedly to herself. Despite her enduring rancour towards Rehmat, she was now beginning to regret involving the police. She should have thought of another way to vent her hatred. She heard Jehan laugh, a sudden, demonic sound that elicited an oath of surprise from the policeman, and she knew that her usual two hours of peace, the freedom she obtained from her crazy sister-in-law while she slept, had been curtailed for that afternoon. She heard doors slamming upstairs and in a few moments, Stewart had come back down. De Witt emerged from Jehan's room, his sparse blond eyebrows raised in silent query.

'Nothing,' Stewart said. 'Some nice clothes, though. Labels are French.'

De Witt looked at Farah. 'We'll find her, don't worry.'

'I'm not worried.'

'You should be, because when we're finished with her, you'll be the next into the jailhouse for helping her.'

'I never wanted to help her,' she said bitterly.

'Then help us.'

'But I don't know where she went. Why don't you try her husband's hotel?'

'He checked out days ago. He keeps moving around. He's not stupid,' said Stewart.

They watched each other. The sun was setting quickly, casting the lower half of the room into shadow. Officer De Witt slammed his fist hard onto the counter and Farah jumped. The sound vibrated in the small room but Stewart waited calmly, and without a sound, his jaw moving continuously beneath his beard.

'Where...is...she?'

Farah opened her mouth to speak, but all they heard was a scream from Jehan's room, a long controlled sound that slowly lengthened and rose in pitch like an orchestrated bar of music, building to a crescendo and exploding finally into a long, hearty peal of manic laughter.

'Quickly, quickly, QUICKLY!!!!' Jehan screamed. 'THEY ARE COMING, SAID MIRIAM, THEY ARE COMING. MIRIAM SAID SO, MIRIAM SAID SO.'

The three people in the kitchen stared at the wall to Jehan's room as though the plaster itself were forming the sounds.

'THEY ARE COMING!!!' Jehan yelled. 'WHERE SHALL I GO? HELP ME, JEHAN, WHERE SHALL I GO, WHERE SHALL I GO?'

There was a silence. De Witt moved to go to the room, but Farah shook her head and he remained still. Jehan's speech had lowered in volume and was now a stream of indistinct muttering. They strained to listen.

'I can't believe it. How did they know? They are coming, Miriam said so, Miriam said so. Miriam phoned. WHERE SHALL I GO, JEHAN, WHERE SHALL I GO?' The recommencement of the shouting startled them all, and the voice had a desperate choke in it as though in exact imitation of the words it was repeating.

'TO THE HARJAN GIRL. THE HARJAN GIRL, THE HARJAN GIRL.' Jehan laughed delightedly. She had evidently found a series of lilting syllables that pleased her, because she continued to recite them in a sing-song voice. 'THE HARJAN GIRL, THE HARJAN GIRL, THE HARJAN GIRL,' she sang blithely. 'The Harjan girl, the Harjan girl. Miriam said so,' she added, suddenly, soberly. 'They are coming. Miriam said so.'

'The Harjan girl?' asked De Witt, frowning. His partner nodded.

'The Bazaar café,' he said. 'You remember. Amina Harjan and Jacob Williams.'

Both men looked at Farah. Her smile was slight, but her eyes held an excited look of triumph.

'What are you waiting for?' she asked them.

'Nothing,' said De Witt and they walked out of the house.

*

It took a few moments for the policemen's presence to be noticed by all the occupants of the café – and there were many, early on this Saturday evening – but one by one, the people at each table noticed the uniformed men standing inside the door, and they stopped chewing, waiting silently, eyes averted, to see what might happen. De Witt looked around the room, but nobody met his eyes. Jacob remained behind the counter, busying his hands with whatever work presented itself, his face impassive and clear of expression. There had been a time when the police had come here regularly to speak to Amina. They had even searched her room and the café a couple of times before, once looking for a black woman that Amina was rumoured to have been involved with, but they found nothing. Jacob was an honest man, but one who could hide his emotions well, and easily. It gave him a relaxed air, as though nothing that might occur in his vicinity, be it a hysterical woman or a pair of impatient police officers, would ever shake his composed exterior. The policemen's arrival had caused a knot in his stomach, but he continued his work as though removing the water spots from his glasses were the only concern on his mind.

The two officers approached him, Stewart walking ahead now.

'Jacob,' he said, nodding.

Jacob nodded back.

'We're looking for someone. A woman.'

Jacob came out from behind the counter, a box of matches in his hand, and walked slowly to one of the paraffin lamps that hung at intervals round the walls of the dining area. He struck a match and held it patiently to the wick, watching as the paraffin drew up the lamp and cast a warm glow on the table beneath. He shook out the match and moved slowly to the next lamp.

'What woman?' he said, his tone politely interested.

Stewart followed him, and watched the next lamp being lit as he spoke. 'An Indian woman. Well dressed, probably. Have you seen her?'

Another match was struck, hissing briefly into the gloom.

'Indians is all we get in here. Why don't you have a look around?' Jacob said. De Witt rolled his eyes at his partner, but they carefully looked over every table anyway. There were no women at all. The café looked inviting now, with the tongues of lamplight licking into the corners and reflecting off the rough polish of the wooden floors and tables.

'Where's Amina?' asked Stewart. The final lamp flared into life, and Jacob returned to his place behind the counter. A low hum of talk began to spread around the room, as people began to eat again. Jacob's methodical lamp-lighting, his apparent lack of concern at the police officers, his measured movements, had reassured them in some way.

'Miss Harjan is asleep.'

De Witt looked impatiently at his watch. 'A little early, isn't it?'

'She'll be getting up to work soon,' Jacob replied. 'She works late on Saturday nights. Why don't you have a seat and wait for her?' He saw the irritation on their faces and he added quickly, 'Or I can go and wake her.'

'She lives here?' De Witt asked his partner.

'She has a room out the back.' Stewart looked at Jacob. 'If it's okay with you, we'll just go and speak to her.'

Jacob said nothing, knowing that it would be okay if they wanted it to be so, and he watched helplessly as the men strode past him, through the kitchen and out to Amina's room.

Chapter Thirteen

T HERE WAS NO delay between the rap on Amina's door, and the entry of the policemen. The room was fully dark now, and in the shadows all they could make out was a long body lying in the bed. They waited in silence and watched Amina's deep, rhythmical breathing. Otherwise she lay perfectly still. Stewart walked round the bed so that he could see her face, and the sound of his boots woke the girl with a start.

'Jacob?' she said, confused.

'Officers Stewart and De Witt.'

Amina sat up at once. She reached for the matches that lay on her bedside table, struck one and applied it to a candle. Then she looked up at the two men revealed to her in the warm light, her eyes still adjusting from the earlier darkness.

'Yes?' she asked politely, as though preparing to take a breakfast order.

'We know she's here,' stated De Witt, with a tone of authority.

Amina looked perplexed. She knew Officer Stewart well – he was as reasonable a policeman as you could get in this place, but she was wary of the other, De Witt, and his gun.

'Who?' she asked him.

'Rehmat Winston.'

'*Who*?'

De Witt sat down on her bed and Amina raised her eyebrows at the presumption and looked at Stewart queryingly. He made no response, just stood impassively, waiting.

'Rehmat Winston,' De Witt repeated. 'Fourteen Boom Street. You know her. She came in here asking you to hide her.'

'Jesus Christ,' said Amina. 'I think I would have noticed.'

'We know she's here.'

'Well, you know more than me, then.'

De Witt leaned in to her. She smelt the acrid odour of sweat and dust on his shirt.

'Don't be smart,' he told her. He got up suddenly and walked around the room. There was no door other than the one that they had used to enter, and no window other than the one that was beside the door. The only furniture in the room besides the bed and the table – which held a wash bowl, a jug and some soap, as well as the candle and two books – was a big wooden closet built into the side wall. Officer Stewart knelt to look beneath the bed, although he knew very well that it was too low to conceal a person. Then he stood up wearily and waited while De Witt went to the closet. Amina remained sitting up in her bed, cross-legged now, watching the two men. She looked bored and vaguely irritated.

Yawning slightly, but audibly enough, she watched De Witt tug at the closet handle.

'Open this up,' he said.

She didn't hear his words because suddenly her heart was pounding so hard that the blood pulsing through her ears blocked out all external sound, but she knew what he wanted. She swung her bare legs from the bed – she was wearing only a man's cotton shirt – and reached for her trousers. Slipping them on, she slid a key from beneath the bed and went to unlock the closet. She moved about methodically, her face showing no trace of concern, when in fact she felt she might pass out at any moment from the strain of trying to slow the adrenaline that poured through her veins. She turned the key with a strong twist of her wrist and flung open the door. De Witt stared at her.

'What is all this stuff?' he asked, frowning.

'Extra stock. From the shop. That's why I lock it,' she said. 'You know these *kaffirs*,' she added with heavy irony. 'They would steal anything.' It was the kind of thing they would ordinarily like to hear, that they could chat about sympathetically, but they caught her tone and knew she was mocking them.

The closet space was shallow but tall, and was stacked top to bottom with tins of jam, bags of flour, beans, lentils and other dry goods. In one corner hung six shirts, three pairs of trousers and a coat. The policemen stepped back, and with a sudden jab of his leg, De Witt kicked the door shut.

'WHERE IS THE BITCH?' he shouted and Amina turned away from him. She tried to reach the front door, but Stewart stood massively in her way.

'Just tell us,' he said.

'I don't even know who you're talking about.' She attempted a smile. 'You know as well as I do that I've had some women in here, but this time even I don't know what...'

De Witt's stinging hand across her neck stopped her from finishing her sentence.

'Stinking queer,' he spat.

A second blow to her body hit her with a force that sent her crashing onto the bed. She lay there with her arms up in front of her, stunned, waiting. Nothing else came. Stewart had grabbed hold of his partner and was pushing him towards the door, the meaning of his shouts lost in the incoherent rage of his speech.

'Leave her,' Stewart was telling him. 'Wait in the car. Go on. Go.'

They heard De Witt stumbling away from the room, around the outside of the café, and in a moment Stewart returned. He stood at the entrance to Amina's room.

'Hey,' he said to her. She was sitting up now. Her neck was sore but she would not touch it while he watched her. She looked down at her hands, deliberately studying the pale outline of the veins, and waited for him to speak.

'Didn't I do you a favour one time?' he said.

She looked at him.

'Yours is the only place in town where your *kaffir* workers eat alongside Indians and Coloureds, and you get away with it. You're on my beat,' he continued. 'And I don't see the point of making an issue of it, so I let it go. I let it go that last time, didn't I?'

'Yes,' she said quietly.

'I could have closed you down any time.'

'Yes.'

'I still can.'

'Yes.'

'So don't you think you owe me one?'

She paused and her eyes looked away to the dark window, considering.

'I suppose so,' she said finally.

'So,' he said, and his tone implied that they both understood the contract just formed between them. 'Is she here?'

Amina looked at him, her eyes clear and open and serious.

'No,' she said.

'Do you know where she is?'

She shrugged helplessly. 'I really don't,' she said. 'I'm sorry.'

He nodded, satisfied at last.

'Okay,' he said. 'Sorry for my colleague, eh?'

Amina waved a dismissive hand. 'Forget it,' she told him, even though she knew she wouldn't. 'Thanks for helping me out. Maybe next time I can do the same for you.'

'*Ja*,' Stewart said. 'Maybe next time.'

Amina lay quietly on her bed for another thirty minutes after they had left, thinking hard, watching the quivering shapes thrown against the walls of her room by the guttering candle. She hated to be laid low by pure physical force, and though she knew that it was De Witt's own weakness that made him hit out, her rationalisations could not reduce her disgust at his behaviour. After she judged that enough time had gone by, she sat up and checked her watch. Then she went to the window.

The lights of the kitchen were opposite, and she could see the outlines of her staff, cooking and washing up. She could also make out the back of Jacob's head as he moved through the kitchen, and she looked again at her watch, and knew he must be wanting to get home. The long days they worked on the weekends tired him. She touched her neck, still red from the officer's hand, then went and sat on her bed and reached down beneath it for the key. She weighed the cold iron in her palm for a moment, and then she went to the front door and slowly opened it.

Outside, she made a brisk, wide circuit of the land around her room and the café, peering carefully into the darkness, straining her ears to hear above the scraping of the crickets that at night invaded even this built-upon area of land. When she was satisfied that the policemen in fact had left, she returned to her room and went directly to the closet, unlocking it and throwing open the doors.

One by one she picked up the bags and tins, swinging each one over to the recess between the closet and the wall, transferring the sugar and flour and lentils back to the place where they were always kept. She worked as she had done the first time, in a steady rhythm, and she soon felt warm, for the bags were heavy, and she paused to undo the top button of her shirt. When she had almost emptied the closet, she straightened up and ran her hand down the edge of the back panel of the wardrobe until her fingers found and pushed into a tiny hollow. With some considerable effort, she pulled her weight against it until the panel slid open.

Rehmat squinted up at her, crouched low in the tiny space,

her arms wrapped defensively about her. Amina leaned against the side of the closet and looked down at her with a wry smile, resting her forehead wearily on one arm.

'They've gone,' said Amina.

Rehmat let out a shaky sigh and looked mutely at Amina, the suggestion of tears touching the edges of her eyes. Without another word, Amina held out a hand and she grasped the long fingers tightly for she had long ago ceased to feel any sensation in her cramped legs and needed all Amina's help just to stand up. Amina supported her as far as the bed where Rehmat sat waiting while the blood began a slow and painful course again through her legs. She rubbed at her calves and the backs of her knees.

'I'm sorry I did this to you,' she said. 'I heard them when they shouted.' She looked more closely at Amina, at the fading red spot on her neck, and gasped.

'Did they hit you?' she asked, appalled.

'No,' she replied. Amina paced up and down a few times. 'They weren't bad. Just frustrated.' She stopped and looked at Rehmat for a long moment, incongruously, as though she were a piece of sculpture, there to be examined and perhaps admired, taking in the details of her eyes and nose and mouth. Disconcerted, Rehmat looked away, and asked her quickly if she hadn't been scared by the policemen.

'Oh no,' said Amina. 'I've had plenty of practice.'

'With the police?' asked Rehmat, surprised.

Amina laughed. 'Yes, I suppose, but I meant I've had plenty of practice with the closet.' Her eyes were smiling and Rehmat smiled too, a little cautiously, uncertain of how to respond. Amina took in her confusion and changed her tone, to one that was more business-like.

'I'll have to get back to work soon,' Amina said.

'Of course – I'm sorry to have caused you so much trouble.'

'No trouble. What will you do now? Where is your husband?'

'I don't know. On a flight to Paris or London, I hope. I phoned him as soon as Miriam phoned me to warn me about the police, and he didn't want to leave me alone, but I persuaded him to go straight to the airport and try to get out. I hope he did. We were both supposed to leave tomorrow morning. Only one more day.'

At her washstand Amina poured some water into the bowl, and began washing her face. She turned to Rehmat as she rubbed the soap into a lather between her hands.

'How did you know to come here?'

'Jehan gave me the idea. The Harjan girl, she kept saying. She's been repeating it on and off for a few days. She must have heard someone talking about you.'

Amina said nothing, and Rehmat continued. 'When the warning call came...'

'From Miriam?' Amina said.

'Yes. The police had been to Delhof.'

Amina washed her face, her expression impassive. Then she reached for her towel and watched Rehmat as she dried herself.

'So how did they know you were here?'

'The police?'

Amina nodded. 'I mean, we're not related. I have a slight

reputation for being in trouble with them but still... Why did they come straight here?

'They must have gone to the house first.'

'So somebody there must have sent them here,' stated Amina simply, and Rehmat frowned.

'No,' she said. 'It's not possible. When I left, only Jehan was home, and she wouldn't even have opened the door.'

'Where was Farah?'

'At the shops. I was expecting her back any time...'

Rehmat heard herself and stopped short and massaged her leg again. She could not look up to meet Amina's eyes. The girl tied back her long curls into a loose ponytail and shrugged on a jacket with a casual motion of her thin shoulders.

'I wouldn't go back there if I were you,' Amina said.

'We don't know if it was Farah. And they'll worry about me,' replied Rehmat.

'Perhaps,' Amina said, without much conviction. 'But apart from anything else, the police are probably watching the house. I think you should stay here tonight. You can read – there are some books over there – and rest. Try to sleep. Tomorrow morning I'll take you to the airport.'

'I can't...'

'Why not?'

'You've already done more than enough. I don't want to put you at risk any longer.'

'What else will you do?' she asked. Rehmat could not answer.

'Don't worry,' said Amina gently. 'Take a shirt from the closet – I think there are even some pyjamas in there.'

Rehmat nodded. There was a sense of safety here in this small, softly lit room, and in the quiet confidence of Amina's voice and her calm directions.

At the door, Amina turned. 'I'm going to make a call to someone I know who works at the airport about getting you on a flight. But your things...'

'Forget them,' said Rehmat. 'It's only my clothes really.'

'What about your passport and tickets?'

'I have them. I made sure I brought them with me when I came.'

'Good. Now try to rest,' Amina repeated.

'I will. Thank you.'

Amina smiled and closed the door behind her and Rehmat began to cry, her sobs a mixture of fear, relief and sorrow.

Fifteen minutes later there was a firm knock at the door. Instinctively, Rehmat froze where she sat on the bed, her stomach a ball of fear, and she tried not to breathe, tried only to listen.

A key was scraping into the lock, turning slowly.

'It's Jacob, ma'am,' called a deep, gentle voice and she stood up quickly, light-headed with relief. She was embarrassed to greet Jacob with her face tear-stained, but he did not look directly at her. He walked inside and placed a tray of covered plates on the bedside table.

'Amina sends you some dinner,' he said. 'Pardon me for walking straight in but I didn't want to just hand them over to you, in case the police are still around.'

'Thank you,' she called after him, but he had already closed and locked the door. The act of eating seemed unimportant to her at this moment, and unappealing. Nevertheless, she uncovered the plates and found the rising scents and warmth stimulated her appetite at once. The dishes were all distinctly South African – she had been sent a plate piled high with a stew of tomato and lamb *breedie*, a square piece of *bobotie*, rich with minced lamb, raisins and spices, and a large slice of milk tart for dessert. A newly opened bottle of soda water stood on one corner of the tray, with an upturned glass balanced on top of it. She poured the drink first, and looked at the food. The bedside table was too small to take more than one plate at a time, so she placed Amina's books and the tray of food onto the floor beside her and brought each dish up to the table in turn.

She consumed the food slowly and with a strange mixture of pleasure and regret. It was food that she remembered from her childhood – not from her father's house, where the food that had been cooked was predominantly Indian – but she recalled it from school and from cafés that she had visited illicitly when she was a teenager. Her emotion constricted her throat and made it difficult to swallow, but she ate anyway, because she knew as she finished the last mouthfuls that it was unlikely that she would ever taste such dishes here in her own country again.

It was almost one o'clock in the morning when Amina locked the back door of the café and walked back to her room. The only breaks in the darkness came from the far, faint glow of a street lamp on the road and from the window of her own room, where a soft light breathed against the curtained pane of glass. Rehmat must be still awake, or else must have left a candle burning. She half hoped that Rehmat would be awake, so that they might talk for a while. Throughout her evening's work at the café, Amina had been considering the events leading to Rehmat's appearance in her room. She knew that Miriam had been visited by the police, but who had alerted them in the first place? She frowned at the thought of Miriam with those men. She knew her to be shy, but she had sensed flashes of strength in her character, and she hoped she had not caused them to harm or threaten her. What it was about Miriam that had caught Amina's interest, she could not quite say. She was attractive, certainly, but so were many other women. Amina intuited a quick intelligence and sensitivity beneath the controlled surface of Miriam's personality, but she was willing to admit that she might be reading too much into their brief meetings. She wondered if her concern would seem justification enough for her to visit Miriam in Delhof. Perhaps not.

Amina hoped that Rehmat would shed some light on the preceding day's events, but she also wanted to talk to this woman about her life, about why and how she had run away from her family for the sake of love. It was a rare event for Amina to find another Indian woman who had dared not to conform to tradition and convention. She reached the door, slipped her key into the lock, and turned it as quietly as she could.

Rehmat was fast asleep on one side of the bed. The candle that still burned on the table lit her even features with a low, trembling light. Amina closed the door soundlessly, and stood watching the woman who lay sleeping before her. Rehmat was very beautiful, Amina decided, and looked very much like her brother. She had thought that Omar was also good-looking, but in her opinion, his regular, clean features were lacking in spirit. There was no openness in his face, and no sense of the unpredictable in his nature. In Amina's eyes, these were the qualities that elevated ordinary beauty to something irresistible. Rehmat was attractive, but Amina's admiration was merely superficial – the appreciation of someone looking at a fine painting, without a wish to hang it in their own house. In a matter of moments, she had buttoned on a clean shirt to sleep in. She had crept to the closet with the intention of wearing the unaccustomed pyjamas, but they were gone, and she assumed that beneath the drawn-up sheet, Rehmat must be wearing them. Amina lifted up the edge of the sheets, and slid slowly beneath them. The sound of her body shifting between the crisp cotton roused Rehmat, but only for a second, long enough for her to turn her head on the pillow, so that now Amina could see her perfect profile.

Amina took a long, deep breath and exhaled slowly and silently, feeling the muscles of her slim body relax in the bed. She turned to look at Rehmat once more, but at that moment, the guttering candle expired, dousing them in a darkness that was as thick as a liquid. Amina turned on her side, closed her eyes, and slipped into sleep to the slumbering breaths of the woman who lay beside her.

Chapter Fourteen

ONLY WHEN SHE had finished the last of her breakfast did Amina fold up the newspaper she had been reading. She was sliding out of her booth when she noticed the large, lumbering frame of a man standing almost over her. He was Indian, but she did not recognise him as a regular customer of the café. She nodded to him politely but he only regarded her nervously, fiddling with his watch strap.

'Miss Harjan?'

'Yes.' She was standing before him now, putting on her jacket, waiting.

'I am Sadru, Rehmat's brother.'

Amina was surprised. He was most unlike either Rehmat or Omar in his features and build. He did not seem to be as articulate either, and appeared to be struggling to address her.

'What can I do for you?'

'My sister. Where is she?'

His tone was almost plaintive, an incongruous tone from such a large man, and Amina glanced around the café to give herself a moment to think. Sadru followed her look with hope, as though it might reveal Rehmat to him. Amina did not think he had had anything to do with calling the police – she was sure his wife had managed that by herself – but Rehmat had come too close to getting away for her to take any chances.

'I don't know,' she said. 'Why do you ask me?'

'Farah told me she came here.'

'Did she really?'

Sadru frowned and his shoulders dropped, as though he sensed that yet another woman was about to run rings around him. Amina smiled, and leaned in towards him so she could lower her voice.

'Listen. She is fine. I promise you. She's not here, but she's fine.'

'Really?' He looked relieved. 'Because, I don't want anything to happen to her, you know. And James has been phoning.'

Amina looked interested. 'Her husband? Where is he?'

'In Nairobi, already. He's flying to Paris tomorrow.' Sadru frowned. 'He didn't waste any time. He just left.'

'Good thing,' said Amina. 'Easier for them both. Listen. Tell James...'

'He's phoning again in an hour,' Sadru interrupted, pointing to his watch.

'Okay. Tell him, she's fine, and that he should just concentrate on getting home? Okay? Will you remember?'

'Concentrate on getting home,' Sadru repeated, earnestly, as though sifting the sentence for a hidden meaning.

'Yes. Anyway,' Amina said, glancing out to her truck. 'If you don't mind excusing me, I have a delivery to make, Mr...'

'Sadru. Please, you must let me thank you for helping us...'

'I didn't do anything.'

He held out a massive hand, which Amina took, while guiding him out through the front door.

'We can never thank you enough, Farah and I...'

'There's really no need. I didn't do anything.' She looked into his face and repeated the words. 'I didn't do anything.'

He frowned. 'No?'

'No. If anyone ever asks you. Okay?'

He nodded, and gave her a wink as he ducked into his car. She watched him lower the window so that he could lean his meaty arm on it, before he revved up the engine and motored out into the road.

Amina watched him go until his car had disappeared completely, in the hope that, if the police were still around, they would follow him instead of her. Then she waved at Jacob through the front door. He gave her an encouraging smile and watched as she went to her truck.

She walked around the vehicle quickly, making her habitual check on the tyres. The roads, especially the side roads, were poor in the Asiatic Bazaar and all the other Indian and Coloured areas, and since the introduction of the Group Areas Act, they had only deteriorated further. Amina rarely had reason to drive into the

African areas but she knew the roads there were much worse, if they existed at all. Once she was satisfied that all was in order, she opened the door and raised a foot to climb in.

'Just a moment.'

She felt the fine hair on the base of her skull prickle as she recognised the voice of Officer De Witt. His hand was on her shoulder. She stepped down again, turned and smiled at the policeman.

'We have to stop meeting like this,' she said. 'People will talk.'

He flashed her a smile that was barely more than a grimace. 'That's something you should already be used to, *ja*? People talking.'

Amina shrugged and looked past the policeman. She frowned as she saw his car parked no more than fifty feet away, across the road – how had she missed it? Officer Stewart was sitting inside the car, but when he saw her looking, he came over to them, his face drawn into a frown. He tipped his cap as he arrived, and spoke with some annoyance to his partner.

'We have things to do. If you've said your good mornings to the lady, we should be on our way.'

De Witt paid little attention. He moved to the rear window of the truck and examined the interior. The back seat was covered with tins and a cardboard box from which various grocery items protruded. The long hollow floor space between the front and back seats was also filled with supplies and covered over with layers of sack cloth.

'Do you always carry so much stuff with you?' he asked, his tone belligerent.

'You know how it is,' replied Amina. 'There's always something to pick up or deliver. Half the time you can't rely on people delivering goods when they say they will. Easier to do it yourself.' She glanced at Officer Stewart for affirmation of this generality, and he nodded politely. She remained very still, trying not to betray her anxiety, trying to slow her movements to give the impression that their interest in her truck was of no concern to her.

'Is there anything else I can do for you gentlemen, or can I get on with my day?' she asked finally and as she spoke, she stepped up behind the wheel. Even as his partner smiled and began to say that they should also be getting on, Officer De Witt yanked open the back door and plunged his fist twice, and with great force, into the sacking that lay across the hollow behind Amina's seat. The girl's heart stopped. De Witt shouted in pain and withdrew his hand, shaking it.

'What the hell have you got in there, rocks?'

'Tinned goods,' Amina replied automatically. She felt dizzy with tension, and started the truck, shifting immediately into first gear. 'I'm sure I'll see you both around,' she called as she pulled away.

De Witt stood nursing his fist and shouting after her. 'Go on,' he yelled. 'If I never see you again, it'll be too damn soon.'

Amina was already too far away to hear the words, but inside the café, Jacob heard the commotion as he poured a cup of coffee for his first customer of the day, and he looked up briefly, and allowed himself a smile.

*

Amina drove down the road at a pace that was sedate and, she hoped, not suspicious, watching the policemen in her rear view mirror. They were walking back to their car, and appeared to be arguing.

'I don't think they're going to follow us,' she called out over her shoulder. 'Are you okay? He punched so hard.'

She was met with no reply other than the sound of the engine, and she looked around at the sacking. Slowing down even more, she flicked back a couple of pieces to find nothing but the tinned goods she had just claimed.

Amina braked slightly but realised she would only draw attention to herself if she stopped.

'Where are you?' she called, as though the missing woman might somehow appear before her.

Amina stared out at the road and tried to think what to do. If she went back, they would see her. Amina had sent Rehmat out to hide in the truck over an hour before. She must have seen the police then. Or did they already have her? A chill grasped her. Maybe that whole exchange just now was a joke on her. That bastard De Witt was probably laughing at her right now.

She had to swerve to avoid an African woman who had stepped out without warning, almost under her wheels. Amina stopped and looked back to check that the woman was okay, only to find that she was running after her, and losing her colourful blanket and headscarf as she came. Without a word she pulled open the door and began clambering up into the truck.

'Give me a hand, would you?' Rehmat said, breathlessly. Amina grasped her wrists, hauled her up and pulled back onto the road at once, pressing the truck to move more quickly. Rehmat sat back, her eyes closed, and took a deep breath. Amina glanced at the blanket which Rehmat still held over her shoulders.

'Tired of the same old Paris fashions?'

Rehmat smiled. 'Yes. Wanted to try something new.'

'What on earth happened?'

'I saw them when I came out,' Rehmat said. 'I had a feeling they might be back, so I crept around and I saw them from behind the tree in the yard.'

'And then?'

'I didn't know what to do,' Rehmat said. 'I started to come back to your room, and then I thought, no, that's the first place they'll come. So I started walking up the road, away from them, and I was hoping that you would start driving, thinking I was in the truck, and see me.'

'I did think you were there,' Amina smiled. 'I thought that you got hurt. That bastard policeman smashed his fist into the sacks and hurt himself on some tins.'

'Which? The one that hit you?'

'Yes.'

'Good,' said Rehmat, and laughed.

She shivered suddenly and turned to look back, but the road behind them was still clear.

'You gave yourself away just now,' she said, after a moment, and Amina frowned and looked into her rear-view mirror but Rehmat smiled.

'No, not with them,' she said. 'With me. You lied to me yesterday. You told me they didn't hit you.'

Amina smiled.

'Why did you lie to me?' Rehmat asked.

Amina shrugged. 'I didn't want you to feel bad.'

'You're very considerate,' Rehmat replied. 'It'll be a lucky man . . . or a lucky person that has you as their partner.'

'A lucky *person*,' repeated Amina with a smile. 'So even you have heard the rumours about me?' She laughed, but Rehmat bit her lip and concentrated on looking from the windscreen before her. After a minute had passed in awkward silence, she spoke.

'What you do and how you live is your own business, and nobody else's,' Rehmat told her, annoyed that her acknowledgement had been cast aside. 'If anyone should understand that, it's me. I was trying to be nice, not make a comment about the way you live.'

Amina glanced at her. 'I know. Don't be angry. I was just surprised, that's all. No one ever gave me such a compliment before.'

Rehmat shrugged slightly then smiled.

'I didn't think you were going to stop back there,' she told Amina. 'I was waving and waving.'

'Sorry, my mind was all over the place. When I realised you weren't in the truck, I panicked. And your disguise confused me.'

Rehmat shook her head. 'This poor African woman. She was walking along with her child, and I came running up and begged her to sell me her scarf and her blanket. She must have thought I was mad.'

'But she gave it to you anyway?'

'You should have seen how much I paid her,' replied Rehmat.

They drove along in silence for few minutes, and Amina kept an eye almost continuously on the road behind her. She felt sure, though, that the officers had given up.

'Your brother Sadru came in the café this morning.'

'Really?'

'He wanted to know where you were, if you were okay. I said I didn't know, but to tell James that you were fine.'

'James is all right?'

Amina nodded. 'He's in Nairobi, so there's nothing to worry about. He's going to Paris tomorrow.'

Rehmat sank back in her seat. 'Thank God,' she said.

'When you've taken off, I'll make sure that he gets your flight details.'

Amina said nothing more, content to just drive and leave Rehmat to her own thoughts. It was several minutes before Rehmat spoke again.

'I feel sorry for my brother,' Rehmat said.

Amina looked at her. 'Sadru?' she asked.

'He's so naïve. He's so...' An edge of anger appeared in her voice. 'Can't he see what she's like?'

'You don't worry about Omar, then?'

'No. Not Omar.' Rehmat laughed. 'Omar is shrewd. He can take care of himself, and he knows what he wants in life. And he is lucky to have a wife like Miriam. Just what he wanted, I'm sure. Someone to live out in the sticks and cook for him.'

'I think she is more than that,' said Amina, a little sharply.

'I'm sure she is,' replied Rehmat, looking at her. 'But whether my brother knows it, or even cares, is another matter.' She reached into her bag and pulled out a cigarette. She held one out to Amina, but the girl shook her head.

'Are you friends with Miriam?' Rehmat asked.

Amina hesitated. 'Not particularly. Why do you ask?'

'I don't know. The way you were in the café...'

'That was only the second time I'd ever seen her,' Amina said.

'Really? Because you didn't talk much, but there seemed to be... I don't know, an understanding between you. Like you get between people who are comfortable with each other.'

Amina shrugged. 'I like her. She seems very intelligent, but she's not used to speaking much. Or being listened to, probably. We talked a bit when I went to work there.' She shifted a little in her seat.

'So you do know her well?'

'Not as well as I'd...' Amina bit off the sentence and looked away. 'I know her a bit. She seems nice.'

Rehmat nodded and took a drag on her cigarette, but Amina's slip had not escaped her.

Several miles later, Amina turned the wheel sharply, veering off onto a smaller, tarred road. 'We're nearly at the airport,' she said.

Rehmat looked at her. 'I'm glad I met you. And not just because you saved my life.'

'I hardly saved your life.'

'You saved me from jail, and that's the same thing,' Rehmat replied. 'Anyway, I'm just glad we met. I hope you always do what you feel is right in your life.'

'I will,' Amina reassured her.

'Good. Because for years, I wondered in the back of my mind whether I had really done the right thing. Eloping. Not because I'm not very happy with James – I am. But because for so long my whole family made me feel I had done something so terrible. It can wear you down.'

Amina smiled. 'If you let it. I took responsibility for myself and my decisions a long time ago, and now I don't have to listen to anyone I don't respect.'

The road narrowed as they entered the airport terminals.

'Do you think they'll have someone here?' Rehmat asked.

'No,' Amina said, with a confidence she did not quite feel. 'Don't worry. I've arranged for someone to take you straight onto the plane without having to check in and all that.'

'How did you manage that?'

Amina just smiled and pulled the truck up to the pavement outside the terminal. Inside, the building teemed with people and Rehmat paused for a moment, taken aback by so many noises and smells and sights after the long, open road with only Amina in her sights and the roar of the truck in her ears. Amina had already darted away and within a few minutes she had returned with her contact. He was a pleasant man, a Cape Malay, and he shook Rehmat's hand cordially before inviting her to follow him through check-in and customs and onto the plane.

'This is where I leave you,' Amina told her. Rehmat nodded and looked at the girl, unable to speak. Amina hated all attempts at goodbyes and, in line with her instincts, hung back from effusiveness but Rehmat quickly stepped forward and hugged her.

'I can never thank you enough,' Rehmat told her. 'I'll never forget what you've done for me.'

She turned away, and looked to the waiting airport official, indicating that she was ready to leave. As they walked into the crowds, she turned to wave but Amina had already placed her hat back on her head and was hurrying back to the truck, for she had decided already that her first task on returning home would be to get Miriam's telephone number, if there was one, and let her know that all was well.

Chapter Fifteen

T HE DAY HAD been cool and overcast, a long, drab day, unremarkable from any of the others that Miriam found flowing surely past. Since Rehmat had left, and the commotion surrounding her departure had died away, their lives had settled once again into the familiar patterns. None of the family had seen her leave, but Amina had left word for them that she had safely boarded her flight. Miriam had wanted to thank Amina for her help, but she had no telephone and no other convincing reason to go to Pretoria; and Omar insisted abruptly that Sadru had thanked her enough for all of them.

As it was the end of the month, they had expected a visit from their landlords, but the long, gleaming car failed to materialise, and early in the evening Miriam changed out of the new cotton dress that she had worn in anticipation of them, and Omar removed his tie. They ate dinner with the children, sitting as usual around the vast wooden table, but the baby was ill tempered and tired, and Miriam put her to bed before the meal was over. They listened to her crying for a few minutes as they ate, until the noise stopped abruptly.

'She is sleeping,' said Sam, and Miriam nodded. Omar said nothing, but ate quickly, as always, and then got up, leaving his plate where it was, and walked over to the single armchair where he picked up his newspaper and began to read. As though released from some kind of spell, Miriam and the children began to talk amongst themselves. Small drips of conversation – a story of what had happened at school, of which teacher said what, a question here, and an explanation there. She spoke quietly, because Omar became irritated at too much noise and when the children's voices rose, excited or questioning, she would hush them, but with smiling reluctance. She liked this time of chatter with her children and when they were finished with their meals, they each picked up their plates and followed her to the sink, where the dishes were deposited. Then came the trek upstairs, leading towards the inevitability of their beds. If she was tired, the struggle to bathe them and make them ready for sleep was a long one. But on days like this, the task was enjoyable to her, their sing-song voices a break from the quiet, brusque tones of her day in the shop, and their trusting faces a relief to her deepening loneliness.

Later that night, she sat with Omar in the back of the kitchen, where both of them had pulled forward their chairs to whatever warmth remained soaked into the black metal of the stove. The silence outside was deep and thick, and she was grateful to be inside where the walls of her home enclosed living people and sounds and movements, however faint they might be. Omar was writing fitfully, doing the shop accounts, with the oil lamp near his elbow, while Miriam sewed a dress for Alisha. She had received the day before, addressed to her alone, a letter from Rehmat, from Paris, and she was tempted to re-read it, although she knew most of the contents by heart now. It was a short letter, a page of thanks for hospitality shown, and for help given. It was written on cream paper of a kind Miriam had never seen before, as thin and as crisp as a layer of onion skin. Miriam glanced at her husband and recalled the black look that had crossed his face when he had realised that the letter was not addressed to him. She decided to keep it until tomorrow and she continued with the sewing. While he did the accounts he disliked distractions, and so the radio was switched off, and she missed the soothing inflections of the unknown man who read stories over the air every evening. She caught only the outside rim of the lamp that he kept at a low burn to conserve the oil, but her young eyes were strong, and she watched the fabric closely as her fingers wove the needle delicately between the turned edges of the cloth. Omar had developed a habit of clearing his throat every minute or two, and she began to make a game of seeing how many stitches she could make before the next scrape of his throat. He looked up at her once, briefly, and her head also raised in response. She met his eyes for a second and almost smiled at her husband, but he looked serious and so she bent her head again to the dim cloth that had slipped away from her fingers.

In that profound quiet, the sudden clattering at the front door of the shop startled them both. In a second, Omar was on his feet.

'What is that?' he asked her, and she watched him, her eyes wide, as she bit off a length of thread with her teeth.

He took up the lamp and went through to the shop, calling for John as he did so.

'John is sick, remember?' she called after him.

The banging came again – someone clearly wanted to be let in – and Miriam dropped her sewing on the chair and followed Omar out to the shop. The noise had stopped, and he was busy opening up the padlocks and grills over the front door.

'What are you doing?' she asked, but then the person outside passed under the light, pacing around impatiently on the porch, and she saw that it was a white man, a farmer she recognised from many months ago as a customer at the shop.

When the door finally opened, a series of muttered curses sailed clearly from the porch through to the back counter, where Miriam stood. The farmer strode into the shop with the air of one who owned it.

'My car.' He pointed outside. 'It's messed up. Both the lights are messed up, and I'm driving in the pitch bloody dark and I can't see a bloody thing.' He stamped his foot like a frustrated child.

'Your car lights stopped working?' repeated Omar, trying to understand.

'*Ja*. I hit a *kaffir*, walking in the middle of the...' he glanced at Miriam and bit off a swear word, '...road, like he owns it, and both my lights got knocked out. I thought I hit him just on the one side, but both my bloody lights are gone.'

Omar went out to the porch and waited for the man to lead the way.

'Where did it happen?' he asked.

'Just here.' He waved out to where the dusty road snaked away into the darkness. 'Two hundred yards. Not even. God, I was glad to see your place.'

They both went out to the car and walked around it slowly, surveying the damage together. The farmer touched a dent beside the broken lamp and then pulled back, holding his fingers away from him.

'Bloody *kaffir*.' He looked around, then wiped his hand on the back of his trousers. 'I don't know why both lamps are out. But I can't get home without any light.'

'I have at least one in the shop.' Omar turned and walked back to the edge of the porch.

'Miriam!' he called.

'Yes.'

'Get the car headlamp. It is on the last shelf, by the big paraffin lamps.'

'Yes.'

The shop was almost completely dark, with only the occasional flicker of Omar's lamp outside casting a thin gleam onto the wooden shelves, but she knew her way around the stock, and she moved carefully along the rows of stacked-up goods, feeling along the shelf above her head, till her fingers had touched on all the lamps, from the tiny candle-like lights to the heavy headlamp at the end. This she pulled down, taking her time, feeling no urgency in spite of the fussing of the men outside. She listened to the rise and fall of their conversation, unable to catch the words, and she felt an unusual sense of control, of calmness, settle upon her. Her mind raced, but her body seemed to move just as it should. She heard again and again in her mind the first words of explanation that the Afrikaaner had given. 'I hit a *kaffir*...' And now his car was messed up. She turned and walked back down the length of the counter and out to the porch, where Omar met her and took the lamp. The farmer looked up, hopeful, pleased.

'*Ja*,' he nodded. 'That looks like the right one.'

He took the light and proceeded to fix it in place.

'Where is he?' The sound of her own voice, barely used for the last several hours, surprised even Miriam herself. The men looked up.

'What?' asked the farmer. She stepped back and looked at Omar. He knew what she was asking, but he said nothing, just stood and held up the lamp.

'The African,' she said quietly. 'Where is he?'

Omar frowned at her, displeased. The farmer just stared, cold-eyed. She took a step back, returned to the shop and took down one of the medium-sized lamps. She was shaking now, from the cold, she thought, and she pulled her cardigan closer around her body. She went into the kitchen, straight to the stove, and stood there, considering. She flicked open the paraffin tin and poured a little into the lamp, then lit it, watching a thin black trail of smoke curl up from the newly wet wick. The thought of the farmer's cool, light eyes made her shudder, and she walked up and down, trying to stop the rage of thought in her mind. He reminded her of the policemen who had threatened her not so long ago. The same carelessness, the same disrespect, the same callousness. The old recollections and new events flew around her head, struggling to form some sense. A man is knocked down – a *kaffir*, a black man, but a man, just the same, and the man who hit him, together with the man whom she was married to, and who was the father of her children, were outside worrying about the dent in the car. The cost of the new lamp. The inconvenience. Are black people really nothing? Did she look in Robert's or John's faces everyday and see no one, no person in there, no heart or soul under the dark skin? What of Amina, whom she liked and admired so much? She was part African. Should she care for her less? She paced again, asking more questions in her mind. Might that African not be hurt, or dead? Might he not have children waiting at home, or a wife, or a mother? Wouldn't they cry to know he had been hit? From outside, she could still catch the short cadences of the men's voices and their conversation. She heard again the rough Afrikaaner accent, harsh and complaining, and then her husband's tone of willing agreement, and without a further thought, she snatched up the lamp, filled a clean jug with water, and went outside by the kitchen door, walking swiftly through the vegetable garden, hoping that it really was too cold, as John had laughingly told her the day before, for many snakes to be out. She stopped only once, at the end of the wooden outhouses behind the garden, and she looked up at the house, at the windows behind which her children slept, and she nearly turned back. With a sense of resolution, though, and with, for some reason, a fleeting thought of Amina Harjan, she started purposefully down the track.

What she expected to find several minutes after the man had been hit, she couldn't have said, even to herself, but she wanted also to be out of the house and away from their voices. The night closed about her, deep and dense like a forest, and she felt for the first time a slight sense of fear. He must be gone already, she thought, the African. But what if he wasn't, and what if he was angry and attacked her? The sound of insects scratching in the blackness became more evident as she moved farther from the house. When she turned to look back now, the night was so pitch dark she could not even see her own home. She was out, away, alone, doing something unthinkable. Still, her body felt controlled and disciplined, and purposefully, she walked on, clutching her lamp and water.

She heard his breathing first, a human sound in the night. She tried to hold her breath, to remain silent, not understanding for a moment that her burning lamp gave her away, and she cursed her heart for banging so loudly against her ribs. She spun around, trying to locate the ragged breathing in the overwhelming darkness, but he had heard her too, and was silent. They waited, both of them together, still and taut, blinded by the night, until an involuntary rasp of pain betrayed him.

She turned in the direction of the sound and walked forward, holding the lamp far out in front of her.

'Hello?' she called, and as she did so, she saw a lean leg slide across the ground and away, out of the circle of her light and into the darkness beyond. She followed it and saw it again, sliding, sticky with blood.

'Wait,' she said and swung the lamp forward, and the man was caught in the pool of light, his breathing hard, his eyes turned away.

'Don't be afraid of me,' she said, and he turned his head, almost shaved of hair and shiny with sweat, and he looked up at her with flashing white eyes that were full of hatred. The force of that hate made her stop short, cut her boldness off dead as though it were a honed razor, and she paused, the jar of water poised in her hand. Miriam swallowed and held out the jug at arm's length, but the man made no attempt to touch it.

'It's water,' she said, and moved towards him. Something brushed behind her and she started, making him jump also, but she realised it was just a bat or some kind of flying insect.

'A bat,' she said out loud. She put the water down on the ground.

'You're hurt, you must let me help you. Otherwise you will not get home.'

No answer from the darkness, just the occasional flash of his eyes, and the feeling of his body there, very near to hers in that vast, empty night. She needed a cloth to bind his leg, a blanket to keep him warm. She looked back towards where she thought the shop was. Should she bring him back to the outhouses and let him stay there? What if Omar found him? What if he stole things?

'I don't need your help,' His voice rasped at her, much nearer than she had thought.

'I can bring you a blanket and a bandage for your leg.'

No reply. An effort was being made; there were heavy breaths and a small groan of pain. He was trying to stand, and she saw his head bob into the light. She put down the lamp and he weaved uncertainly on his feet. Without thinking, she moved forward and grasped his arm, uncovered even in that cold, and he leaned on her for one second, his tall body against her slim frame, before he stood upright again. She immediately let go of him, blushing in the dark, amazed at her audacity. If her family ever knew she had touched a strange man in such a way, they would be scandalised. No matter what the circumstances.

'Let me get you some...'

'I don't need your help,' he said, his voice stronger now and hard. He looked at her with contempt, then he turned and limped away from her.

She felt like crying, overwhelmed by the dark night, the hatred, the blood. Did he see her as white? As someone as bad as the farmer? She began to walk back to the shop and saw the water jug before her, untouched. Stopping to pick it up, she half ran the short distance back, till she came within sight of the *stoep*. The farmer's car was gone, and the house seemed completely dark. She walked silently round to the front, and saw Omar's light in the shop, his shadow moving back and forth among the sacks of goods. She hurried back to the kitchen door, stopped at the step and plunged her hands into the water, rubbing furiously to remove the blood that she could smell on her fingers. Then she threw out the water and reached up for the door handle. It was locked. She tried again, and this time saw her husband's lamp swing into the far end of the kitchen from the shop and come down to the back door where she stood, tense and still. Omar held the lamp up to the window and looked out at her, then turned the key in the lock and stood back to let her enter.

She surprised herself when she walked in as normal, as though she were returning from the garden in broad daylight. She went to the table, put down the lamp, straightened her cardigan, and pulled up a sleeve that she now noticed had blood on it.

'Where have you been?' he said quietly.

'In the laundry room,' she replied. 'I wanted to get a clean blanket.' Her tone was calm and steady, but the lie did not ring true and she knew it. For one thing, she wasn't holding any blanket. He came to where she stood, and he leaned in to her. She put up her hands, thinking he was going to strike her, but he only sniffed at her as a dog sniffs an unfamiliar object. She knew immediately what he would smell, that he would sense the faint, sweet odour of the injured man's sweat and blood on her clothing, and this time when he stepped forward again he hit her. The strike was hard and she staggered back, bruising her hip against the table, and she kept her hands up for the next blow. It hit her across the face despite her shielding, splitting her lip and causing a thin stream of blood to course down her chin and neck. For the first time since she had re-entered the house, she became aware that the baby was crying in the room above.

He hit her four times and it was a shock to her, that he had come to this at last. She stood against the counter, arms up over her face, and when he stopped she could not look at him. Neither could he look at her. Instead he put down the oil lamp and went upstairs without another word.

She had always dreaded this moment; not out of physical fear, though certainly she had been scared. But because she knew it would be a terrible thing to have to understand about your husband, that he would really hit you, and she had always thought when she was younger that hitting was the one thing that she would never tolerate. But now it had happened and she knew that she would go upstairs when he had calmed down. What else was there to do with the children in their beds, and no other place to go to? She knew him better than he knew himself, knew he would hate what he had just done. She could visualise him in the bathroom upstairs, washing his hands as though that would remove the taint of the violence; combing back his hair without meeting his own eyes in the mirror. She tasted the blood filling her mouth, and it tasted as she imagined metal would taste, cool and sharp. Blood like his, like the injured African's, there on the road.

Miriam straightened up and waited until her dizziness had passed, and then she went to the pump and put her head beneath it, until the drying blood had washed away. She was freezing cold and her limbs were stiff and she was shaking. With legs like lead, she walked up the stairs to the baby's room, but when she opened the door and looked, she realised that the crying had stopped. She walked tiredly over to the cot and watched the child sleeping now, her chubby pink fists raised, as if in fight, above her head. Miriam felt like weeping, but she did not. She wiped her hand absently upon her skirt, then reached down with the tips of her fingers and stroked the soft, dark down on the baby's head. 'Sleep,' she said to the child, and she watched her for a while and then went to face Omar.

Chapter Sixteen

ROBERT PULLED AND heaved at the wooden door to the cellar as Miriam stood nearby, watching the boy struggling.

'Didn't you just go down there last week?' she asked him.

'Yes, Madam. It was okay then,' he confirmed. 'Let me keep trying, Madam. It is just stuck from the rain.'

Miriam nodded and went back out to the shop, where Christina, the maid at the Weston farm, was still looking leisurely through the merchandise on offer. Although they sold mostly basic items, Christina eagerly looked forward to her weekly visits here and always noticed anything new.

'Can I help you find anything?' Miriam asked. She glanced back and watched as Robert pulled with all his weight at the cellar door. The wood creaked loudly, and then slowly began to move upwards. Miriam smiled.

'No, not to worry, Missus,' replied Christina. 'I'm just looking at these fabrics. I'm thinking of a new dress one of these days.'

Miriam nodded, barely listening. 'Take your time, Christina,' she said, and she went back to see how Robert was doing.

In the black square that lay open in the floor, only the top rungs of a wooden ladder were visible. Robert stood with his feet right at the edge of the darkness beneath them.

'I will go down there, Madam,' he said, preparing to descend but Miriam's voice held him back.

'No,' she said. 'I know what I'm looking for. I'll go down.'

'But there are many spiders there, Madam,' Robert replied, with only a trace of a smile. Miriam considered this information for a moment and then looked at the boy, who was grinning now. 'Sometimes there are snakes also,' he added.

'I'm looking for a box of books,' Miriam told him. 'The books I used to have when I was a girl. They are novels,' she added.

'I know books,' replied Robert. 'I can find them.'

He was small and lithe and he scrambled down the ladder in a few seconds, pausing on the last rung before dropping down to the cellar floor with a thud. He waited with patience for a few moments, until his eyes adjusted to the close darkness around him. Then he went directly to a stack of boxes that had stood undisturbed in the back of the cellar for as long as he could recall.

Out in the shop, the bell was ringing. Miriam hurried into the shop and looked at Christina, who still held the bell in her hand.

'I thought you had all gone home,' Christina said, laughing nervously.

'We live here,' Miriam said, and raised her eyes to the ceiling where she could hear the steps of her husband. No doubt the insistent ringing had roused him from his afternoon sleep. She moved swiftly halfway up the stairs, and saw Omar on his way back from the bathroom.

'I'm sorry,' she said. 'I was outside with Robert and Christina kept ringing the bell.'

He nodded, still groggy with sleep.

'Go back,' Miriam urged him in a low voice. 'Sleep for a while. I'll wake you soon.'

'I'm up now,' he said irritably.

Miriam looked defeated. 'All right,' she said. 'But you don't have to rush. Take your time.'

He glanced at her, suspicious at her insistence, but she was already running back down the stairs.

At last Christina was gone, and Miriam returned at once to the cellar door. Within seconds a cardboard box appeared, followed by the head of Robert. He pushed it onto the floor with some effort, and presented it to Miriam with a sweep of his hand.

'Books, Madam.'

Miriam kneeled down and pulled the box open. They were indeed her books, the ones that she had brought with her by boat from India and then by truck from Pretoria.

'You forgot them, Madam?' asked Robert, watching as Miriam emptied them from the box and touched them all, one by one.

'Yes,' she replied. 'Until someone reminded me.'

She sorted through them quickly, not taking the time to open them or recall the last time they had been read. Those recollections and re-readings she would save for another day when she was lonely again in the quiet of the late evening. She piled them all around her – there must have been fifteen books in all – and picked up *Far From the Madding Crowd* and *Jane Eyre*, but settled finally upon *Little Women*, which she remembered well from her school days. As a schoolgirl, she had always imagined herself as the fiery, independent character Jo, but when she thought about it now, it was someone else that she pictured in that role.

Miriam carried the book into the shop. She could hear Omar's steps upstairs and she knew also that her children would be returning from school at any moment. She placed the book gently on the counter and searched some drawers, finding a sheet of brown paper and some string. She looked longingly for a moment at the festive wrapping paper that lay in sheets at the other end of the counter, but she knew that Omar would miss it if she were to use some. She lifted the cover of the book, and revealed a soft, white page, slightly spotted with damp, but clean all the same. A page for writing upon, for leaving an inscription on.

Miriam went to get a pen. This pen she then held poised above the flyleaf for at least three minutes, while she hesitated as to the best words to send to the recipient. Finally the pen moved down:

'To the lover'

Miriam wrote, and then paused. She scrutinised the strokes made by her pen on the page and seemed satisfied that the letters were neatly made. She had been good at English handwriting at school, all those years ago. She leaned over and wrote again, completing the sentence:

'To the lover of books,
    Love
    Miriam'

She had stopped again at the word 'love', uncertain whether 'regards' or something similar might not be better. But then she had decided that for anyone else she would have had little hesitation signing with love, and saw no reason to be so tentative now. She waited for the black ink to dry, blowing on it a little anxiously when she became aware again of Omar's footsteps. She heard him say something to Robert and heard the boy come downstairs.

She shut the book and deftly wrapped it. Then the string was passed twice around the parcel and secured in a bow, and she quickly wrote in block capitals the address in Pretoria.

'Robert,' she called, and the boy came in from the kitchen. 'Here,' she said, holding the parcel out to him. 'Take this.' From her purse she extracted more money than she believed the postage would cost and handed it to him.

'Take this to the Post Office tomorrow, okay?'

'Okay, Madam.' He carefully turned over the package. 'Is it a book?'

'Yes,' she replied, and for the first time she allowed herself to feel some hesitation at this idea of hers. She heard Omar's step on the stairs and held out her hand to Robert, wanting suddenly to take the book back. He held onto it tightly, however, and whispered reassuringly that he would post it for her the next morning. Then he was gone, attending to the vegetables in the sink, with the book safely in his pocket and Miriam turned to the stairs just in time to greet her husband.

*

The parcel lay in the Post Office for two weeks before it was eventually collected with the mail. Miss Smith, the postmistress, had been forced to keep it outside Amina's post box because of its size, and she had kept it beside her, and had become used to the sight of it among the rubber stamps and books of coupons, and after a while had ceased to recognise it as something waiting to be delivered.

She noticed it again, finally, when she spilt some red ink on its outer wrapping. It was covered unassumingly in smooth brown paper and tied with plain string, and when Miss Smith knocked over the ink and saw the spreading blot of red, she picked up the package and muttered to herself in Afrikaans that at the age of sixty-three she was losing her mind already, and what hope was there for the rest of her old age? She turned the parcel over in her hands, which were freckled from younger days spent as much as possible in the sun, then placed it right before her in the little window from which she served customers, because she knew that Jacob Williams would be in again today, and that he would be able to pass it on, at last, to Amina.

It was just past eleven o'clock when Jacob came into the post office to collect the mail for the café. He came twice a week, on Tuesdays and Fridays, and Amina left the mail collection to him, partly because she usually forgot about it altogether, and partly because she had been with him to the Post Office once, and she had noticed that he and Miss Smith seemed to enjoy a mild flirtation of some kind.

'Morning, ma'am,' said Jacob, tipping his hat to the post-mistress. She smiled and her eyes seemed to him to be more blue than ever. They were like crackling neon, Jacob decided as he watched her, not like any colour he had ever seen in nature.

'Good morning, Mr Williams,' she replied and she asked after his health, and he asked after hers, and they chatted for a few minutes across the counter, before another customer came in. The man saw Jacob leaning against the Whites Only counter, smiling at the postmistress, and he frowned. Jacob turned and moved smartly over to the counter from which Coloured people were supposed to be served and he waited patiently while Miss Smith, who was the only Post Office employee present in the mornings, served the newcomer. She tore off strips of stamps with efficiency, and ignored the angry stare of her customer.

'It's warm out, isn't it?' she said to the man, and she looked at him over the steel rims of her spectacles, noting the sweat that dripped down the side of his head. Inside the Post Office it was cool and quiet, with only the reassuring sounds of Miss Smith's rubber stamps and till echoing into the atmosphere. The windows were high up in the walls and they cast broad squares of sunlight into the room, but the area around the counters was shaded. On the ceiling, two fans whirred gently, producing soft currents of air that circled above them.

The man used his sleeve to wipe his forehead. 'You can say that again,' he muttered in reply, and he looked up at Jacob who was studying the notices that were posted on the wall beyond. Miss Smith pushed some stamps across the glass divide in the centre of the counter, and told the man the price. She waited with her hand on the till, but he was still watching Jacob. She felt a prick of nervous tension in the tips of her fingers.

'Hey, boy,' he called across the room and for a moment, despite being the only other customer of the Post Office, Jacob did not understand that the words were directed at him.

'Hey!' the man called again. Jacob looked up and raised his eyebrows. 'Get me some water, boy,' he said and jerked his head in the direction of the drinking fountain which stood in the back corner. Jacob watched him, and ran his hand over his head. By nature, he was not a man who made decisions quickly, and in this particular circumstance he found he suddenly had a lot to think about. Jacob would gladly have walked a mile to bring a glass of water to someone who asked him politely, but there was no way he would answer the disrespect which had just been shown. To be called 'boy' by someone twenty years his junior was too much. But then again, he hated to make trouble. And he hated to do so in front of Miss Smith.

'Go on,' shouted the man. 'You understand English don't you?'

Jacob burned with anger and embarrassment but his body remained relaxed and still. He looked completely at ease, although he could not quite bring himself to look at Miss Smith. The postmistress, however, was not looking at him. She had already moved out to the other side of the counter.

'There's no need for that,' she said sharply to the customer. 'I am the employee here and I will get you the water if you are incapable of getting it yourself.'

Miss Smith had spent twenty years of her life teaching mathematics in a secondary school and was still accustomed to treating people who were younger than she as ageing pupils, to be guided, praised or reprimanded as the situation required. She moved briskly to the water fountain, filled a glass beaker with tepid water and held it out to the man.

'Here you are,' she said.

He was incredulous. 'What's the matter with you, lady? Haven't you heard of *apartheid*?'

For a moment, as she looked into his face, Miss Smith saw the face of her only son, who lived in England now. There was no real resemblance between this man and the boy of whom she was so proud, but they could have been the same age, and a shudder caught the postmistress as she saw the surprise in the eyes before her, and she felt keenly how easily a young mind could be educated into ignorance. She blinked, realising the man was still staring at her and she remembered his question, the tail-ends of his words still echoing in the high corners of the room.

'Yes, I have heard of *apartheid*,' she replied. 'And I don't much care for it, thank you.'

He made no move to take the water, so she placed it back down by the fountain, and asked him again for the money that he owed for his postage stamps. Abruptly, he fished the coins from his pocket, ignored Miss Smith's outstretched palm, and tossed them onto the counter. They landed with a clatter that broke the tense silence of the room, and a single coin skipped to the floor, where it rolled away beneath a chair. Then the man walked out, stopping to mutter an oath at Jacob who was on his knees, retrieving the coin before Miss Smith should be forced to do that too. The door shut with a crash.

Jacob stood up slowly and handed Miss Smith the money.

'Thank you,' she said softly, and she held onto his hand for a moment longer than was necessary. 'We are all of us losing our dignity as human beings in this place, aren't we?' she said.

'Some of us more quickly than others,' Jacob replied, looking down.

'Don't you believe it for a second.' Her tone was fierce. 'It's people like him that lose the most...'

'Perhaps.'

Miss Smith moved quickly away behind the counter and was relieved to recognise the parcel that sat before her.

'Mr Williams,' she called to him. 'I have a parcel here for you. Or rather, for young Miss Harjan.' She looked up apologetically. 'It's been here for rather a long time, I'm afraid. A couple of weeks. I kept forgetting to give it to you. Here.'

She held the package out to him, and Jacob was grateful to her for her business-like tone, for giving him something to look at so he did not have to look at her just yet. He took it and turned it over.

'No return address,' he commented, pointlessly.

'No,' Miss Smith agreed. 'Maybe it's from a secret *paramour*,' she added, but then she remembered all the rumours she had heard about Amina's personal life and she reddened, cursing herself again inwardly for being absent-minded and tactless.

'I'd better be going back. Work to do,' said Jacob, sensing that the kindest thing for both of them would be to bring the visit to an end. He raised his hat and moved across to the door.

'Good morning,' he said.

'Mr Williams!' Jacob turned and waited, and Miss Smith hesitated for a moment, undecided whether to apologise for the incident or not.

'I'll see you again soon,' he said, reading her look. She watched him over the tops of her spectacles and smiled suddenly, her blue eyes crinkling at the corners.

'Make sure you do,' she said and Jacob smiled back before closing the door.

Jacob walked into the café to find that it had filled up considerably in his absence. Amina's eyes met his by way of greeting and he raised the parcel that he held in his right hand before he placed it down on the counter.

She was talking to some customers, and while she waited to take their order she glanced over at the package. It looked plainly wrapped in brown paper and string, and she wondered if it was from her mother.

'Are your *breedies* fresh?' someone asked her, and she fixed them with a smile that was tinged with surprise.

'All our food is always fresh,' she said. She finished taking the order, then picked up the package as she walked over to the kitchen. She called the order through the rectangular serving hatch and waited for a shout back to confirm it was understood. The handwriting on the front of the paper, she noticed, was not that of her mother or her father. As she reached for a knife to slit the string, a glass dropped, splintering noisily on the wooden floor behind the counter. There was a moment's hush before people began talking again.

Jacob stood staring at the glass, wondering how it had slipped from his hands. Amina watched him, and realised that she had never seen him break anything before, not even a plate. She also noticed that his hands were shaking, very slightly. One of the waitresses was already at Jacob's feet, with a short brush and a pan, and within a very few moments, all evidence of the broken glass had gone. No one was interested any more. Only Jacob still looked at the floor.

'What is it?' Amina appeared at his side.

'It slipped. I was polishing it. Sorry.'

'Not the glass,' Amina said softly. 'What's the matter?'

Jacob used the cloth he still held to wipe over the shining counter. 'Nothing,' he replied. She let him work for a few moments, waiting patiently until he spoke again.

'Some Afrikaaner in the Post Office,' he said finally, avoiding her gaze. 'He called me "boy" and ordered me to get him water. A young fellow.'

Amina sighed irritably. 'What's the matter with the world these days?'

Jacob shrugged. 'I don't know.'

'Come and sit with me,' she said to him. Jacob put down his cloth and followed her.

'There are people waiting,' he told her. 'We should be helping.'

'Doris and Mary will handle it,' she replied, watching the waitresses as they moved from table to table.

Amina carried a cup of coffee to the booth and placed it in front of Jacob, then sat down.

'I wonder what's in this?' she asked, placing the parcel down between them. She wanted to give him time to settle, to gather himself, so she cut through the thin string with the knife and quickly pulled away the paper wrapping. Before her lay a book. It was old, with a powder blue jacket and fine lettering.

'*Little Women.*' Jacob read the words upside down. 'Who's it from?'

'I don't know,' Amina said, a little too quickly, and when she looked up at him she was smiling.

'No letter?' asked Jacob.

'No letter.'

'Maybe there's something written inside,' he suggested helpfully.

Amina seemed to find this unlikely and appeared reluctant to open the front cover of the book. Jacob noted that her eyes were shining – she seemed hardly able to keep still.

'Jacob, don't let those idiots get you down. They're ignorant.'

'I know,' he said. 'It's not worth worrying about, but I was embarrassed.'

She nodded. 'Miss Smith?'

'Yes.'

He stood up from the table, and smiled at her.

'Thank you for calming me down,' he said. 'And enjoy your book.'

He walked away, over to where a group of people were waiting at the door. When he had seated them, he turned back and saw that Amina was still sitting at the booth, reading the inside of the book, and smiling to herself.

Chapter Seventeen

Amina was still enjoying the fact of her newly received book when a telephone call came through from her mother. In her blissful state she could not imagine that it might be bad news, and it took a few minutes for her to recognise that her mother's subdued tone sounded more than usually depressed. When Mrs Harjan finally stumbled through the news that Amina's grandmother had passed away, it seemed so unreal that Amina made her repeat it.

'How did it happen?' Amina asked.

'A heart attack.'

'Just like that?'

There was a long pause. 'I think it was the shock,' said her mother's quavering voice. 'Those people came again, and she found out...'

'What people?' There was no reply and Amina tried again:

'Found out what, Mum?'

There was a crackle and a sound of weeping, Amina thought, and the line went dead. She looked up at Jacob who had been watching her as she spoke.

'My grandmother is dead,' she said.

Her parents were sitting at the kitchen table when Amina walked in. She had lingered outside, making the walk from her truck deliberately slow and measured, uncertain of how to greet her father in the wake of his mother's death. He had always been a man of such little outward emotion that she had no idea how he would behave now that his mother was laid out in an upstairs room, never to rise again. For her own part, Amina felt vaguely guilty that she had felt so little in these hours immediately following her grandmother's death. Their lives had never crossed much until this recent visit. Her grandfather had been alive until three years before, and had lived with his wife in their own apartment, never with his children. Amina had grown up knowing her grandmother only as a visitor, and one that she had never particularly liked.

She stopped just outside the back door and deposited the two bags of flour she had brought for her mother – she would not take them inside where her father might see them, in case he should become aware that all his groceries were not bought from his wife's meagre housekeeping money.

Her parents looked up when she turned the door handle. She leaned down to take the tentative kiss that her mother offered to her forehead and she looked over at her father. Their eyes met for an instant before he glanced back down to the cup of tea that sat cooling before him. She did not go to him for a greeting – it was not the custom between them – but pulled another chair to the table and sat down.

'Do you want some tea?' her mother asked.

Amina shook her head. She watched as her mother got up and went to the stove where a large pot of *daal* sat simmering. The lentils were ladled into three plates and Amina stood up to carry them one by one to the table. A plate of *rotlis* followed.

Amina sat down again and considered her plate. 'How did it happen?' she asked finally.

Her mother regarded her with a tragic air and, for some reason that she could not specify, Amina immediately felt guilty.

'She had a heart attack,' said her father, flatly. He picked up his tea cup and sipped at the liquid with the air of a man who has said everything that is on his mind.

'Oh,' said Amina, although this much she already knew. She waited a few moments, but nobody seemed eager to continue the discussion.

'What brought it on?' she asked tentatively.

Her mother glanced up at her again, with that same indefinable look, and Amina swallowed. Still, nobody spoke, and she waited with growing unease, and some impatience.

'We had a visit,' her mother offered at last. She sniffed, as though this sentence were somehow self-explanatory.

'A visit?' repeated Amina.

Mrs Harjan nodded. 'The Alis,' she said.

The family of the suitable boy. Amina stared at her mother, for she had long ago forgotten about them, and was wondering how they could be connected to her grandmother's demise.

'They came yesterday evening, to give their reply.'

'Reply?' repeated Amina, before she realised what her mother meant.

'About you.' Mrs Harjan's eyes filled with tears. 'They refused you for their son.'

Amina would have felt relieved had she felt at all concerned about the prospect of marriage to this boy, but as it was, the news that she was apparently not good enough for the young man was neither a surprise nor an inconvenience.

'Why did they only reply now?' she asked.

Her mother sniffed. 'I think they were avoiding us. Because they were refusing you. Your grandmother kept calling them though, until they had to come.'

The last words were swallowed under a sob from Mrs Harjan, and in desperation, Amina looked at her father, who was spooning up his food and listening impassively as his wife spoke. Amina was hungry and looked down at her plate, wondering whether she might start eating, despite the fact that her mother had not yet finished her story. The girl took a large, clean handkerchief from her pocket.

'She was shocked that they refused?' Amina prompted.

Mrs Harjan shook her head and dabbed her eyes, unable, it seemed, to speak. She sniffed heartily, and finally saw the handkerchief that Amina waved before her. She took it and blew her nose.

'They told her about your business. With the Coloured man.

With Jacob,' she added, more politely, as she saw the fierce look that passed through her daughter's eyes.

'And then they told her that you were not...not feminine enough.'

This last sentence was punctuated by sobs, and ended with Mrs Harjan burying her face fully in the handkerchief.

'You see!' she cried suddenly, raising her head. 'It is things like this that make them say that!' She held up the generous square of white cotton accusingly. 'What girl carries around a hankie like this? This is a man's hankie. It's not right.'

Amina pushed her plate away and glanced briefly at her father. He had stopped eating and was looking at her now, but without reproach, and his unmoving expression calmed her briefly. He glanced at his sobbing wife, without any sign of feeling, and then his eyes went back to his daughter.

'Your grandmother always ate too much,' he said in a flat tone. 'And she never did any exercise. For her heart.'

Amina was grateful and looked down at the table.

'Come on,' he told her. 'Eat.'

Nobody had realised at first that Amina's grandmother was dead. She had listened with growing horror to the Ali family as they listed the reasons for their refusal and she had seemed to choke upon her tea. Then she had clasped at her ample chest and cried for some water. At that point the visitors had decided to leave and once they had gone the old lady had called for her son and told him to send for Amina at once, because the girl needed some discipline now, and then she changed her mind and decided she would rather that he sent for the doctor because she was dying from shock.

Mr Harjan was used to his mother's dramatic insistences; she had been assuring her immediate family that her death was imminent for the last thirty years. It was a means of attracting attention in times of stress and anger and illness and it had worked for the first couple of years, but not for the last twenty-eight. Mr Harjan therefore listened to his mother and then left the room, only stopping in the kitchen to ask his wife to take the old lady some tea and a glass of water when she was ready.

When Mrs Harjan sent Rosemary in with the tea, the old lady appeared to be sleeping, so Rosemary poured out a cup of the milky brew and left her to rest. When Mrs Harjan went to check on her mother-in-law a few minutes later, she found that the old woman was indeed asleep in her chair, doubtless worn out from all the dramatic railing. She straightened the tea cup on the tray before her and went away, returning an hour later to call her for dinner. She had not moved an inch from her previous position and Mrs Harjan noticed that she looked rather pale. She went over to touch her on the shoulder and the old lady slumped forward, nose first, into the tea and biscuits. Mrs Harjan gave a little cry, and then found she could produce no further sound. She began to pray fervently in her mind for help. Within seconds God sent her Rosemary, who had been peeling potatoes in the kitchen, but Rosemary only stopped at the door for a moment, just long enough to realise that the old lady was not drinking directly from the tea cup but had died and fallen into it, before she ran into the garden screaming.

*

'I don't have time to go driving around the countryside for some old woman we didn't even know,' said Omar as he strode back into the shop.

Miriam followed him. 'It's not for the old lady. She's dead already. It's for the family. You know Mr Harjan.'

'Hardly,' he said, pacing around as though looking for a physical escape from the conversation.

'You are always the one telling me and the children about our responsibilities and our traditions, and now you won't even go and give your condolences?'

'Don't shout at me.' Even though she had not been raising her voice, Omar looked accusingly at her and she fell silent. He began leafing through an order book, flipping back the pages with an audible snapping sound.

'That family don't mix with any of us and yet when it suits them they expect everyone to come running.'

Miriam took a breath and made a final attempt. 'They don't expect anything. But it's the least we can do.'

'I don't owe these people anything!' he shouted at her.

'Yes, you do,' she said quietly. 'Yes, you do. Amina Harjan saved your sister, remember?'

Omar threw the book across the room and it crashed against the wall, several feet away from Miriam. She stared at it for a moment, then she picked it up, smoothed down the bent pages, and placed it on the counter top. Without looking at Omar again, she went back to her kitchen.

All the floors of the downstairs rooms in the Harjan house were covered over with white sheets. Upon these sheets sat various people from the surrounding community, who had arrived to pay their condolences and provide support for the grieving family. Most of those present were women, and most of these were older women, for whom a death, particularly one that did not emotionally affect them, was an opportunity not to missed. It was a chance for them to get together, to fuss, to cook and to reminisce about the deceased person, even one they had not really known.

Mr Harjan was extremely unhappy. His immediate instinct upon finding these strangers overrunning his house was to turn around and return to his business, but he soon found that this would not do at all, and that he, the bereaved son, was expected to be in the house at all times.

So he sat resignedly upon one of his dining room chairs (his favourite armchair having been given up some time ago to a succession of visiting old people) and accepted the continuous murmurings of condolence. People would tell him that he should be happy that his mother had gone to a place where she could rest peacefully, and he would nod while his eyes moved to the ceiling and he envisioned the old lady's massive body in its final repose on the bed upstairs.

From the kitchen there issued an unceasing undertone of female voices, that would bubble up now and then like an unwatched pot before quietening down again. In the midst of these women was Mrs Harjan, busily taking stock of the dishes that her new friends had brought her – for traditionally, no cooking took place in the house of the deceased. From time to time she shook her head and recited once more, at the request of her friends and acquaintances, the circumstances of her mother-in-law's death. She left out the details of Amina's rejection by the family of the suitable boy, but the death scene itself became embellished bit by bit, the dramatic re-telling being polished like glowing silver with each recitation. Then there were the omens to be discussed – almost everyone who had seen or spoken to the old lady in the week before her death now realised that she had said something that struck them as strange.

'She told me, you know, just last week, that she was tired of life.'

'She said to me, only the other day, that when God decided to call her she would be ready. It was as though she knew.'

And so it continued. When Omar and Miriam arrived at dusk on the second day, Omar went to shake hands and mutter his condolences to Mr Harjan before retiring to a corner amongst the quietly talking men. He could hear that they were discussing Malan, his government, and the voting laws. At least he would be able to catch up on the latest news of the National Party, and find out whether the newest *apartheid* laws might affect his business. His interest in his country's politics had always been predicated on the practical rather than the ethical.

In the meantime, Miriam went directly to the kitchen, where she was quickly swallowed up by the milling women who were getting ready to serve dinner. Miriam placed down the plate of samosas that she had brought as her contribution to the kitchen. The women fell on them, put them into the oven, then continued tasting, comparing, preparing – but Amina, Miriam noticed at once, was not among them. She waited a little and helped to begin serving the plates of food that were taken in to where the men sat, and then she quietly spoke to Mrs Harjan and asked her if Amina were not here, as she would like to pay her condolences. Mrs Harjan stopped what she was doing and looked at Miriam. She did not know her, but seemed pleased that this young, conservative-looking woman could be one of her daughter's friends.

'She is upstairs,' said Mrs Harjan, almost in a whisper. 'Go up, if you like – and please – see if she will come down.'

Miriam looked at the pleading eyes and tried to nod reassuringly. She left the kitchen and moved quietly out into the hall. There were no electric lights switched on out here, and only the remaining faint streaks of twilight lit the gloomy walls. Miriam shivered and looked up to the stairs, the top of which were already cast into darkness. She walked up slowly, hoping that she would find Amina before she found her grandmother's body.

A glow of light spread from a small room to her right as she reached the top of the stairs, and Miriam put her head around the door. A cushion had been placed on the floor and an open book lay beside it, but other than that the room was empty. Something in the hush and the darkness that pervaded the upstairs rooms – perhaps her awareness that the dead body was here somewhere – prevented Miriam from calling out to Amina. Instead she moved back into the hallway and waited uncertainly for a moment.

All the other doors were shut except for the room that lay on her left – here the door was ajar, although the room lay in darkness. With silent steps, Miriam walked to the entrance and looked in. For a moment or two she could see nothing, her eyes still dulled to darkness from the light in the other room. There was a smell, though, a pungent, sweet odour that Miriam could not identify, but which seemed distantly familiar to her. She blinked again and this time she saw a pair of eyes – intent, piercing eyes which were all she saw at first of the girl sitting on the floor and Miriam jumped, before she made out the outline of a *shalwaar kameez*. Despite the traditional dress and the vaguely tamed hair, she realised in an instant that the girl was in fact Amina. The dark intensity of her stare made her recognisable to Miriam, as did the slow smile that moved over her face when Amina also recognised the intruder facing her. She jumped up from her seat against the wall, and went to the door.

'You scared me,' she said. 'I thought for a minute that my grandmother had returned to check on me.' She waved a hand to her side, and Miriam saw the old lady's body lying on the bed beside her.

'God forgive us,' said Miriam instinctively, and she backed out of the room as hastily as she could. Amina followed her, shutting the door behind them before turning to Miriam with an amused expression in her eyes.

'I thought you'd seen her there.'

Miriam shook her head and knew then that she had recognised that odour from her days as a girl in Bombay, and that the odour was that of death. Two of her aunts had died in quick succession when she was fourteen years old, and that same, tainted smell had lingered over their bodies. She felt sick for a moment, and dizzy, and she reached out her hand to lean against the wall, but before she could do so she felt a firm hand on her elbow, and another on her back, supportive and strong.

'Are you okay?' Amina asked.

Miriam nodded and smiled, embarrassed at her weakness, but Amina quickly drew her towards the lighted room.

'I didn't expect to see you here today,' she said. 'I didn't know you knew my parents.'

'I don't,' Miriam said. 'We came to see you. To offer our condolences.'

'That's kind. Nobody else came especially to see me. Probably because they all think I killed my own grandmother with my trousers and my lifestyle,' she added with an ironic tone.

Miriam looked at her. Amina looked pretty in her outfit, tall and straight-backed, with an elegance that fitted the long flowing outfit, but she also looked like a stranger. Amina watched the movement of Miriam's eyes and smiled.

'I can't tell whether you approve of my clothes or not. From your expression.'

Miriam blushed. 'Neither. It is not for me to approve or disapprove...'

'No, tell me. What do you think?'

'It looks very nice.'

'It's a nice outfit,' said Amina, purposely misreading the comment.

'I mean,' stammered Miriam, 'that you look very nice in it.'

'Ah,' said Amina. 'That's different.'

Miriam laughed nervously and looked about her, avoiding the girl's gaze.

'So,' Amina continued. 'You prefer me in traditional clothes?'

Miriam frowned. The girl's tone was hard to read – at times she felt she was being teased, and at others as though she were being tested.

'No,' Miriam replied. 'You look nice in these clothes, but you are tall and thin and . . . and nice-looking and you would look fine in anything. But,' she took a breath, and avoided Amina's intent eyes, 'you don't look like yourself.'

Amina's laugh seemed to warm the cool silence of the room. 'I'm glad you said that, because I don't feel like myself.' She looked ruefully down at the gold stitching and the coloured cloth.

'But I have to please a person who, God rest her soul, is not even able to see me.'

'It sounds ridiculous, when you say it like that.'

'I know.' Amina offered Miriam a seat, but she shook her head and remained standing while Amina sat down cross-legged upon her cushion. 'I keep looking at the accepted conventions from the wrong angle – and once you've done that, you can't ever go back to seeing things the old way.'

'Maybe you are not seeing from the wrong angle,' suggested Miriam, not sure of her argument but determined nevertheless to hold up her end of the conversation.

'Everybody else thinks I am.'

Miriam said nothing, and Amina watched her, amused.

'Do you think I am right and everyone else is wrong?' Amina pressed.

'Perhaps. I don't know what you are talking about in particular.

But just because everyone believes something does not make it right.'

'But what people think puts pressure on you to accept things, doesn't it? I mean, why did you get married?'

Miriam was surprised. 'What do you mean?'

'Did you see your husband and fall in love, and know you wanted to be with him for the rest of your life?'

There was a small window in the room, and against the lamplight it was simply a black square with nothing visible through it. Even so, Miriam took a step towards it and studied the darkness as though it were the view she had waited all her life to see. Amina was silent, watching the floor and Miriam's shoes.

'No,' Miriam replied quietly.

'Then why did you get married?'

Miriam turned to her with a slight smile and a shrug, as though already acknowledging her defeat in an argument that had barely started.

'He saw me a few times and proposed, and my family accepted for me,' she said. 'That's what you want to hear, isn't it? I married him because they told me to. But it never occurred to me, Amina, to question it. I got married because everyone expected me to.'

The uttering of Amina's name had made Miriam self-conscious, and she turned again to look through the opaque window.

'Well, it occurred to me to question it,' said Amina.

'I know.'

The girl looked down, dissatisfied, and her eyes rested on the opened book which lay beside her.

'I didn't thank you for the book,' she said. 'I liked the inscription a lot.'

Miriam blushed, but tried to sound casual. 'You don't have to thank me. I should be thanking you. You made me think about all the books I had brought with me from Bombay.'

'From Bombay?'

'Yes. I know, it's a long way to drag a box of books, but my husband didn't know – he thought it was part of my essential possessions. In a way, it was. I loved those books as a girl and bringing them with me made me feel less homesick. I felt as though I were bringing some friends with me. Even if they were only characters in novels.'

When she turned away from the window, Miriam found that Amina was listening with great care, and her gaze made Miriam feel nervous again.

'Listen to me, talking away,' she said, with a slight laugh. 'I am here to give you my condolences, not tell you my life story.'

'I like to hear it,' said Amina, but speaking of condolences had reminded Miriam of Mrs Harjan's words.

'Your mother wants you to come downstairs.'

Amina sighed.

'Come on,' Miriam coaxed. 'My husband would like to see you as well.'

Amina tried not to look too doubtful about this last comment.

'He would,' repeated Miriam. 'To thank you.'

'For what?'

'You know for what. For Rehmat. What you did was…'

'Nothing,' said Amina, standing up. 'It was nothing. Anyone else would have done the same.'

'I didn't,' Miriam said, and again she was looking out of the window, so that Amina could not see her eyes.

'You warned her they were coming for her,' said Amina, 'and because of that, she had time to come to me. You did your part, and then handed her over. We were like runners in one of those relay races.' She laughed, pleased with her analogy, but Miriam shook her head.

'I didn't do my part. All I did was betray her, and then wait while you saved her.'

'Would you come with me?' Amina said. 'I want to change back into my usual clothes before we go downstairs.'

Miriam followed Amina out to the room next door, and waited while the girl pulled the long blouse over her head and picked up a shirt from the bed.

'You think you betrayed Rehmat? Because you told the police she was in Pretoria?' Amina asked.

'Yes.'

'They didn't hurt you, did they?'

'No. They didn't touch me. They were taking my children away. To the station.' She could see the gleam of Amina's skin in the darkness, and the flash of her eyes. The girl was already pulling on a pair of trousers.

'Then you did the right thing,' Amina told her. 'Rehmat knew she was taking a risk coming back here. There is no reason for your children to suffer because of that.'

Miriam nodded, as though conceding the point. 'But then, there was no reason for you to risk yourself either.'

'I am an adult,' Amina said. 'And I can make my own decisions, unlike Sam and Alisha. And my reasons for taking the risk were that I hate *apartheid* and its stupid laws and I hate seeing the police get away with bullying people.'

Amina looked up and began buttoning her shirt. Miriam turned away quickly, conscious that she had been watching the girl.

'I think we should go downstairs now,' she said.

Amina nodded and walked past Miriam to lead the way.

'You know, Amina,' Miriam said suddenly. 'I would like to be more like you.'

Amina was already at the doorway, but she stopped at this and turned back, until they were standing so close that even in that darkness, Miriam could see the amusement in her eyes.

'Be careful what you wish for,' she said, and smiled.

Chapter Eighteen

'JACOB,' SAID AMINA. 'I have an idea.'
'What is it?'
'Indian food.'

Jacob smiled to himself and sighed, both at the same time. The two of them sat in the café, drinking coffee. It was early morning and it was quiet; the short minutes of calm before the breakfast clients arrived, although today they expected fewer people because of the heavy rain. It had been raining steadily for three days, and the water fell now onto large pools that already lay on the ground, and spread like molten glass over the roads and sidewalks. The rain was warm and smelled strangely of grass, Jacob thought, a smell he remembered from a childhood that had passed fifty years ago. He liked to hear the metallic sound it made when it dripped from the roof and hit the puddles beneath. He listened also to the drumming sound of it on the roof, and felt comforted by the warmth and light in the café.

Amina waited, humming a tune under her breath, watching his slow smile, noting the hand that went up to brush over his cropped hair, a sure indication that he was thinking about what she had just said. Jacob was a man of routine, who generally disliked too much disruption. Amina's ideas nearly always meant a disruption of some kind, but on the other hand, they were almost always brilliant. He was sitting in the wooden chair that had come to be his favourite spot, by the gramophone that Amina kept running all day, and when he was ready, he looked back at his business partner.

'Curries?' he asked.

'Yes, and all sorts of things. Samosas, rice pilaus, biryani. That's what we should serve. I mean, as well as what we have already.'

Jacob reached for his coffee cup, which sat high above him on the wooden counter top. He took a sip of the black brew and considered. He knew it was his role to think out the possible problems whenever Amina came up with an idea. Her natural optimism rarely allowed any thoughts of setbacks or failure into her head, and while he enjoyed this trait in her, it also exasperated him at times.

'Most of our customers are Indians,' he said. 'Why would they want the same kind of food they get at home?'

'People love what they know. And anyway, I don't say it would be just any food – it would have to be good. First rate.'

'I don't know...'

'Maybe even just one special every day. How about that? One

Indian dish each day?' She frowned, thinking. 'Or maybe a few dishes one day a week?'

He looked at her eyes, alight with enthusiasm.

'Jacob, look. The men who are working around here, who can't get home for lunch. Even the women, who want a break from cooking two meals a day. They would all come.'

Jacob looked less sceptical at this, but a sudden thought brought the frown back to his face.

'Our girls,' he said, nodding towards the kitchen, 'they don't know the first thing about making a proper Indian curry. Who's going to do the cooking?'

Amina looked at him and smiled, in a way that made his misgivings suddenly return.

'Don't worry,' she told him. 'I've already thought of that.'

Still the warm rain fell, and Amina cursed silently as the wheels of her truck ground and spun with difficulty up the wide dirt road that was the main street of Delhof. She peered through her dripping windscreen, pausing once in a while to wipe at the condensation with an old cloth.

'What a place,' she muttered to herself. She was feeling uncharacteristically nervous today, as she drove out to try to secure the services of a new cook. It was a Tuesday and she hoped that the rain had not prevented Omar from making his usual trip to Pretoria, for if he was at the shop, she would have an uphill struggle to persuade Miriam to cook for the café. She had overheard some gossip in the café about Omar and Farah – it was interesting how her own community were often careless within her hearing, as though assuming that such an outsider as she would not know or care about the people they spoke of. The talk corresponded with what she had already suspected about his nights away and so, before leaving that morning, she had driven past Farah's house but had not seen his car there. Perhaps people were being too hard on him, but somehow she doubted it.

In a few minutes the shop came into sight through the misty glass, and she drove slowly up the path and parked as close as she could to the *stoep*. Even the few steps she had to take through the sheeting rain proved to be too much however – she appeared in the doorway with her curling hair damp against her head and drops of rain on her face and sprinkling the shoulders of her jacket. She found that she was the only occupant of the shop which, on this gloomy afternoon, was lit solely by one paraffin lamp, which cast a pale yellow glow that reflected off the counters. Amina wiped her face with the ends of her sleeves and pushed back her hair.

'Shop!' she called. There was a light tapping of shoes on the stairs and Miriam came hurrying into the room. She held in her hand a baby's bottle, half full of milk, and she looked at the girl, surprised and speechless.

'You're feeding her,' Amina said, looking at the milk. 'Go ahead. I can wait.'

Miriam only nodded, then disappeared back to the kitchen, where she sat feeding the baby and wondering why seeing Amina unexpectedly should throw her into such confusion that she had stood before her like an idiot, unable to speak.

In the meantime, Amina walked about the shop looking at the items on sale. She felt lighter now, relieved that Omar was not around. She became aware of a soft issuing of music in the room and, looking around, found a wireless set in the corner. She turned it up slightly, and hummed along with a Doris Day tune. '*Once I had a secret love...*' sang the radio, and Amina smiled to hear the words. She picked up a coloured hair tie that hung with others on a piece of cardboard by the till and tied back her damp hair. Checking the back of the card, she noted the price and fished in her pocket, leaving a pile of coins by the till in case she forgot to pay later. She leaned back against the counter, then, and read three times through the headlines of the magazines that were racked in front of her until Miriam suddenly appeared again, the baby in her arms.

'Hello,' Miriam said. She seemed more composed now that she was busying herself with the child. 'Sorry to make you wait. I was surprised. I didn't expect you to be passing here.'

'I wasn't passing. I came especially to see you.'

'Oh.'

'She's gorgeous,' Amina said, smiling at the baby. 'Can I hold her?'

'Of course,' replied Miriam, and she held the child out. Salma went to Amina, as she did to everyone, without complaint, although Amina held her with some awkwardness at first. She stood looking from Miriam to the baby, and then began to walk around the shop, pointing out items of interest to the child as she went. 'Look at the sweeties,' she said, 'and look here, here's a hammer and nails, and here is a cup and saucer, look...' The child looked only at Amina however, a serious expression on her little face, and then she leaned towards her and grasped an escaped lock of curly hair in her tiny fingers. Amina laughed and spun the child around. The baby smelled clean and fragrant, and she held the child closer for a few moments, kissing her finally on her forehead.

'She's beautiful,' she said to Miriam.

Miriam was smiling at her. 'I know.'

Amina felt self-conscious before Miriam's gaze, and she took the baby to the open front door where they stood looking out at the rain, staring at the water while she racked her brain for something to say to Miriam.

'Terrible weather we've been having,' she said at last, with such formality that Miriam laughed. Amina blushed.

'You're right,' said Miriam, containing her smile. 'It has been terrible.' She walked over to the counter and picked up her apron. She was caught in the glow of the lamp light now, and Amina patted the baby's back and watched Miriam, a slight frown on her face. She had never in her life felt so disconcerted by anyone, and as she stood in the gloom by the open door, she examined Miriam as though she were a framed picture on a wall. She watched her slender hands place the apron around her waist, saw the slim muscles that flickered like thin fish beneath the skin of her forearm. She watched the lighted face intent on tying the bow, watched the shadowed angles of her cheekbones, and the long eyelashes that brushed the tops of her cheeks when she blinked. Miriam felt the eyes upon her and looked up. The shop was dark beyond the circle of the lamp, and she walked away from the light, towards the door.

'I can't believe you drove through all this rain,' she said. The baby was restless, and Amina handed her back. Miriam felt the girl's hands brushing hers as the child moved between them and wondered for a moment why she was so aware of such small things where Amina was concerned.

'I'm used to driving in the rain.'

'Oh, yes. I forgot that you used to do taxi-driving,' replied Miriam.

'I still do,' Amina corrected. 'I'm leaving again next week, in fact. To Cape Town.'

'Cape Town,' Miriam repeated, and the tone of wonder in her voice made Amina turn to look at her again. 'What is it like, in Cape Town?' asked Miriam.

'It's beautiful,' Amina said. 'Lovely small towns. And the mountains and the beaches. There are some beautiful beaches – especially if you're White.' She paused and looked out again.

'I don't stay there long,' she said. 'I like the drive more than anything – even when it's not picturesque, like the Garden Route, there are always things to see. Even driving past townships, you see all these people living very different lives from your own.'

Miriam held the baby close and thought that Amina herself lived a very different life from her own.

'You've been on the Garden Route?' she asked, her tone wistful.

Amina nodded. 'Twice,' she said.

Miriam turned and sat the baby down amongst her toys on the floor behind the counter, pausing to touch her soft hair.

'I've never been anywhere,' she said, straightening up. 'Only to Pretoria.'

Miriam hardly noticed the girl move, but suddenly Amina was standing right before her, with only the counter top between them.

'Come with me to Cape Town,' she offered, and her tone was one that Miriam recognised from before, flirtatious and laughing. She was looking Miriam directly in the eyes, and then she looked, disconcertingly, at her mouth. Miriam pulled back, for Amina was standing so close to her that she could catch the fresh scent of her, a scent that she still remembered well from the night the girl had stayed over. Miriam said nothing, but came out from behind the counter and went back to her spot by the open door.

'Come with me,' said Amina again, more serious this time. 'It would be company for me. And we could take turns with the driving.'

'I can't drive,' said Miriam.

Amina considered this. 'Well, I don't really need help with the driving . . .'

'I can't go with you,' Miriam told her abruptly. 'I have a husband and three children and a shop to look after.' She looked away, and they were both silent, listening to the rain and the blues tune that floated out from the radio.

'Okay,' said Amina quietly, to pacify the sudden irritation, and she sat down on the window sill and looked up at Miriam. 'Okay. Anyway, that's not what I came here to ask you.'

'I see,' said Miriam, although she did not. She did not want Amina to think badly of her, and was embarrassed at her moment of ill temper, which had come of frustration. She wanted nothing more than to see Cape Town, but she was trapped in this vast, limited square of countryside forever.

'I haven't even offered you tea,' Miriam said. 'Or a cold drink...?'

Amina shook her head. 'I'm fine. But I have something to ask you. About the café. We're doing well, but business has been a bit slow recently and we're planning on starting up something new.'

She paused and took a breath, for seeing Miriam's eyes fixed upon her always seemed to unsettle her.

'Anyway,' she continued. 'We're going to start serving Indian food. You know, maybe once or twice a week, just a couple of specials for lunch and dinner.'

'That's a good idea,' said Miriam. 'Indian men love to eat their own food, and when they can't get home for lunch they can come to you.'

'Exactly what I was telling Jacob.'

'So...?' asked Miriam

'So...we need a cook. But not just anyone, we need someone who cooks very well; better than usual.'

Miriam watched her, unable still to see the connection.

'I want you to cook for the café,' said Amina.

'Me?'

Amina smiled. 'Yes.'

'But you don't even know how I cook...'

'Yes, I do. I had lunch and dinner here, remember?'

'Daal! Potato curry!' exclaimed Miriam, appalled. 'Peasant food.'

Amina raised an eyebrow and Miriam smiled. 'I didn't mean it like that. It's what we eat most days. It's just that...'

'What?'

'Potato curry is nothing.'

'It's not nothing, and it tasted wonderful,' replied Amina. Her earlier awkwardness had fallen away and she spoke decisively. For her part, Miriam felt an excitement at the idea of working at the café – at being away from the shop, at doing something new and useful – but she was immediately filled with the certainty that she would not be able to take the job.

'I have to work in the shop...' she told Amina.

'We'd pay you well. Of course.'

'My children...'

'You'd only be at the café in the morning to cook.'

'My husband wouldn't like it...'

'I'm offering the job to you, not your husband.'

Miriam shifted uneasily at this last remark, turning her head to the doorway that led to the house, and Amina realised that they were not alone after all.

'Where is he?' she asked.

'Sleeping. He'll be down soon. I can hear him.' She pointed vaguely to the ceiling and Amina looked up, aware now of the muffled sounds from upstairs that she had assumed came from Robert. She looked away, and Miriam watched her from the corner of her eye, not sure of what to say next.

'You surprise me,' Amina told her, after a moment. She had turned aside and was looking once more at the rain. 'I thought you had a fearless streak in you. I thought you had the inclination to fight the world if you had to.'

Miriam stared at her. 'What are you talking about? How would you know if I am fearless or not?'

'I heard,' Amina said simply.

'What did you hear?' Miriam walked right up to the girl, trying to catch from her expression some idea of what she was trying to say.

'Wasn't it you who went out in the middle of the night to help an African who had been hit by a car?'

Miriam was astounded. Amina looked at her and could not help but smile at her stunned expression. Miriam glanced back at the inner shop door, then turned again to Amina, her voice low.

'How could you possibly know about that? There are only two people who know – me and my husband.'

'Three.'

'What?'

'Three people.' She smiled at Miriam. 'I know this government likes to tell us they're savages, but the Africans can speak as well as we can.'

Amina expected her to look shocked again, but this time, Miriam just laughed. It was still unfathomable to her how the words of that particular African could have reached Amina Harjan, but she accepted it as a fact immediately, and she realised that the more she came to know this girl, the less she was surprised by anything she said or did.

Within moments, two customers ran in from the rain, startling both women. They were African workers from the Weston farm, sent for some bags of mealie corn, and so when Omar came into his shop a few moments later, he found his wife serving the two workers from behind the counter, and Amina Harjan sitting on the window sill, watching the rain. His wife did not look up at him, but seemed slightly flustered and his eyes moved back to Amina, to whom he nodded a curt greeting. He went to where Miriam stood and took over at the till, and once the purchases had been rung up and the men had left, he looked expectantly at his wife.

'Do you want some tea?' she asked him.

'Not now,' he said. 'Was it busy?'

'No, not really.'

'Where's Robert?'

'Cleaning upstairs,' she said. 'Didn't you see him?'

'Yes. I forgot.' He looked at Amina. 'How are you?' he asked her, but what he meant was to ask what she was doing there, and she realised that at once, and decided to dispense with any small talk.

'I came to see if Miriam would cook for the café. Only now and then,' she added, for she knew she did not stand much chance against a man like this. Omar probably did not care whether or not his wife wanted to work, and he would definitely not wish people to think his wife had to work for a living – in that respect he was like so many of the men she knew.

Sure enough, Omar looked displeased, but refrained from refusing on his wife's behalf at once.

'What did you say?' he asked Miriam.

'I said that there was the shop, and the children to look after, and that . . .' she paused and glanced at him, but avoided Amina's gaze, 'that you probably wouldn't like it.'

Omar nodded, satisfied. 'My wife understands me,' he said, almost smiling at Amina. 'She doesn't need to work. The shop is doing well and she has plenty to do here.'

Amina stood up. 'It's not a question of need,' she said, her tone cool beneath her politeness. 'It's a question of my finding an excellent cook.'

Nobody responded. Omar walked over to the radio and switched it off. Amina watched him and considered whether to make one last attempt.

'It would only be one or two mornings a week,' she said, rapidly reorganising her weekly menu in her head. 'And it's a quick drive to Pretoria from here.'

'No,' he said, sharply, and Miriam burned with embarrassment. Omar regretted the slip into heavy-handedness and tried at once to mask the authoritative manner of his refusal.

'Unfortunately, my wife doesn't drive. I've told her time and again to take lessons, but she never wanted to. If only she had...' he said with a casual shrug of his shoulders.

Miriam listened to his poor excuses and felt sick. She watched the floor, and wished that Amina would leave so that she would not have to face her any more.

'Oh, that's great,' said Amina cheerfully. 'I teach driving myself.'

'Since when?' asked Omar, frowning.

Amina waved a dismissive hand. 'For years. I've taught several people. Listen,' she said, working swiftly, for she knew when to cut her losses, 'forget the cooking job – if it's not possible, it's not possible. But if you want to learn to drive, I'll be happy to come up once a week and teach you for a couple of hours.' She looked at Miriam kindly.

Miriam was stunned, and inwardly pleased at the way Amina

had circled Omar to get to this compromise, but her awareness of the stiff attitude of her husband kept her from smiling. On the other hand, she did not want to appear so weak before Amina again.

'Okay,' Miriam said, looking squarely at Amina for the first time since Omar had come into the shop. 'Okay, thank you.' She hesitated for only a moment before delivering the final shot.

'My husband has been telling me to learn for ages,' she said. Omar cleared his throat but could think of nothing to say. His eyes remained fixed on the paperwork that lay before him, and Miriam felt the silence from him, and knew that his anger ran very deep. She did not let herself think of the possible consequences now, though, but waited patiently as Amina prepared to leave.

'Then it's settled,' Amina said, and she stood up and began buttoning up her jacket. 'I'm taxi-driving next week,' she said, 'but I'll see you after that?'

Miriam nodded and Amina said goodbye to them both, before looking out at the rain once more.

'Do you want to wait until it stops?' asked Miriam courteously.

Amina grinned and looked at the sky. 'I think I'd have to move in here for quite a while,' she said. She ran down the steps and got into her truck. Wiping at the condensation on the windscreen, she thought about what she had just done; the lengths she had gone to just to see Miriam on a regular basis. Under pretence of wiping the glass, she covertly watched the woman who stood in the doorway, wishing that it would not have to be nearly two weeks before they met again. She also knew that she should not be allowing herself to feel that way. The elation she had felt in sidling past Omar's subtle bullying gave way slowly to a sense of misgiving, and even despair. She turned over the engine, frowning at these thoughts of hers, and with much spinning of wheels, she drove slowly away.

Chapter Nineteen

AMINA HAD SPENT a long hour trying to correct the rattle on the exhaust of the car she was to drive to Cape Town, and nothing she tried seemed to help. She ducked into the driver's seat to switch the engine on once more, and stepped on the gas pedal, only to hear a familiar metallic rumbling from the rear of the car.

'It's definitely rattling less,' Jacob called encouragingly. He was watching her from where he stood, leaning against the open front door of the café. Amina heard him but continued to watch the exhaust, then wiped her forehead with the back of her hand and walked slowly to the front of the car where she leaned inside the window and turned off the engine. There were few vehicles around at this time on a Sunday morning, and they could hear birds piping in the trees behind the café. Amina sighed and fixed the exhaust pipe with a black stare. Then she swung back her leg and kicked it. She kicked with huge force, as though the frustrations of the entire world were pent up in her foot, and Jacob winced at the sound. She gave no sign of being in pain, but her lip trembled slightly, and she would not look up.

For three days now she had been in a strange mood. Jacob felt he knew Amina better than most people, and he could honestly say that his business partner was not herself. He had seen her upset before – but her bouts of sorrow or anger had never lasted for this long. Of more concern to him was the fact that this latest mood of hers had arrived without any obvious cause. He had tried to raise her spirits by talking over the new Indian menu, but such conversations did not seem to help. In fact, she seemed to have lost her enthusiasm for the idea, even as Jacob was deciding it was just what they needed. He lingered on the steps of the cafe, unwilling to leave her and go back inside, yet unable to think of anything helpful to say. Still she stared at the car and would not look at him. She raised her hand to push back her hair, but the hand stopped slightly on the way down. This running of her hand through the tangle of curls was such a characteristic and frequent gesture that the slightest change in the angle of her arm was noticeable to Jacob, and he realised by the unusual jerk of her hand, and the poorly disguised lingering of that hand by her face, that she was crying and trying covertly to wipe away her tears.

Jacob stepped down and walked towards her, nodding a greeting to an incoming customer as he went.

'Hey,' he said softly, as he reached Amina's shoulder. 'Maybe you should postpone this trip. Take the next job that comes up...'

She did not look up, only cleared her throat. 'A trip away is just what I need right now,' she said abruptly. He waited for further explanation, but none came. Instead, she touched his arm by way of acknowledging his concern and then turned and walked back to her room.

The people she was driving to Cape Town were two Afrikaaner businessmen. They seemed surprised and intrigued at being driven by a young Indian girl, but from the start Amina did not encourage much talk between them. She was polite, but nothing more. Originally, she used to take these driving jobs because she often became restless in one place, because she liked to see the countryside, and because she liked to meet new people. This time, however, she did not care much about the drive, or the job, or the businessmen who sat passively in the back seat. She met them with the same lack of interest that had marked her experience of everything in her world for the last several days. It was a form of mental and emotional lethargy she had never experienced before, but one that she found had descended on her like a summer shower, lightly, and without announcement. In the very back of her mind she was wholly aware that there was one person other than herself who had contributed most to her mood, and over the passing hours she had let herself consider more and more the future options that might be open to her. This introspection had only worsened her temper however, because the more she had considered the situation, the more she was coming to realise the impossibility of the route her heart was choosing for her.

They began the drive early on a Monday morning, and

although the day was clear and fresh, their progress was slower than usual because the smaller roads had been affected by the recent rain. Amina did not look out from her side windows often and when she did, she noticed very little. Occasionally she slowed down and pointed out to her passengers some landmark that had been deemed significant by someone else long before her; the men looked and thanked her and perhaps asked a question or two which she answered as well as she could. The rest of the time she drove in silence, her mind dark and drawn in.

By the evening of the first day she found that several hours had passed by without her noticing. She had been so immersed in thought that she had not noticed the road flying past, or even the route they had taken. More and more she was being held to physical reality only by the few mechanical motions that she had to go through as a driver. She changed gears, looked into mirrors, avoided the odd pothole which had appeared after the rain. And whenever the men asked her to, she stopped at a café or restaurant for lunch or dinner. At these stops, they did not ask her to join them, even to buy a sandwich, for her countenance was not open and her eyes did not meet theirs. In any event, such a lunch, with all three of them around a table, would not be possible in this time of segregation. Amina had no appetite at all, but ate at irregular intervals because she knew she should. At these times, she was forced to find which part of a room she might sit in to eat, or at which counter she would be served as a non-White. She had mistakenly sat down at lunchtime at a table marked as 'Whites Only' and had been asked to move by the waitress. She had looked at the woman's expression, which was polite and slightly embarrassed, and it had taken her a moment to realise what she meant. The waitress was saying something, which Amina did not hear, but she followed the woman's hand with her eyes and saw a shiny new notice on the alcove above her, thoughtfully written in both Afrikaans and English, that barred her from that area of the restaurant. Amina had nodded and stood up and walked outside, and had not bothered any further with trying to get some lunch.

When they stopped again at dusk, they were only about four hours away from the city. Amina was directed by her passengers to stop at a small restaurant that stood pale and luminous in a tiny town made up of one dusty street. The restaurant was built in the Cape Dutch style, with a thatched roof, and it advertised traditional cooking: *Home-Cooked Breedies and Boboeties Served Here!* As she looked at the whitewashed café and the lush green landscapes that surrounded it, Amina felt as though she were in another country, a land far removed from the brown, dusty surroundings of Pretoria, and she felt simultaneously relieved and homesick. The men went inside to eat and Amina sat for a minute in the car and then went round to the side door of the restaurant, where a few Africans, who looked as though they worked in the kitchens, sat on the steps, talking together. She nodded to them and asked where she could get some food.

'You can go inside, lady,' offered one of the Africans. He looked her up and down. 'They serve Indians.'

'I don't want to eat inside,' Amina said. 'I just want a sandwich or something.'

The man shrugged. 'You want a plate of *breedie*, lady?'

'Yes, thank you.'

He got up and disappeared inside and Amina waited, lingering near the others. A White woman, evidently the owner, appeared in the doorway.

'Come on,' she said to the workers. 'What do you think this is? There are customers waiting inside.' They all jumped up and moved back in through the door, edging past the woman. She paused in the doorway and looked at Amina for a moment.

'Are you looking for work?' she asked pleasantly.

'No,' Amina said and turned away.

She was wondering whether the African worker had forgotten her now that there were two White customers in the restaurant but within a couple of minutes the man appeared at the kitchen door and handed her a large platter of food.

'Thank you,' she said, and now that she caught the aroma of the stew, she realised how hungry she was. 'How much do I owe you?'

Once she had paid, she walked away with her plate and looked for somewhere quiet to sit. It was a warm night, but the late evening heat was stirred now and then by passing breaths of wind. There was a wide porch on the opposite side of the road that belonged to a drugstore that had long since closed for the day. Here she sat and balanced the plate on her knees, looking about her in an effort to keep her mind from straying once more to the mistress of the only shop in Delhof. There were some children playing down the road – they had paused briefly to watch her as she crossed their path, but they had now returned to their game, tossing a ball back and forth, even though the twilight was deepening and they must have been barely able to see it.

Amina ate quickly, then retraced her steps across the road to the door of the kitchen, which appeared now as a rectangle of orange light in the darkness. She glanced inside, but the cooks were busy and did not notice her. Leaving her plate on the top step she returned to her seat on the porch so that she might watch the front door of the restaurant and see the men when they emerged.

She looked for the children, but they had gone now, and she imagined them back in their houses, being bathed and given dinner. She had never thought about having children, but wondered now how her life would be if she did have them. Completely different, she decided. More routine, more settled. She would not be able to take off for a few days as she was doing now. She nodded to herself, but the thought had not comforted her quite as much as she had hoped it would.

In her shirt pocket was a pack of cigarettes. She shook one free and rolled it back and forth between her long fingers. She had not smoked at all in two years and rarely before that. She held the cigarette between her lips, taking some comfort in the feel of it, while she searched for her matches. Around her, the evening grew darker, the sky a deep ink blue. She could hear faintly the sound of insects, even on the main road where she sat. A car rolled by, its wheels crunching softly on the gravel-specked road. The hiss of her match against the rough wood of the porch was replaced by a burst of light, and she watched the flame as it twisted in the dusk. It looked to her like a taunting demon, dancing and stretching before her eyes. She quickly applied it to the cigarette and shook it out.

As she smoked, she concentrated very hard on Miriam and on not thinking about her. After a while she began to realise that, as a strategy, this was somewhat counter-productive.

'You're an idiot, Amina,' she said out loud. She allowed herself a smile. 'And now you're talking to yourself.' She frowned. 'You need to be logical,' she continued, somehow reassured to hear a human voice in the dark, even if it were only her own. 'Be logical. Make a list. For and Against. Pros and Cons.' She nodded, happy to have made a practical decision and she got up to get a pen and paper from the car. As she approached, however, the men emerged, and so she walked round the car, checking the tyres and giving the exhaust pipe a cursory glance while they got back in for the final leg of the drive.

'Ready to go?' she asked them, and they nodded.

'How far is it?' one of them asked.

'About four hours,' she replied. 'Not long.'

'Did you eat something?' the other man asked.

'Yes,' she said. 'Thank you.'

They fell silent, and Amina went back to her lists. Miriam – For and Against. The night was pitch black now, the road lit only by the tunnels of light thrown forward by the headlamps. She drove with one finger on the lamp control, ready to dip the beams should anyone come along the opposite way, but the road she had chosen was not a major route, and other cars were few and far between. She glanced into the mirror at her passengers. One was already asleep, while the other stared out of the side window.

She wanted to begin positively, with her 'Reasons For' list, but nothing came immediately to mind. Nothing practical in any event. She knew she had fallen for Miriam much harder than she had ever fallen for anyone and that her days were spent looking forward to the times when she might see her again. But practical considerations eluded her. She moved on to the 'Reasons Against'. Her mind became suddenly crowded. The most obvious point was that Miriam was a woman, but this consideration had ceased to hold much importance for Amina some time ago. She decided to skip it and move on. 'Married' was the word that occurred to her next. This one was less easy to dismiss, as were children (three), Indian, family, scandal and the question of what right did she have to expect someone else to live against the accepted conventions of the whole world?

She stopped making the list, and instead just drove, listening to the sound of the road as it roared along beneath them, blocking all thought and feeling until she heard the unexpected sound of Miriam's voice. What was most surprising was that it sounded so true and so real in Amina's head. Over the past week, she had been trying hard to recall every gesture and expression and tone of Miriam's, and each time the nuances had become more and more elusive to her. And yet here it was, that soft, low voice as real as though she were in the seat next to her.

'My husband has been telling me to learn to drive for ages,' said the voice, softly spoken and yet filled with a new strength, and Amina smiled at the recollection. Those words of Miriam's had delighted her, and she had had to try very hard not to smile until after she had left the shop that day.

'Come with me,' she remembered herself saying. 'Come to Cape Town...'

'I have a husband, three children and a shop to look after; I can't just leave...' The abrupt tone of the sentence depressed Amina at once.

She watched the road, swallowed ahead of her by the blackness of the night, and she pressed her foot a little harder on the gas pedal, as though she might somehow be able to catch up to the darkness that always lay just ahead of her, and be covered up by it. She switched on the radio, keeping the volume low, concentrating on listening to the crackling music that it produced. Then she grasped the wheel firmly in both hands and decided to forget about list-making for good, because right at that moment she could not think of any reasons why she should not just do what she had promised herself some time before and forget about Miriam entirely.

Chapter Twenty

MIRIAM HAD LONG since stopped counting days, and was instead counting hours. After much consideration and uncertainty, she had decided that lunchtime on Tuesday should be the hour she should count towards, for Amina knew Omar's routine by now, and she would surely wait until Tuesday, when he went to Pretoria, to come to give the promised driving lesson.

She awoke in the thin darkness of pre-dawn, and was relieved when edges of daylight became visible beneath the curtains because she had lain awake for some time, not moving, waiting until it should be light enough outside to justify getting up. Downstairs, she went through her usual preparations; she waved to John as he went home after another night watching the shop; she chatted to Robert, then to her children as she helped them wash and dress; she fed the baby, and then

Omar, watching him silently as he ate a bowl of porridge.

'What's the matter?' he asked her. 'Why aren't you eating?'

She looked down at her plate.

'I don't know. My stomach feels funny,' she said. It was true, but although she would not admit it, even to herself, it was not a case of any illness, but merely a flutter of nervousness that pulsed through her, simultaneously leaving her with an edgy energy. Her children were somehow washed and breakfasted and on their way to school without even noticing the time passing, and Omar also felt a restlessness infecting him from the woman sitting opposite.

'Are you sick?' he asked, before he left.

'I'm fine,' Miriam replied – and she looked fine, her husband noticed with a frown. She smiled as she handed him his jacket, and her eyes seemed to laugh.

'Have a good trip,' she said, and he realised that for a long time now, she had not said those words to him when he left her on a Tuesday. He had been dimly aware that she suspected something about his nights away; probably she even knew the truth. Nothing, however, would ever be articulated between them; even if she should think of speaking about it, he would not allow such a conversation to happen.

His eyes were slightly narrowed as he watched her, and he touched his collar, then checked his tie. It was a gesture she had seen him make a thousand times; he had a particular way of grasping the knot of his tie between his thumb and forefinger. It was a delicate movement – he had a fastidiousness about him when it came to little details that Miriam had always liked. His nails were always kept neatly and squarely cut, and when he put his pen down while doing accounts, he always made sure that it was aligned exactly with the book.

Miriam followed her husband outside. She knew that he would skip the top step when he walked down to the car; that he would start the engine and straighten the mirror without a glance at her; that he would only look up briefly as he pulled away, because somewhere inside himself he felt bad about going. She knew every detail about his every mannerism, and yet today she felt as though she were watching a stranger. It must be me, she thought to herself; nothing about him has changed.

She waved as he drove slowly away, and watched from the side of her eye as two workers from the Weston farm came walking across the scrubby grass towards the shop. She was pleased they had come, for she sensed that this particular morning would pass even more slowly than all the others that had come before.

As usual, Farah had woken up at four a.m. that morning to see her husband off for his two-day trip to the markets. She would not have bothered to get up at all, were it not for the fact that he moved around so heavily, which made sleeping through his rituals of washing and dressing impossible. He also liked her to rise with him and prepare him some breakfast, which she grudgingly did each week. Anyway, some untrusting part of her liked to watch him drive away in his truck, and to know that he was really gone before his brother arrived later in the day. Today she yawned widely at the window as she watched him leave, and then she turned and went back upstairs where she would sleep for two more hours before rising again to send her children to school, feed her crazy sister-in-law, and get ready for Omar.

By ten o'clock that morning, she had seen to everyone in her household, and was heating water for a bath when she heard the key turn in the lock downstairs. She slipped on a robe, a pale silk garment that Rehmat had left behind, and walked slowly down the stairs, a smile playing on her lips.

'You're early...' she said, and stopped abruptly. Sadru was staring at her, his mouth slightly open.

'You're very early!' she continued as carelessly as she could. 'What happened?' She tied the robe more tightly around herself and watched him from the stairs.

Sadru shook his head and continued to stare. 'They... they are closed.'

'Closed?'

He nodded.

'The market?'

Sadru nodded again.

Farah began to get irritable. 'Why are they closed?'

'Some demonstration. Day of action by the blacks.'

'Bloody *kaffirs*,' noted Farah, and she went back upstairs. She took off the robe and stepped into the bath, her mind racing. There was no way to get hold of Omar. He would have left the shop over two hours ago and would already be here in Pretoria, having meetings with whomever it was he did his weekly business. She considered her predicament for a few minutes, then shrugged and sank as far into the meagre inches of warm water as she could. There was a knock at the bathroom door. Her husband. She had already forgotten him.

'What?' she shouted. There was no reply, and she smiled, knowing he wanted her to invite him in. She heard his feet shuffling outside the door.

'I want some more breakfast,' he said suddenly, his tone petulant.

'Then wait a minute,' she told him, and she closed her eyes and leaned back down in the bath.

At noon, Miriam walked out to the *stoep* once more and looked at the empty road. She listened and waited. There was the piping of the birds above her, and then the slow rumble of the day's solitary train. It was a familiar sound to her, the faraway hum of the engine, and she raised her hand to her eyes and looked to the east where she knew the train would appear at any moment.

With a long, distant clatter it ambled past her, along the horizon ahead, and she thought of how she had laughed with Amina to think of her children running out to catch sight of it, and she smiled slightly and raised a hand to wave at it before she went back inside to stir once more at the warm pots of food that sat on the stove.

The café, much to Amina's dissatisfaction, had been mostly empty all morning. Irritably, she walked up and down the polished floor, watching from the corner of her eye the only occupied table and trying not to think.

'If you've got somewhere to go, just go,' Jacob called to her. 'I can manage here.'

Amina waved her hand impatiently. 'I don't want to go anywhere,' she said.

Yes, you do, thought Jacob; and he went back to the letter that he was writing. He was not a man who communicated well on paper, his writing style being even less effusive than his speech, but he knew he ought to write to his sisters and his uncle, and besides, he had found that having a newly finished letter provided an excellent reason to visit the post office, where Miss Smith would sell him the required stamps. He never asked for more stamps than he needed, and Miss Smith never offered to sell him a supply, and she had smiled to herself when she had noticed that recently he had begun to send letters almost daily, although he never had a letter to post on the same day that he came to collect the mail. She always sold him his single stamp with great seriousness, however, and never for a moment acknowledged to Jacob that she suspected the reason for his sudden literary turn. She too was pleased to be able to see him and talk with him each day.

The long scratching of a record being roughly placed on the gramophone made Jacob shudder inwardly. He turned to look behind him.

'Sorry,' Amina said.

A tune by Cole Porter came wheezing out, the notes warbling a little until the record settled down. Amina listened for two seconds and then became bored. She went into the kitchen, where she poked around and checked on the cook before emerging again into the café.

'I need to go out,' she announced to Jacob, her tone suddenly rather too casual after the nervous energy of the morning. 'Is it okay?'

Jacob looked up, his face impassive. 'That's what I've been telling you,' he said.

She picked up her hat and spent a few minutes looking for her keys before she found them already clasped in her hand.

'I'll be back in a few hours,' she called, but this time Jacob did not even look up, only raised a hand in acknowledgement.

Amina felt a sense of release at having chosen some course of action, even if she had not yet convinced herself of her destination. She drove slowly, watching a certain upcoming side street narrowly. With a sudden grasp of the steering wheel, she turned into it and parked. Even from here, she could see Omar's car outside his brother's house; he had just arrived. She instinctively shrank down in her seat as she watched him get out of the car, shrugging off his jacket, which he left draped on the back seat. She was too far up the road to be noticed, however, and she watched him loosen his tie and walk quickly up the short pathway before placing his own key in the lock. Amina pushed back a stray curl and looked at herself in the rear-view mirror. Her eyes looked sad, and her cheekbones were darkly shadowed. She had lost weight in the last couple of weeks.

'You're a bad man,' she said under her breath, looking again at the door through which Omar had disappeared. 'You give me all sorts of ideas about how to spend a Tuesday afternoon.'

For the first time in several days, Amina smiled to herself. Then she ground back the stiff gears and turned the truck around, veering back onto the main road, where she was able to drive at her usual high speed, until she took the small road that was the route to Delhof.

Miriam rocked the baby back and forth and only when she heard the quick, caught breaths of sleep from her child did she allow herself to look again at the clock. It was one-thirty, and she went downstairs to take the food off the stove.

When Omar walked through the door and saw his brother stretched on the couch, half-asleep, he took a step back. He stared at Sadru from the doorway, eyes wide and alert with shock. For the second time that morning, Sadru felt he must surely be dreaming. He had just got over the surprise of coming home to find his wife dressed as though she worked in a brothel. Now he was confronted with the sight of his own brother bursting through the front door in the middle of the day. A dim idea began to rise like curls of smoke in the back of Sadru's mind, but before he could formulate anything clearly, he heard Farah's voice echo stridently from the stairs.

'My God, *bhai*! Were you just going to surprise us like this? How nice to see you! What made you stop here today? Did you know Sadru was back?'

'No, I didn't,' replied Omar, truthfully. He avoided Farah's eyes and grimaced a smile in Sadru's direction. 'I finished early today,' he continued, 'so I thought I'd stop and say hello . . .'

Sadru swung his legs down from the couch and rubbed at his eyes sleepily. 'I finished early too. Day of action by the Blacks.'

'Ah.' Omar nodded. He walked in and sat down. He felt in

control again, and thanked Farah with his usual distant politeness when she brought him a glass of Coke.

'She'll make some lunch,' said Sadru. 'You'll stay won't you?'

Omar sipped his drink and considered a moment.

'No, thanks. I should get back to the shop,' he said.

'How is business, *bhai*? Busy?'

'Not bad,' Omar said.

Sadru sat forward in his chair and listened, attentive to his younger brother. He felt ashamed of the thought that had barely crossed his mind a few moments ago, and as he looked at Omar now, he felt a glow of affection for his well-dressed brother, and resolved always to do his best to make him feel at home in his house.

Chapter Twenty-One

ROBERT HAD BEEN put to work cleaning the ironwork of the security gate that closed over the front door every night. The polish was thick and black, and he concentrated hard on his work, so that he would not get the staining substance onto his clothes. He was barely aware, therefore, of the truck that rumbled up the track and passed the shop before stopping about ten yards further up, and he only glanced up when he heard brisk steps walking back towards him. Amina's eyes were focused beyond him, on the shop, and as he opened his mouth to greet her, she put her finger to her own lips.

'I want to surprise them,' she whispered. 'Where are they?'

'Sir has gone to Pretoria,' he whispered back, and Amina feigned surprise and even a slight disappointment. 'Madam is in the shop,' added Robert encouragingly.

Madam was indeed in the shop, sitting on a stool behind the

counter. Her head was bowed and still and Amina crept inside and watched her, surmising that she must be reading.

'Is it love poetry, or the rules of the road?' Amina asked.

Miriam jumped, and then with a smile, she lifted her hand to show the book of poetry that Amina had given her.

'I didn't think you were coming,' she said.

'It was sort of busy at the café this morning...'

'Was it?' Miriam asked, with genuine interest, but Amina looked away.

'Well, no. It wasn't. Not really. I just...I wasn't sure if I should come.'

Miriam came out from behind the counter and kissed Amina on the cheek, a gesture that she made a little too carelessly, as though emphasising its role as a greeting.

'Of course you should have come. Who else is going to teach me to drive? I've been waiting for you all day.'

'Have you?' The idea seemed to please Amina.

'Yes.'

'Well, let's start then. Before your husband returns.' The last comment was added with the timing of a question, and Miriam knew it at once.

'He won't be back until tomorrow,' she said, and to cover the blush that rose to her face, she walked briskly out of the shop to where Amina's truck stood waiting.

Robert had not been able to finish the blacking of the door, before his mistress had asked him to start preparing some soup for dinner. Although it was only three o'clock, and although there were already three pots of food sitting untouched on the stove top, he thought it better not to say anything. Her voice was firm and her manner direct. He nodded and went in to wash his hands and start preparing the vegetables.

Miriam waited patiently by the truck while Amina tugged at the seat, trying to slide it forward. She managed to move it about two inches and then stood aside for Miriam to get in.

'Sorry. The seats are old and don't move much any more.'

Miriam climbed in and sat with her legs almost at full stretch, her feet over the pedals. She placed both hands on the wheel moving it gently from side to side and looking straight ahead of her, as though she were already in motion on the open road. Amina watched her with an amused air.

'It goes even better when the engine's switched on,' Amina said as she walked around to the passenger side. The truck was old, but scrupulously clean, Miriam noted. There was no dust on the dashboard, and even the floor had brush marks where it had recently been scrubbed. She wondered briefly if the effort had been made especially for her, but she looked at the small stack of neatly folded maps and papers beneath the dashboard and she looked at Amina's clothes as the girl got into the passenger seat. They were a little worn but spotless, as they always were, and she realised that the girl had an innate attention to surroundings and her person that reminded her a little of Omar.

'To begin, let's show you the basic pedals,' said Amina, a slightly formal tone in her voice now that she had assumed the role of driving instructor. She reached across Miriam to point at the floor beneath her, and Miriam caught once again that now familiar scent of her skin and clothes.

'This,' said Amina, 'is the gas pedal. The accelerator.'

Miriam nodded.

'This,' she said, moving her pointing finger along, 'is the...'

'Brake?' suggested Miriam. Amina looked at her.

'Yes. And this...?'

'The clutch.'

Amina sat back in her seat and smiled. 'Do you secretly know how to drive?' she asked.

'Why would I ask for lessons if I knew?'

Amina shrugged, her eyes dancing. 'I don't know. Maybe you just wanted to see me.'

Miriam looked down. 'I don't know how to drive, but my husband showed me the pedals when he started to teach me once. There are only three. It's not difficult to remember.'

'Such confidence!' Amina commented. 'Let's hope they are not difficult to remember at forty miles an hour.'

After a quick tour of the gears, lights and ignition, the truck was started up, and trembled beneath them. The sun had dropped lower and hit the glass, so that when Miriam tried to look at Amina, her eyes were flooded with light and colour.

'Now. Do you know your way around each gear?'

Miriam did not.

'Okay. Around here is where first gear should be, which is the gear you use to get started. Try to find it.'

Miriam tried.

'You have to push down the clutch first,' Amina said. 'Hold

the clutch down with your foot while you find the gear.'

Miriam did this, and slid into gear. The truck shuddered.

'No. That's third. It's a difficult one to find...' Miriam shifted and pushed, without success.

'I can't do it,' she said finally, sitting back.

'Yes, you can. Let me show you.' Amina's hand closed over Miriam's, and they slowly manoeuvred the gear stick together, sliding easily into first.

'See?' said Amina.

Miriam nodded, although in fact she did not see, because her heart had almost stopped in the instant that Amina's hand touched hers, and all she had been aware of after that was the way the long fingers so easily took control of hers.

'You can let go of the clutch now,' said Amina, very softly, and Miriam removed her foot. The truck lurched forward and stalled.

'Sorry,' Miriam said and she looked across to find that she was being watched intently. She swallowed and looked away.

The few seconds that followed seemed to expand in Miriam's mind, filling up all her senses, until she could hear nothing but a roaring and a pounding which she later realised had come from her own blood and her own ears. The scent of the girl next to her was no longer an ephemeral thing to be caught at passing moments, but had turned into the very air around her. It was all she was aware of, and the reason was that Amina was leaning over her, closely, so close that for a moment Miriam felt the soft folds of the cotton shirt brush her chin, and then her forehead, except that it was not the shirt that touched her head, but Amina's lips.

Miriam was no longer breathing and she waited with utter stillness as the lips moved slowly down, barely touching her cheeks before they were finally upon her mouth.

Miriam felt the searing sun on her closed eyelids, and the feather touch of the lips on hers. She jerked her head suddenly and pulled away as though she had been stung. Her hand went to her mouth and she stared at Amina.

'What are you doing?'

Amina opened her hands as though to say that Miriam already knew the answer to that question.

'We can't do this.'

'We can,' replied Amina, with a sigh, 'but we probably shouldn't.'

Miriam swallowed and looked down. She felt as though she might cry at any moment.

'You wanted me to do it,' Amina said gently.

Miriam said nothing, and Amina reached out a hand to touch her shoulder reassuringly when something – a sound, or perhaps just an instinct – made her look out of the rear window of the truck and back towards the shop.

Robert had been surprised to see his boss home so early from his trip to town, and he had smiled at him and asked if he wanted some tea. Omar only glared and asked him where his mistress was. Robert had got as far as the words 'driving lessons' when he felt the stinging weight of an open palm across his face, followed by the rough kick of a boot administered to his legs. He fell, and remained lying on the floor for a few minutes, held there more by fear and shock than by pain, and he went over and over in his mind the short exchange he had just had with his boss, trying to understand what he might have said wrong.

By the time Omar strode out to the truck, the women inside were sitting as far apart as possible, and seemed extraordinarily interested in the workings of the dashboard.

'Stay calm,' Amina ordered, as he tapped on the window. Miriam fumbled for the handle and began to wind it down even as Omar yanked the door open. His reddened face stared in at them, but he said nothing as he struggled to control the rage that had flared up within him. As he watched the two women, he was dimly aware that later he would look back at his behaviour in the last hour, at the careering drive back from Pretoria and at the violence he had used on Robert, and his logical mind would not be able to pinpoint what it was he had been angry about. He would not easily realise that his anger was not anger at all, but a combination of the tension he had felt at nearly being caught with Farah, the guilt he felt towards his amiable, trusting brother, and the fear that he was slowly losing control of his wife.

'Hello,' he said to them, in a polite tone so far removed from the one they had expected from his eyes and manner that they both looked at him in surprise.

'Hello,' said Amina. 'We were having a driving lesson.'

Omar nodded, but did not offer the possibility of continuing. He held the door open and waited for Miriam to get out. Amina jumped out of the passenger side, then noticed that Miriam had made not the slightest movement, but was just sitting there, her right hand still on the wheel.

'Miriam…' Amina began gently, sensing the defiant attitude of the motionless body beside her. 'Let's go…'

'We haven't finished our lesson yet,' Miriam announced, turning to her husband.

'Get out of the car,' he shouted.

'Come on,' said Amina quietly.

Miriam got out of the car.

Omar continued to hold open the door to the driver's seat as Amina walked around. Her eyes moved to Omar's hand, grasping Miriam's upper arm, and she saw a bruise there; the first time she had seen it. She glanced at Miriam before she got into the truck, for she did not want to leave her in the hands of a man full of rage, and yet she did not see how she could reasonably stay. Miriam was looking down at the ground, however, and Amina could not communicate with her.

The girl put her hand on the wheel and a foot up on the running board and turned her attention to Omar.

'How has your day been?' she asked him.

The question was so unexpected and so out of place in the tense atmosphere that both Omar and Miriam looked at Amina. Omar's expression as he watched the girl was strange, she thought, and Amina felt certain that she could see an edge of relief in his eyes, as though she had somehow offered him a way out of his anger.

'It was okay. It wasn't the best day I've ever had,' he added.

Her eyes remained on his for a moment, and she gave a half-shrug of comradeship that again caught him off balance. Then she glanced again at Miriam, and this time, Miriam nodded just slightly, and thanked her for coming. Amina swung up into the driver's seat and turned the ignition key. She took her time turning the truck around, wishing she could be certain that she was making the right decision in leaving. When she finally drove slowly down the track she was simultaneously relieved and jealous to note that Omar had in fact put his arm protectively around Miriam's shoulders.

Miriam's first reaction was to pull away from her husband's touch. She was tired of his anger and his coldness and in any event, any show of affection, even one as hesitant as this, was so out of character that it only made her suspicious.

He felt her withdrawal and pulled back his arm.

'I want to talk to you,' he heard himself say, with a tremendous effort, but she kept on walking ahead of him and as he watched her disappear out of the aching sunlight into the cool depths of the shop, he realised that he had spoken so softly that she could never have heard him. He touched his forehead with a sigh, looked at his watch, and then at the empty landscape around him. His children – their children – would be back from school at any moment, and in the tiny block of time still left to him, he had to find a way to break the habit of a lifetime and talk to his wife.

In the empty kitchen, a pot of vegetable soup was simmering on the stove.

'Where is that boy?' asked Miriam, with some irritation.

Omar hung his jacket over the back of a chair and sat down.

'Probably avoiding me. I was angry with him earlier.'

The unaccustomed frankness of this answer caused Miriam to look her husband in the face for the first time since that morning.

She remembered how she had seen him off; the excitement that had been coursing through her at the thought that Amina might come; the way she had genuinely wished him to have a good day. Why had she wished him well, when deep down she had known what he was leaving her to do? Perhaps because today, for the first time since they had been married, she had felt that her life did not have to depend on his.

She looked at him now and blushed as she thought of how Amina had kissed her in the car. She cleared her throat, trying to clear her embarrassment, and she went to stir the soup as she spoke to him:

'Why were you angry with him?'

Omar said nothing.

She finished stirring and he counted in his head as she tapped the spoon three times against the side of the pot, as she always did, and then she turned towards him and asked him again, her eyes not quite on his, but lingering instead over the legs of the chair upon which he was sitting.

'Why were you angry with him?' Her voice was small and full of the tension that came of holding back tears. 'Why are you always angry with all of us?'

Still he said nothing.

'It is I who should be angry with you.' It was the first time she had ever come close to mentioning his affair, and she knew she was treading upon dangerous ground, but she kept going because she did not care any more what he might do to her.

'How can you keep doing this to me. *With her!*'

'It is finished,' he said.

'What?'

'It is finished. I am not going to see her again.' She stared at him in shock, and only after a moment did she register the sound of the school bus stopping at the end of the track.

Omar had heard it too and got up, taking up his jacket to cover his shaking hands.

'Don't hate me,' he said to her, so quietly that she was not even sure she had heard him correctly. He turned and went quickly towards the stairs, and she did not have time to tell him that she did not hate him before her children ran inside, eager to tell their mother about their day.

Chapter Twenty-Two

'I ASKED MISS SMITH to have dinner with me,' Jacob said, smiling.

Amina regarded him with a confused air. It was early morning, and she had been awake for much of the night, with only a brief interlude of sleep that had come so full of nightmares that she had been glad to wake up again. At dawn she had risen, bathed, and prepared herself some strong tea in the kitchen. Then she sat in the empty restaurant and sipped slowly while reading the newspaper headlines. There had been more arrests of demonstrators in the last week and a black man, she noted, had been detained in prison on suspicion of consorting with a white woman.

'You asked her to have dinner?' she repeated.

'Yes.'

'What did she say?'

'She said yes.'

Jacob was smiling so broadly that Amina could not help but congratulate him. He was outwardly a quiet man and, at the age of sixty seemed at peace with himself and contented with his life. And Amina knew how hard-won that contentment was. At the age of thirty-five he had fallen in love with a young woman in Cape Town. She had recognised in him a nobility of spirit that she loved passionately, and they were soon married. They had each worked hard during the days and had relished each evening, spent talking and planning and learning together. They had lived in such happiness for four years that Jacob had never once felt his feet upon the ground, and had thanked God every day for sending him such a person to share his life with. The only, irrational shadow over his joy was the small fear that no one could really be as happy in the world as he was, and the larger fear that his wife would somehow be taken from him.

A week after their fourth wedding anniversary, she had been killed in a matter of moments by a brain haemorrhage, and after her death Jacob had been unable to speak so much as one word to anyone for three and a half years. Slowly, and with much painstaking effort, his speech had come back to him, but within his own mind and heart he had changed out of all recognition.

Amina watched him, quietly moved at his obvious happiness. And yet she could not keep the serious expression from her eyes as she listened to Jacob describe the conversation he had had with the postmistress.

'Jacob...' She sighed and looked out of the window. Their

waitresses were coming up the road, ready for the first breakfast shift.

'What is it?'

'Do you know what you are getting yourself into?'

Jacob nodded. 'Yes, I believe I do.'

'I was just reading about this kind of thing in the paper,' she went on. 'It's not a safe way to live, however wonderful she might be.'

Jacob got up from the booth.

'This kind of thing?' he said and she winced at the implication she now heard in her own words.

'I'm just saying that you should be careful. We don't live in a place where certain ordinary human relationships are acceptable.'

'Do you think I don't know that already?' He turned away, but she called his name with an apologetic tone and he came back, to find that she could only look at him.

'I never thought I'd have to hear something like this from you,' he said simply.

'Something like what?'

'It's not a safe way to live?' he repeated. 'It's not *acceptable*? Since when have you known anything about an acceptable way to live? If you lived the way you were supposed to, and only went with people you were supposed to go with, you'd be married to some nice Indian boy by now.'

Jacob's voice had risen, and the waitresses who had just arrived stopped awkwardly at the door.

'Don't, Jacob,' said Amina in a hushed voice. 'Sit down. Please?'

Jacob sat, and Amina noticed his fingers tremble as he reached for his coffee cup.

'I know you like her, Jacob, but in the real world, you could get both of you into a lot of trouble. That's all.'

'It's not right,' he said.

'I know.'

'They have no right to keep us from seeing who we want to see.'

'I know, Jacob.'

He sipped at his coffee and said nothing further until the waitresses had put on their aprons and made their way into the kitchen to get some breakfast. Then he looked back at her. To Amina's relief, his eyes contained again something of their usual sparkle.

'Amina, I know you mean well, and I will be careful. I'm not stupid. But life is short, and I don't want to end it alone and unhappy because I had to live by someone else's rules. You of all people should understand that.'

Amina sighed and pushed her hair back from her face. Jacob saw clearly the shadows beneath her eyes.

'Of course I understand,' she said. 'But even I've been wondering lately whether it is always worth doing exactly what you want...' She paused as if biting off her sentence, and then added the final words, in a low voice:

'...and going after people you shouldn't really go after. However strongly you feel about them.'

Jacob ran a thoughtful hand over his head and tried to decide what to tell her, because she watched him with such questioning eyes that he knew for certain that she was no longer talking about him.

'It is worth it,' he said finally. 'You, more than anyone, my young friend, have taught me that, and I'll tell you something else.'

Amina waited.

'If you start changing now, I'll never forgive you.' With that, he stood up and went to open the door for the first of the morning's customers.

So it was that later that morning, Amina found herself sitting in her truck, at the top of the road where Sadru and Farah lived, waiting for any sign of Omar. She knew that he would probably come to Pretoria for business but she had no way of checking on this unless she saw him arrive at his brother's house. Impatiently she sat, humming to herself, and watching the street. A couple of women left their houses to go shopping, but in general the street was quiet. The children had gone to school, the husbands had left for work, and only the wives and mothers remained, cleaning or cooking or, thought Amina, waiting for their brothers-in-law to visit.

Omar arrived sooner than she had expected, and she instinctively lowered her shoulders when she saw him, trying to make herself small behind the wheel. She was many yards up the road, though, and he was not looking for her. She watched as he climbed out of the car, but this time he did not leave his jacket in the back seat. Although the day was hot, he reached in and put the coat on, buttoning up the front, and checking his tie.

'Oh no,' said Amina, under her breath. 'Why are you all dressed up? Are you planning to break it off? Does this mean you won't be long?' She stared at him, waiting for a response that she herself would have to guess.

She drummed her fingers on the steering wheel. She knew she could drive quickly, but even if she raced to Delhof, Omar would surely be shortly behind her, and there would not be enough time to tell Miriam the things she wanted to say.

Amina turned on the ignition and pushed the pick-up into reverse. Looking over her shoulder she careered to the end of the street and around the corner, pulling up by a group of Coloured boys who were playing cricket on the pavement by the road.

'Hey,' she called as she jumped down from the truck.

A small boy with thin arms and a button nose stood up from his batting stance and regarded her coolly.

'You want to make some money?' she asked him.

'How much?' he replied.

She laughed. 'You'll go far.'

She reached into her trouser pocket, extracted a shiny coin, and held it out. The boy dropped his bat and came over, only to see her long fingers close over the coin as he reached for it.

'What do you want, lady?' he asked in a polite tone. His voice was high and had the strong sing-song accent that Jacob had had when she had first met him. The boy's family had probably come here from Cape Town. She leaned down so that her eyes were level with his.

'Do you know how to let the air out of tyres?' she asked.

The boy looked insulted. 'Of course.'

'I mean properly. So they can't be pumped again?

'Of course, lady.'

'Okay,' she said. 'I need you to do it to two tyres, the ones on the road.'

He looked around. 'Which car?'

Amina grasped his shoulder and walked him around the corner, pausing to tell his friends, who were following her with widened eyes, to stay where they were.

'There,' she said, pointing far down the road. 'The green one. The one in front of the bike.'

'I can see it.'

'Good. Go straight there, undo the caps, and for God's sake, run like hell all the way back. There's bound to be some bored old lady watching the street. Okay? You *run* back.'

'Okay,' he said with some impatience. 'Where's the money?'

'When you get back,' she said, smiling. 'I'll be in my truck around the corner.'

He looked suspicious, but the money was gleaming in her palm, and so he nodded, and after checking that he was ready, Amina gave him an encouraging pat on the shoulder before sending him on his way and retreating to the corner. The boy ran like a hare, thin legs flying, and in no time he was crouched by the wheels, working at the caps. A few moments later, he was flying back, with the predicted shouts from a neighbour at his back, and Amina was getting into her pick-up and starting the engine. He rounded the corner like a tiny greyhound, to find that the unknown lady was already pulling away. Her arm swung out of the truck as she passed him, and their palms touched for a second to exchange the money, and the boy was left looking in surprise and pleasure at two silver coins in his small hand. When he looked up again, all he could see was a cloud of dust obscuring the distant pick-up as it roared along towards Delhof.

Sam had woken up that morning with a fever and a sore throat, and Miriam had taken one look at the child and had known that he would be unable to go to school. She put him gently back in his bed, made him eat a few spoons of porridge and talked to him for a while. Miriam had been counting through each day of the past week, living only with the idea of getting as far as Tuesday once more, so that again she might live through the torment of waiting and wondering if Amina would come. Now, on the appointed morning, her son was ill, and her attention was almost entirely diverted to the boy, to watching over his thin, bony frame.

Omar looked in at the child's door before leaving for Pretoria. 'He doesn't look so sick,' he commented.

Miriam was sitting by Sam's bed and had put her hand to his forehead for the tenth time that morning.

'He's burning,' she said. She had become used, in the last seven days, to using only as many words are were entirely necessary for basic communication with her husband. Even to state 'He has a fever' or 'His forehead is burning,' felt to her to be one or two words too many.

Omar had done nothing wrong in the past seven days. On the contrary, he had seemed overly aware of her, and as considerate as she had imagined him capable of being. He had tried to show her some affection, had not lost his temper more than once or twice, had even caught himself when issuing her with orders, but the truth was, the change in his behaviour made little difference to Miriam now because she no longer much cared.

She had never before swung between such extremes of happiness and despair in the space of one week, one day, or even one hour. In a week of mind-crowding confusion, she had searched for something that she could do regularly, something that would give her a basis of routine separate from those she had built around her husband and children. So she had got into a habit of reading a chapter or two from one of her old books, and she read with a sense of escapism that was familiar to her from her schooldays, but also with great care and attention, as if the subtle metre and the words themselves might somehow be holding signs for her.

She was already absorbed in her reading this morning as she watched the shop, before Omar had even left. He stopped on his way out and looked at his wife, unused to seeing her seated at this time of the day, and longing inwardly for the reassurance of her usual movement and bustle.

'I'm going,' he said, and beneath its deep tone, his voice held that familiar plea for attention that now irritated her as she looked up from her book.

'Okay,' she said. And then she remembered that it was Tuesday, and she looked back at him.

'I'll see you tomorrow,' she said, too nonchalantly, but he looked pleased, as though he had been waiting for this opportunity to surprise her.

'No,' he said, with a half-smile. 'I'll be back this afternoon.'

She had not responded with the gratitude he had hoped to see, and so he turned and left, and she watched him go, wishing for once that he would not be hurrying back.

At about two o'clock that afternoon, just as it began to rain, Amina Harjan came roaring through the main street of Delhof, with the fleeting thought that every time she passed this place it looked less and less like a town, and more and more like a few buildings strung together along a strip of dirt. The rapid movement of her truck brought to the few ramshackle stores and houses as much excitement as they had seen for a while, and she tooted her horn at a group of ragged-looking children who stood in a row with some solemnity and waved to her as she passed. She smiled, but only briefly, for her stomach was churning. She took a deep breath and began humming a tune to stop herself from thinking, and she was still humming when she pulled up outside the shop.

Miriam had been waiting for her but at the critical moment, she found that her thoughts were away from Amina. There were three people waiting to be served in the shop when the girl walked in, and Amina found herself having to hold back the first breathless sentences she had willed herself to speak immediately in case she should lose her nerve later. Miriam saw her at once and Amina smiled to notice that she blushed and avoided looking at her again as she continued to serve her customers. The room had darkened under the rain and Amina watched as Miriam switched on a lamp, so that she could better see the roll of material she was cutting. Her angular hands grasped the large shears a little awkwardly, but the line she cut was straight and smooth, and the waiting customer looked satisfied.

The tableau continued, Amina watching as each person was served, and money was exchanged along with some pleasantries and news. Robert helped on one side of the counter, and within ten minutes the shop was empty again.

'You look very thoughtful,' said Miriam, clearing her throat.

Amina smiled and glanced out of the window. 'I was just thinking, we always seem to meet when it's raining.'

'Yes,' said Miriam. She hesitated. 'These dark, rainy afternoons remind me of you now.'

Amina looked at Robert, and greeted him politely, and Miriam read the meaning of her look as she removed her apron.

'Robert, mind the shop please.'

'Yes, madam.'

'And the baby.'

'Yes, madam.'

Amina had not noticed the cradle, tucked behind the counter, as though the child too were keeping watch over the shop with her mother.

'Amina, will you come up with me? Sam is sick in bed. I want to check on him.'

Amina's eyebrows raised – she had not expected to find a sick child at home with them. She wished she had brought a toy, or a book or something for the boy. She liked him, and had noticed that despite being the eldest, he was often overshadowed by his talkative sister. Amina followed Miriam's light steps up the stairs, her eyes focused on the back of her slim ankles, and at the top they stopped at the open door to her son's room. They waited and listened, one behind the other, Amina's lean frame watching over

Miriam's shoulder. The child was asleep, and Amina's eyes went to Miriam's face as she watched her son. The girl looked down, frowning slightly, then stepped back from the door, silently, and Miriam turned to her, pulling the door of Sam's room closed behind her.

The movement brought her close to Amina, and the girl did not step back. Instead, she just waited, her eyes fixed on Miriam's, a few faint lines of concern feathered across her forehead. Her hand moved to her hair and then back again. The gesture was an awkward one, and Miriam knew the girl was extremely nervous.

Miriam watched her. 'You didn't come here to give me a driving lesson, did you?' she said.

'No.'

'I didn't think so. What did you come for?'

For the briefest moment, Amina's eyes, when they came up to meet Miriam's, contained that flash of mischievous suggestion that Miriam recognised so well from her early exchanges with the girl.

'To see you,' she replied, her eyes intent again. 'And to talk to you. I have to tell you something.'

Miriam felt her heart moving down her body until it came to rest somewhere near the base of her stomach. So, she thought, this is how it ends, before it even begins. She pointed to the open door of her own bedroom, and Amina went in, and waited awkwardly for Miriam to follow. She came in behind her and sat down on her bed and waited.

Amina cleared her throat and then rolled up her shirt sleeves, as though preparing to take part in a fight. Miriam watched the slender, tanned arms slowly revealed, and watched as Amina took an audible breath.

'When I kissed you the other day,' Amina began, 'I did it because I couldn't stop myself any more.'

Miriam felt her face flush and Amina smiled slightly again, that roguish smile that somehow reassured Miriam because it was familiar. Then she bit her lip and leaned on the dresser next to her with such ostentatious casualness that she looked completely ill at ease. Miriam touched the bedspread.

'Do you want to sit down?' she asked.

Amina took her place beside Miriam. She said something else then, something that Miriam could not hear. She was conscious of nothing except the bare arm of the girl that was lying so very close to her own. They were not touching, except for the outer fold of Amina's shirt which barely brushed against Miriam's shoulder, but she could feel the warmth of Amina's skin and when the girl moved slightly, she felt her own arm shiver.

'Did you hear me?'

Miriam looked up, startled.

'I love you,' repeated Amina. Miriam found she couldn't breathe, but her face must have remained expectant, because Amina continued, her tone earnest and desperate:

'I've tried and tried, Miriam, I really have, to forget you, and not think about you, and not be in love with you, but I can't help it. I can't. And I know you feel the same. Or similar,' she added, qualifying her presumption.

'I don't,' Miriam said, in a small voice. 'How can I? It's not right. I am married, and you are a girl.'

'Yes, you do. I know it. Otherwise I wouldn't be here.'

Miriam looked down at her hands. She could hear the pattering rain, and Amina's voice, the voice she now spent all her days longing to hear, speaking gently above it, and she could feel the heat from her body, and she could smell the fresh scent of her hair. She wanted to look at her, but she could not make herself look up, could not raise her head to find those eyes and that mouth only an inch away from hers.

'I should never have let you come,' Miriam said, so quietly that Amina had to lean even closer to hear her.

'Miriam,' Amina said.

'Yes?'

'Miriam, look at me.'

Miriam looked.

'I have to ask you something.' Miriam's head fell again, but this time, Amina caught her chin with a finger, and turned the reluctant face towards hers again.

'Do you love me?'

There was no reply.

'Whose is the first face that appears before you when you wake in the morning?'

Amina's.

'Who is the last person you think about before you sleep at night?'

Amina.

'Miriam, do you love me?'

'Yes.'

'I wish you would say something,' Amina sighed, and Miriam realised that her reply had been so whispered that the girl had not even heard it. 'Anything. Even tell me to go away.' She ran her hand across her eyes.

'I said...yes,' repeated Miriam, and Amina stared at her and Miriam felt the months of coiled-up fear and tension pooling inside her, and felt the hot tears come streaming down her face. Amina put an arm around her and pulled her back onto the bed where she lay holding her, stroking her head, waiting, feeling the tears fall wet against her neck.

'It's okay. It'll be fine. Everything will be fine.' They lay like this for a few minutes, until Miriam laughed. Amina turned her head and smiled.

'What is it?'

'Nothing. Just...I'm happy here with you.'

'Then stay with me all the time.'

Miriam looked into the girl's eyes, hopeful and sincere and so young, and she felt the cool clarity of her logical mind returning. Abruptly she sat up and edged forward so that she was sitting on the corner of the bed.

'I can't, Amina. I can't even stay with you for a day. Or an hour.'

'Why not?'

'Do you really have to ask?' Miriam's voice was full of desperation.

Amina got up with deliberation and walked up and down the room, pausing to look back at Miriam and the bed where she sat.

Her husband's bed. On the dresser was a new photograph of the whole family, evidently taken just after Salma was born. She made herself stop and examine it. Omar stood behind the chair in which his wife sat with the baby. He looked handsome, if cold, and his jacket and tie were immaculate. Miriam was looking away from the camera, at her new baby, and Sam and Alisha stood on one side of her, their father's hand resting firmly on his son's shoulder.

Amina looked away, then made herself look back. She felt sick again, and jumped when she felt Miriam's hand on her arm.

'I have a husband. Three children, who I will never leave.'

'I don't want you to leave them,' said Amina, her tone defiant.

Miriam almost laughed. 'What should I do, bring them with me?'

'Yes.'

'What you want to do is crazy. We would be outcasts. Where would we live? How would we live?'

'I have money. I make a lot with the business. We could move – away from here.' Her hand went to her curls, making them even more unruly.

'You've always wanted to see Cape Town,' she said to Miriam, with a short laugh. Her eyes were flickering all over the room, as though she saw it now as a prison cell, and she carried on talking, explaining how things could be, in a voice that grasped for breath during even short sentences.

'I'll look after you and the children...'

'Stop it, please.'

'I'm serious. I know you think I don't know what I'm talking about, but I've lived this way, my own way, all my life. It can be done, Miriam, it can...'

'Amina, please stop...'

The girl looked at her, eyes desperate, her strong, straight shoulders lowered, and Miriam felt a rush of love and pity.

'Come here,' she said, and she pulled Amina to her, and held her head down against her shoulder and listened to the girl's erratic breathing, and closed her eyes and kissed the forehead that was level with her mouth. Her lips touched Amina's hair, then the sharp planes of her cheekbones and her closed eyes, and she tasted salt there, and knew the girl was crying, and she kissed her, looking for something, her mouth, and when she found it, she kissed her again, with some hesitancy at first, but then with a delicate decision. She pulled away quickly, before she should allow herself to fall too deeply in, and held the girl's head down against her neck. For a long moment they stood like this, until Miriam turned to look at the clock.

'Alisha,' she said. 'She'll be back any minute.'

Amina nodded and reached to touch Miriam's cheek, but Miriam pulled away.

'I can't. This is wrong.'

'Because we are women?' said Amina, through clenched teeth.

'Because I am married.'

'To a man you don't love.'

Miriam reached up and kissed her softly on the cheek and then on her neck, breathing in the clean scent that she now wondered if she would ever know again. She could not allow herself to look into Amina's eyes and still do what she intended to do, so she simply stood before her, and looked at her chin and mouth and at the bones that ran from her long neck to her shoulders, and she touched the open neck of Amina's shirt and the clear buttons that held back her cuffs.

'I can't,' she said again and then she closed her eyes, turned her head and walked out of the room and down the stairs, through the kitchen and out of the back door, where she paced up and down, staring at the grass beneath her feet, blurred through her falling tears.

By the time she had recovered herself enough to go back into the house, her daughter was waiting for her at the kitchen table, her son was descending the stairs, bright-eyed after his sleep, and Amina had left without leaving any trace that she had ever come.

Chapter Twenty-Three

JACOB WAS BECOMING nervous. He looked again at his watch, straightened his tie and checked for the third time that his shoes were shined. He watched three more customers enter the restaurant, then walked to the front door and looked out at the street. She was nowhere to be seen, but that did not mean she was not coming. Streetlights were few beyond the corner and she might arrive at any moment out of the early evening darkness.

He went back inside and took over from Doris the lighting of the candle lamps that hung on all the café walls. He stopped to greet the occupants of one table, and then, just as he had decided to take his chances and leave, he heard the familiar sound of the truck pulling to a stop. The hasty slam of the door made him instantly wary. He turned to see her walk in, and she looked for him too, as she always did. He nodded, and saw her pause and take in his formal clothes, his suit and tie, and his newly cut hair.

Amina did not see or hear the people who greeted her as she passed through the café. She stopped at the end of the room and sat down in the booth nearest the kitchen, where Jacob joined her.

'Sorry I got so late,' she said. 'I had a problem.'

Her tone did not invite further enquiry. Jacob took in the shadows beneath her eyes, the slight lowering of the usually erect shoulders.

'It's okay,' he replied. 'I was just going...'

'Where?'

Jacob looked surprised at her sharp tone. 'To dinner,' he replied. 'With Madeleine Smith. Remember?'

'Oh, yes.' Amina ran a hand over her eyes and then looked up at him from where she sat slumped down in her seat.

'Where are you going to take her to dinner?' she asked. Her voice was neutral but Jacob knew she had thought of the very problem he had hoped she would overlook.

Jacob hesitated. 'I wasn't sure what to do,' he said. 'I suppose, to my place.'

Amina did not respond for a few seconds, except to look at him with great seriousness.

'Where else can we go?' he said.

'I don't know. What if your neighbours see?'

'They won't say anything...'

'What if they do?'

'They won't.'

'They might. What if they catch you? What if they catch *her*? Is that what you want?'

'Amina, if you have problems, you can always talk to me about them, but don't take them out on me.' Jacob stood up, and pulled at his jacket. 'I'm late to collect her,' he said.

'I'm not taking anything out on you,' Amina added, trying to not to snap at him. 'But you're living in a dream world, Jacob, and I hate to have to say things like this, and ruin things for you, but someone has to see things as they are.'

'Will you be okay if I leave now?' Jacob asked. Amina sighed and looked at him.

'Of course. Go on. And I hope you have a nice time with her. Really.'

'Thank you,' Jacob replied, and without looking back at her, he left.

At the Post Office, Miss Smith had not quite finished closing up. She had been listening for Jacob, and when she heard his step and voice out front, she called a greeting to him. He called back and waited in the shadows of the high, darkened room, his hat in his hands, wondering how it was that such a familiar place could look so different at night. The amber light of a street lamp fell into the room from the high windows, and half illuminated a metal sign indicating the section that was for non-Whites. Without thinking, Jacob took a step back so that he stood fully inside his own area. Miss Smith's face popped up from behind the counter.

'Sorry, Jacob. I seem to be so behind this evening. We had a run of deliveries this afternoon that just set me right back.'

'It's no problem,' said Jacob. She disappeared again, and he heard her locking up some doors at the back before the sounds stopped. Jacob peered into the darkness.

'Are you okay, Miss Smith?'

He heard her laugh echo across to him.

'I think at this stage we should drop "Miss Smith" and start using "Madeleine",' she said. 'Jacob?'

'Yes, Madeleine?'

'Can you help me with this padlock please?'

Jacob moved quickly behind the counter, to where the figure of Madeleine Smith was bent over the lock. He held out his hand for the padlock, and as he knelt to place it on the door, he stopped and looked at the postmistress.

'What is it?' she asked him.

'I think I made a big mistake, Madeleine.'

She did not look surprised or concerned – she only waited calmly for him to continue.

'I didn't think about things properly. About where we could go, who might see us, what people might think... I just thought it would be nice, and now I've begun to realise, just on the way here, what I'm doing.'

'What *we're* doing,' she corrected.

Jacob was grateful for that response, but dismissed it quickly from his mind. He looked again at the small, determined woman who stood expectantly before him.

'Why are you doing this?' he asked. 'You must have thought about it, before I did...'

'I like you,' she said, her voice matter-of-fact. 'I like you very much. And I don't like rules. Not the kind of rules they would have us live by now, anyway.'

He had no time to reply for they heard the main door open and shut.

'Hello!' The call came from the front of the Post Office.

'Hello?' she called back.

'Officer David here, ma'am.'

'Postmistress Smith here, sir!' she replied, in a parody of his officious tone.

The policeman cleared his throat. 'Are you all right, ma'am? I was driving by and I saw the door ajar.'

'I'm fine,' she said, moving forward to the counter. The round spot of a flashlight played briefly over her face.

'Sorry to trouble you,' the policeman said, but the sweep of the torch beam caught on something, and he trained it onto the darkness behind Miss Smith. Jacob's outline was illuminated, and the policeman frowned.

'Who's there?'

Miss Smith hesitated for a moment – she could not quite take the measure of the young man before her.

'This is Jacob,' she said.

The policeman seemed uninterested in introductions.

'The section where you are is for Whites only,' he said.

'He was helping me lock up,' said Miss Smith sharply, as Jacob came forward.

'Well, he shouldn't be there. Who is he anyway?' asked the policeman, arrogant now, his torch moving down to light up the formal clothes of the Coloured man who stood before him. His light flicked over to the postmistress and her smart skirt suit and he frowned.

Miss Smith glanced at Jacob, who stood unmoving in the glare of the torch as it flickered over the bars of the counter, and an image of him standing like that behind the bars of a prison cell passed through her mind. She turned again to the policeman.

'He's my driver,' she said.

At the café, two customers started an argument about an item on their bill and Doris, despite having worked at the café for over a year, was not quite sure what to do to about it because, unusually, neither Jacob nor Amina was there. She sent one of the younger girls out to knock on the door of Amina's room, but the girl returned to the restaurant in two minutes with the message that Doris should take off the bill whatever was being contended, and that no one should disturb Amina again.

'You look familiar,' said the policeman, watching Jacob carefully.

Miss Smith sighed with some irritation.

'Officer, are we going to stand here all night? I've had a long day and I would like to go home.'

The policeman stood back and lowered his torch.

'Come then. I'll walk you out.' He held open the front door for Miss Smith and then for Jacob, and held his torch over the lock while she secured it. Then he walked alongside her up the road while Jacob followed a few steps behind. Miss Smith stopped at her car and rummaged in her bag for the keys.

'Why doesn't your driver keep the keys?' the officer asked.

'I prefer to keep them,' she answered.

'I know what you mean,' he said with a smile. 'Better to be safe than sorry, *ja*?'

'Quite.'

She handed the keys to Jacob who opened the rear door and waited while Miss Smith got in. Then he walked somewhat stiffly round to the driver's side and sat down. His knees were cramped – he was after all much taller than Miss Smith – but he started the engine and reversed the car, ready to pull away. Not once did he take his eyes from the windshield before him.

'All right, ma'am!' called the policeman, and Miss Smith raised a hand to him before Jacob drove away.

When Amina's father walked into the café that evening, he felt a strange sense of depression float down on him. He was a man of such equanimity that any extreme of emotion tended to confuse him, and he looked around him in case the café itself should yield up a reason for the heaviness that invaded his heart. But everything looked as normal. The thick darkness that lay over the street outside had been banished inside, with candles and lamps. The glow was attractive from the doorway, and yet... he felt a change, something missing. There was no music playing this evening, he noticed, and he glanced to the gramophone he had given Amina such a long time ago. For an instant, he recalled the joy that had lit her face when he had presented it to her, and how he had been so overwhelmed by that face that he had gruffly brushed aside her thanks and gone to his chair to read his newspaper, all the while beaming inwardly at his daughter's pleasure.

He looked about for Amina but could not see her. Neither could he see Jacob, and he realised then what was missing in the atmosphere of the place tonight. He walked towards the kitchen, meaning to go out to Amina's room, but Doris stopped him and asked if he would like to sit down. He introduced himself and the waitress stared at him in surprise.

'Her father, eh? You look like her,' she said.

'She looks like me,' he corrected, and without another word he pointed enquiringly towards the back with his hat, and Doris stood aside to let him pass.

Under the low throb of the car engine, Jacob sighed. He looked into the rear mirror, where his eyes met Madeleine Smith's. She looked back at him with a strange expression, somewhere between a frown and a smile of reassurance.

'He's still behind us, somewhere,' Jacob told her.

'I didn't see his car,' she replied.

'He has a motorbike.'

'I see.'

Jacob drove on towards the area where he knew Madeleine Smith must live. He did not speak, for he had no idea what to say. He had not felt such profound sadness for a long time. After a few minutes, she spoke again:

'Where are we going?'

He did not reply at once, but continued to look out at the road before him.

'Where do you live?' he asked, his tone gentle, trying to atone for the implication she might take from the question.

'Five one two Cortell Street,' she said. 'It's off the main road at...'

'I think I know it,' he said.

'Is he still following us?' she asked, her voice barely carrying now from the back seat. Jacob looked up into the mirror again and met her look. He shook his head.

When they arrived Jacob rolled the car gently to a stop outside the small block of newly constructed apartments. Not long ago this area had housed an Indian community, but they had been made to move.

'My son bought it for me,' Miss Smith said, watching Jacob's eyes take in the apartment.

'It's very nice.'

He opened the door for her and offered her his hand. Once she was outside, facing him, he handed her back the keys.

'I'll be going now,' he said, his tone and manner formal.

'Jacob, I'm so terribly sorry for what happened. I was afraid. I'm ashamed to say it, but I was afraid of that young policeman, and what he might do to you if he suspected.'

'I know,' replied Jacob, looking at her more kindly. 'I don't blame you. I don't. But I can't...'

She waited, but he was unable to articulate himself.

'It's quite all right,' she said finally. 'I understand. I'm sorry though.'

He wanted to tell her that he was sorry too, but he could not speak. He re-buttoned his jacket, and then held out his hand.

'Good-bye, Miss Smith,' he said.

'Jacob, you know my name.'

Jacob nodded. 'Good-bye, Madeleine,' he said.

'Good-bye, Jacob. Good-bye.'

She waited outside and watched him as he turned and began the walk back to the main road. She opened her mouth to ask if she could not drive him back, but she knew that he would refuse, so she remained silent, peering at the erect figure disappearing through the darkness. She lifted her hand in farewell when she thought he had at last turned his head to look back, only to realise with some regret, that in fact, he had not.

Amina was trying to decide which of her belongings to take with her and which to leave behind when there was a second knock on the door. She looked up irritably.

'I thought I told you not to disturb me!'

There was a short pause before the handle turned, very slowly. Amina heard the click and watched in disbelief as the door opened despite her shouted warning. Her father's sallow face poked round it, to be followed at once by the rest of his gaunt frame.

'I don't want to disturb you,' he said.

Amina stared for a moment, then shook herself into speech.

'You're not,' she replied. She motioned to her father to come in, and quickly moved to slide her suitcase off her bed, in the vain hope that he might not notice it.

'I thought it was Doris or one of the girls,' she said.

He didn't respond, and she offered him her only chair, lighting a lamp to supplement the poor flicker of candlelight that she had preferred until now.

'Can I get you something? Something to eat? Some tea?'

He shook his head. He did not look at her directly; he rarely met the eyes of anyone around him, even on the few occasions that he was involved in a conversation. He did notice, however, that his daughter's face looked thin. The shadows cast by the sharp angles of her cheekbones, and her wide, tired eyes gave her expression a strange, unworldly quality that unsettled him.

'Is everything all right, Dad?'

'Everything's fine.' He cleared his throat. 'We haven't heard from you for three weeks,' he added, knowing that she must be wondering what he was doing there. 'Your mother was worried.'

'There's been a lot going on. I haven't even noticed the time going by.'

'I know you're busy, but it would be nice if you phoned your mother.'

'Yes,' she said quietly. She felt like crying suddenly, like running to her father and asking him to look after her and make everything better. But she did not remember a time when she had done that, even as a small child. She searched for something to ask him to break the silence that was looming in the room and to cover her distress.

'Why didn't you just phone me?' The question had just occurred to her.

Mr Harjan looked uncomfortable. 'I wanted to see you. To check you are really okay.'

'I'm fine.'

She saw his eyes move to her half-packed case.

'I've been having a strange few weeks, that's all. Things haven't been going too well.'

'With the business?'

'No...'

'I didn't think so,' Mr Harjan said, and he sat forward in his chair, looking down at the floor. Amina waited without moving, to see if he would explain his last comment. He did not.

'It's hard to explain...' she began, but he raised a hand to stop her.

'Don't explain,' he told her. 'People like to make sure your mother and I know everything that they think is happening with you. They wouldn't like us to miss out.'

Amina closed her eyes against the sudden idea that her parents had all along known more about her life than she had imagined. Of course, she knew people talked about her, and that her parents must have suspected, but they had never mentioned anything to her, and she had never considered the issue long enough for it to concern her.

She looked helplessly at her father, but he was not looking at her. He continued to study his shoes. After a few seconds, he spoke again:

'This time, people are talking about her, not just you. They know her as well.'

'Miriam? They have no right to say anything about her. Who even knows that we're friends?' She paused. Farah, for one, would delight in spreading gossip. Omar might have complained to her. 'It's only because she is friends with me that they make assumptions,' Amina continued. 'Don't people have anything better to do?'

'No, they don't,' replied her father with a faint smile. 'That's why I avoid them.'

He sat back again, so that Amina could better see his face.

'Amina?'

'Yes, Dad?'

'I've never interfered with your life before, have I?'

'No.'

'Well, I just have to say this.'

Amina looked up at him expectantly, and he caught the glint of tears in her eyes.

'She's married, Amina,' he said. 'It's no good.'

'He hits her!' she burst out angrily.

Her father looked displeased and Amina was unsure whether his response was to her tone or her allegation.

'Then go and fetch her,' he said, as firmly as she had ever heard him speak. She stared at him, shocked.

'What?'

'Go and get her. If you are that serious, do it. I can't help you, but I won't stop you.'

Amina felt the tears burning on her cheeks and cursed herself for crying. Her father's words had touched her, but also made her even more aware of the difficulty of her situation.

'She won't just leave like that...'

'So you're running away?'

Amina wiped her eyes. 'I just need some time. Please, Dad, I just need some time away from here, to think.'

He stood up and walked the length of the room, which for him was about six steps.

'Do you need money?' he asked, stopping alongside her.

She shook her head. She did not need money, and would not have taken anything from her father even if she had, for he had very little of his own.

'Will you come and see your mother before you go?'

Amina nodded.

'Okay.' He walked to the small window and looked out.

'You shouldn't go,' he said simply.

She gave a short laugh. 'Why not?'

He scratched his forehead. 'For one thing, your mother will miss you.' Amina almost smiled. So will you, she thought, even though you won't say it.

'And for another thing...' He turned again to look at her, and saw in her vivid, intent eyes a determination and strength that he did not recognise in himself, but which he admired anyway.

'What, Dad?' she asked.

He looked down again and walked to the door.

'If she should come to her senses, and if you have gone away, how will she know where to find you?'

He turned the door handle and said something else, some form of farewell, which she did not hear because she was thinking. When she broke from her reverie, she realised that he was gone, and she looked around, wondering if she could have dreamt the whole episode, so out of character did it seem to her. He had left some money on her washstand, however, a trace that made her realise that he really had come, and had said what she had heard him say. She lay back on her bed and closed her eyes for a while, and when she sat up again, she looked at the half-filled suitcase for a minute or two. Then she pushed it back under the bed, and got up to return to the café.

Chapter Twenty-Four

M IRIAM HAD NO trouble getting her children to sleep that evening. Sam had come down to eat dinner with them and was worn out from the chattering of his sister. Even Alisha went to bed quietly, noticing an unfamiliar sadness about her mother and a redness in her eyes that she was at a loss to understand. Miriam read her a story, and then went to check on the baby, but Salma was already asleep. She too had joined them at dinner, gurgling in her high chair and was now tired as well, it seemed. Miriam watched her youngest child – she slept on her side, with her tiny arms held out in front of her, chubby hands formed into loose fists, breathing ragged but even. She leaned into the cot to smell her clean fragrance, and then felt tears in her eyes. Quietly, she closed the door and went downstairs, into the dim light of the kitchen. Beyond the windows, the night was already black, and she let herself acknowledge for the first time that her husband had not returned that afternoon, as he had said he would.

She went to the window and looked out, knowing that she did not much care that he had decided to stay the night with his sister-in-law. She was relieved. She was miserable and did not want to have to see him, look after him and sleep beside him while she felt like this. She leaned against the glass pane to catch sight of John's glowing coals, keeping watch with him out on the porch, and then she looked back at the darkness ahead. There was a faint smear of light somewhere out above the trees that stood to the right of the track, a light that was drawing closer and closer, and she watched and waited with a breathless hope as a set of headlights appeared. When the vehicle at last came into view and she realised that it was her husband, she felt the metallic taste of her own tears of disappointment coursing down her cheeks.

She had brushed away all those tears by the time he entered. He walked in and stood before her with some arrogance, as though expecting her to be grateful for his arrival. He had struggled to get home that evening, knowing that she would be doubting him again, and he presented himself almost with a flourish now that he was at the end of his journey. She waited for him to speak.

'I have been trying to get back here since four o'clock this afternoon,' he informed her, his voice dramatic.

She watched as he loosened his tie and removed his jacket, draping it carefully over the back of the chair that was always his when they ate at the kitchen table. He rubbed his eyes with one hand and sat down.

'Do you want some food?' she asked. He gave a brief nod and continued with his story.

'You won't believe what happened to me. When I went to leave, both my tyres were down. Two of them.'

'Both tyres had punctures?' she asked, her tone carrying only the barest hint of disbelief.

'No,' he said irritably. 'Both of them had been let down. Some little brat had let the air out. So, of course, I only had one spare, and I had to call Mackies Repairs and wait for two hours till they came with another one. What a day.'

She placed his food in front of him before going to fetch a Coke. She removed the bottle cap and left it beside him with a glass. She did not pour it, as he liked to do that himself. She sat down and tried to think of something to ask him, something to pass the time until she could be in bed upstairs, lying silently with her own thoughts.

'Where are the children? In bed already?'

She nodded. 'Who let the tyres down?'

He looked up from his food with a look of satisfaction. 'Some Coloured kid,' he said. 'I caught him. They were playing round the corner.'

'Why?'

Omar shrugged. 'He wouldn't say. Kept telling me he just did it for fun. The brat. He felt my hand.'

Miriam flinched. 'How can you just...'

'Not badly,' he replied, waving his fork. 'Just enough to make him sorry. On his backside.'

Miriam stood up, and got herself a bottle of Coke. When

she came back to the table, his manner had changed and he was watching her with a slight frown on his forehead.

'Did you have your driving lesson today?' he asked, casually taking another mouthful of food.

'No,' she replied and she reassured herself inwardly that she was in fact telling the truth.

'So they're finished with?'

She could not look at him for she felt a burning in her eyes, so she walked over to the window and looked out at the track where his car now stood, a dark, bulky shape looming in the night. Behind her, she heard him scoop up another forkful of food. His insouciant tone combined with the sound of his chewing irritated her.

'No,' she said, finally. He said nothing to that, but she could hear that he had put down his fork and was no longer eating. When she turned she looked first at his plate, which was still half-full. Omar was watching her, his face serious, his look narrow.

'What do you mean?'

'I mean that I need to be able to drive if I am going to be able to work.'

The anger rose visibly in his face like a wave, and she watched without much concern as it ebbed away slowly, as though she were watching a science experiment. She saw his mouth twitch as he fought to control the words that must be fighting to come tumbling out.

'You work here,' was what he said at last.

'And I will still work here. All I want is two or three mornings a week to go and cook...' She did not add 'in Pretoria' or 'at the café' for she knew that he was perfectly aware of what she meant.

He scraped back his chair with a noise that echoed in the high darkness of the kitchen. Walking over to the sink he almost tossed his plate there, irritably throwing his fork after it as though to emphasise to her that she had ruined his meal. When he turned to look at his wife, she had not stepped back into a corner, nor was her face lined with concern about what his next movement might be. Instead, she looked coolly back at him, interested, waiting.

Miriam saw Omar's brows pull together and she almost smiled at the confusion on his face. When he spoke, his tone was harsh.

'Why do you want to work there?'

'Why not? The hours are flexible and short, and it is work that I know how to do. I have no other skills,' she replied, fiercely. 'I must do what I can.'

'You don't *need* to work.' His fist came down on the iron sink with such force that Miriam winced at the pain he must have felt.

'Yes, I do.'

He moved forward, very quickly, and swiped at her with an open palm, but she must have been expecting it, and she dodged out to one side, so that he caught her with only the edge of his hand, on her neck. She felt almost no pain from the blow, but her heart was pounding fast. She turned to face him, and instinctively took a few steps back. He stood there, waiting, almost daring her to speak up again. She did not, for the moment, but to his surprise she regained those few steps she had just given up, and now stood almost in front of his face. Outside, John passed before the window on his walk up and down the patio, and was perturbed to see the master and his wife facing each other like two boxers, intent and alert, each waiting for the first strike.

Omar watched her, his limbs taut, his eyes flat and cloaked over, so that she could not read them. She did not need money, she did not need food. What need did she have to work? He wanted to ask, but did not, because, somewhere, very deep inside himself, he felt that her reasons were not reasons he could counter, even if he were ever willing to hear them.

Miriam cleared her throat and tried to speak calmly. She would not raise her voice and wake the children, but neither would she be afraid of him any more.

'It is just two mornings a week. That's all. Teach me to drive.'

He cut her off impatiently with a gesture of his hand, as though he could not bear to hear any more.

'There is nothing more to say.' His voice rose. '*You will not be my wife and work.*'

'You want to divorce me?'

Omar stared at her open mouthed. He had overcome a moment of weakness when he had almost felt like giving in, but he had now uttered his final decree, and she was not listening. He made a sudden jerking movement forward, and Miriam moved back just as quickly, expecting the open hand again. But he seemed to pull back, tired perhaps of swinging at thin air.

'*You will not be my wife and work!*' he shouted, slamming his hand instead against the wall.

She could see the anger coiling in his body, making his movements harsh and abrupt, but she still ignored the instinctive movement of her own legs, which were trying to carry her out of harm's way.

'What about the children?' she continued. 'Do you want them to suffer? Do you want to send me back to Bombay? All because you will not let me out of your sight for two mornings in the week?'

She stopped, suddenly aware that her voice was unnaturally loud, and she watched as he turned around to the table, picking up his glass this time. He hurled it at her and she felt the hiss of it and saw the glistening edges of it as it flew past her eye, before it hit the wall behind her, splintering into pieces that sprayed out onto the floor.

'*I will never teach you to drive,*' he shouted, and she saw tiny spits of saliva spray out from his mouth. His hair was tousled, for he had shaken his head fiercely when refusing her, and his face was red and lined. She knew he hated feeling out of control. When he had hit her previously, he had always gone straight to the bathroom to cool and clean himself. To make neat his appearance once again.

'You don't have to,' she said, and she saw his face relax slightly, saw him fall upon her words, desperate for an excuse to stop his own madness.

'I'll take the bus,' she added, almost laughing at her own daring. She watched his face, appalled, and yet somehow removed, for it moved through so many expressions so quickly, that she felt as though it could not be real. He turned again and picked up a chair.

This time she moved away, and towards the stairs, shouting at him to stop or the children would wake. He threw it in her direction, but with no real attempt to hit her, and it crashed down, taking with it a plate that was sitting on the edge of the table.

In the silence that followed, Miriam waited by the stairs. She waited, feeling nothing, hoping that he would look at her and see that she was not scared, that she would still look him in the eye. But he only stood with his hands resting on the table, his head hanging down, spent. She turned and went lightly up the stairs. On the top landing, Alisha stood listening, eyes wide open.

'It's okay,' Miriam told her. 'Your father dropped his glass, that's all. Go back to bed.' She steered the child into her room, and waited while she got back into bed. 'Sleep. I'll come back to check on you. Go to sleep.'

She stood alone on the landing for a moment, overcome at once with the desire to weep. But instead, she went back down the stairs. Omar was sitting down, his head in his hands and he did not look up as she walked in. She took the chair right beside him and sat watching him. He shifted in his seat, uncomfortable with her proximity and somehow disarmed by it, by the fact of his wife sitting a hair's breadth away from him, even though she must be worried that he might hit her.

In a minute or two, he turned towards her, but without looking at her. He straightened his tie, his lower lip caught slightly between his teeth, as though he were literally chewing over the problem.

'I don't like it,' he said, quietly, almost to himself. 'If I don't like it, that should be enough.'

She summoned the courage to talk back to him yet one more time.

'It's not enough,' she told him. 'It has never been enough, but I never told you before.' Her face was flushed, not with fear or tension, but with embarrassment, as though this moment of speaking her thoughts to her husband was a revelation of herself akin to being caught dancing naked in the street. He was staring at her and she held his look. Please don't be afraid of me, she thought to herself.

'Will you teach me to drive, please?' she asked him, her voice almost a whisper. There was rain falling now, they could hear its light tapping on the roof. Omar studied his nails, and considered his options. She was offering him a compromise, he felt, but his pride would not allow him to take hold of it so easily.

'For what?'

'You know for what.'

He stood up abruptly, pushing back his chair so hard that it fell over. Why would she not give up the idea of work and be satisfied with the driving?

'You will not drive,' he said evenly. 'And you will not work.'

'I'll take the bus,' she repeated.

He laughed, a rough-edged sound in the night. 'That bus will take two hours to get there.'

'I don't care.' She paused. 'I'm your wife. Why don't you want me to be happy?'

He heard the tears in her voice, but he was looking away, out of the black, rain-streaked window, and did not say anything in reply. They both stayed still for a few moments, in absolute quiet, and then she went to get the dust pan and brush from below the sink, carrying it over to where the broken glass lay.

He spun around. 'Leave it,' he ordered. 'Leave it.' He could not bear to watch her cleaning up the glass that was meant to hit her, and making him feel bad.

She kneeled down carefully and began brushing.

'LEAVE IT!' he shouted. 'Robert will do it.'

She dropped the pan and brush and left them where they lay. She could see that the anger was seeping out of him slowly, and that now he would hate himself as well as her. He was looking at her strangely, his attitude almost defeated, and she thought for a moment that he might actually say something, or reach out a hand to her. But he turned away and, without another word, walked steadily up the stairs. She heard him reach the landing, heard a pause, and then the closing of the bathroom door.

She looked down at the brush, and at the splinters of glass which lay like a miniature field of sparkling crystal at her feet. She stepped across them carefully and went into the dark shop. In the slight moonlight that filtered through the rain clouds, she went behind the counter and felt below it for the pen and the pad of paper that he always kept there. When she had found them, she carried them into the kitchen and sat down at the table, stopping to right the chair that he had toppled over. Her letter to Amina was brief and business-like; just as the acceptance of a job should be, she thought. She toyed with adding a further paragraph of explanation at the end, but decided against it. The night was late already, and she wanted to be up early the next morning to catch the first mail to Pretoria.

THE END

SHAMIM SARIF recently wrote and directed the motion picture adaptation of her own novel, The World Unseen. She is also the writer/director of the feature film I Can't Think Straight, which is based on her novel of the same name. She is the author of a further novel, Despite the Falling Snow.

She lives in London with her partner Hanan and their two children.

ACCLAIM FOR DESPITE THE FALLING SNOW
by
Shamim Sarif

❧ "Despite the Falling Snow by Shamim Sarif, one of our most outstanding young novelists, is my novel of the year: its delicate artistry and immense compass reaches back to the labyrinthine heart of Soviet Russia.' STEVIE DAVIES, THE INDEPENDENT

❧ 'Sarif's thrilling new novel makes me think of the 'The English Patient' and 'The French Lieutenant's Woman'. Like those books, it has at its core an unforgettable love story. Yet Sarif also understands the human cost exacted by totalitarian systems. And she knows that the worst betrayals are those committed by the ones we love. Her novel is immensely powerful – and deeply moving.' STEVE YARBROUGH, AUTHOR OF THE OXYGEN MAN

❧ 'A perfectly balanced novel of love and tragedy...brutally shocking. The beauty of the streets of Moscow, the bejewelled architecture of the metro stations, is all a majestic backdrop to a play of mistrust and deception, where friends, even the best of friends, can turn against each other in fear.' WATERSTONES MAGAZINE

❧ 'This story is, quite literally, breathtaking.' THE GOOD BOOK GUIDE

❧ 'Explores love and tragic loss with the pace of a thriller and a style that is gentle and flowing, a hypnotic combination that eases between the US and 1950s Moscow. . . . A pure delight, highly recommended.' THE BOOKSELLER

❧ 'An intriguing story of love, betrayal, anguish and despair . . . Shamim Sarif brings her characters to life with a delicacy of touch evocative of the intensity of their passions. An enthralling read.' DAILY DISPATCH

❧ 'A compelling read, flicking expertly between the tragic present and tumultuous past...Haunting at times, Shamim's elegant prose weaves a poignant tale indeed.' CRUSH BOOKS

❧ 'Shamim Sarif's intense and elegant first novel drew on her South African roots. This one shows that her cultural compass can stretch even wider without dulling the delicacy of her gaze....Highly readable.' THE INDEPENDENT